FINDING NAOMI

DIANE HAWLEY NAGATOMO

Black Rose Writing | Texas

ISBN: 978-1-68513-507-2
PUBLISHED BY BLACK ROSE WRITING
www.blackrosewriting.com

Printed in the United States of America
Suggested Retail Price (SRP) $21.95

Finding Naomi is printed in Baskerville

*As a planet-friendly publisher, Black Rose Writing does its best to eliminate unnecessary waste to reduce paper usage and energy costs, while never compromising the reading experience. As a result, the final word count vs. page count may not meet common expectations.

For Karen, Debbie, and Mary D
—friends forever!

PRAISE FOR
FINDING NAOMI

"A delightful novel by a skilled storyteller, Japan and the American Midwest blend seamlessly in this fast-paced modern-day fairy tale."
–Karen Hill Anton, author of *A Thousand Graces*

"In *Finding Naomi*, Nagatomo whisks the reader from the neon-lit alleys of Tokyo to the windswept plains of Nebraska, getting all the details just right. I was rooting for Naomi all the way as she dealt with complicated family issues and smalltown rivalries, and I loved meeting the well-drawn and sometimes quirky characters who surround her. Nagatomo's second novel will satisfy existing fans and bring in new ones."
–Suzanne Kamata, author of *The Baseball Widow, Candy Cane Crush,* and *Cinnamon Beach*

"Fresh off the success of her widely acclaimed debut novel, *The Butterfly Café,* Diane Hawley Nagatomo delivers another page-turner with *Finding Naomi.* Set partly in Tokyo and partly in rural Nebraska, the book takes the reader on a rollercoaster ride of twists and turns as we follow the protagonist's search for identity and happiness. As a long-term American resident of Tokyo, Nagatomo deftly details the striking differences between Japan's megacity and the American heartland credibly and humorously."
–John Rucynski, editor of *A Passion for Japan: A Collection of Personal Narratives*

"Nagatomo once more skillfully weaves an engaging cast into newfound family, friends, and love. With small-town feels, character growth, and a satisfying story, I couldn't put this page-turner down."
–Lena Gibson, award-winning author of *The Wish, The Edge of Life: Love and Survival During the Apocalypse,* and *The Train Hoppers* series

"Nagatomo's latest work is for the interculturally curious, but also those who love a roller-coaster yarn. Furthermore, it is the kind of heart-warming book that makes you want to go home, hug your loved ones, and live happily ever after! Expect a few moist-eyed moments."
–Thomas Lockley, author of *African Samurai: The True Story of Yasuke, a Legendary Black Warrior in Feudal Japan* and *A Gentleman from Japan: The Untold Story of an Incredible Journey from Asia to Queen Elizabeth's Court*

We hope you enjoyed reading this title from:

Subscribe to our mailing list – *The Rosevine* – and receive **FREE** books, daily deals, and stay current with news about upcoming releases and our hottest authors. Scan the QR code below to sign up.

Already a subscriber? Please accept a sincere thank you for being a fan of Black Rose Writing authors.

"From Tokyo to the American Midwest, Nagatomo leads readers on a journey full of twists and turns through loss, betrayal, forgiveness, and love. Along the way she elucidates the sometimes-surprising, often-hilarious cultural differences between Japan and America, especially when it comes to romance and the unpredictable complications that result. *Finding Naomi* is a smart, entertaining novel that highlights Nagatomo's many talents as a storyteller."
–David Joiner, author of *The Heron Catchers* and *Kanagawa*

"She's only gone and done it again! In her second novel, *Finding Naomi,* Diane Nagatomo has once again crafted a tale bound to warm the cockles of your heart and bring a tear to your eye. Bi-racial Naomi has grown up in Japan not knowing her American father – or her mother, who committed suicide when she was a child. Learning her father has died and left her property in Nebraska in his will, Naomi makes her way to the States. As in all good novels, the trick is in the title. In discovering her American identity, Naomi finds herself–and happiness and fulfilment."
–Lea O'Harra, author of *Imperfect Strangers, Progeny,* and *Lady First*

"Nagatomo's delightful international romance bridges two cultures, asking the question: if given a chance to remake yourself, does love deserve a second chance too?"
–Cam Torrens, award-winning author of *Stable, False Summit,* and *Scorched*

"A compelling blend of intrigue, romance, and cultural exploration that will leave you thoroughly entertained and enlightened."
–Niamh McAnally, author of *The Writer on the Water* and *Following Sunshine*

"Part literary fiction, love story, and a suspenseful mystery, Diane Nagatomo in *Finding Naomi* brings forth an eclectic cast of well-framed characters, a story that grips and does not let go, and a grand finale sure to impress."
–Michael J. Summers, author of *Cherry Blossoms in Winter: A Riveting Soldier's Story of the Korean War, Friendship, and Love in Post-War Japan*

"Part women's fiction and part romance, with elements of mystery and crime thrown in for extra flavor, this entertaining novel will appeal to readers across these genres."
–Ruth Stevens, author of *My Year of Casual Acquaintances*

"The author's description of life in a small town – complete with local gossip, nosiness, and back-stabbing is right on... Finding Naomi is an edge-of-your-seat, eye-opening page-turner."
–Muriel Ellis Pritchett, author of *Aliens Spurlock*

FINDING NAOMI

PART ONE

CHAPTER ONE

Because Naomi hadn't gotten home until nearly dawn, she didn't hear the banging on her door at first. Her next-door neighbor certainly did, though—she already had her big busybody nose poking out her own door, checking to see why the police would show up at eight on a Sunday morning.

Oh, great, Naomi thought woozily. Something else that woman could complain to the landlord about.

"Miss Kihara?" asked the taller officer in a quiet voice.

"*Hai,*" she confirmed. "Yes, that's me." Naomi covered her mouth, attempting to mask last night's tequila. Did that idiot Tyler get himself in some sort of trouble after their stupid argument? She caught a glimpse of herself in the mirror above the shoe cupboard. Yesterday's mascara made her look like a deranged panda.

"We are sorry to inform you," he said in a quiet and official manner, "that your father took ill last night. Unfortunately, he passed away before an ambulance could get him to a hospital."

Naomi rubbed her eyes. "I think you might have the wrong person."

"His dinner companions did not know whom to call," he said, as if she hadn't spoken. "But we found this address in his briefcase."

"*This* address?" Naomi opened the door wider, using it as a barrier to prevent Mrs. Fukuda from listening. But doing so gave the cops a sweeping view of her studio apartment: the rumpled futon, the low *kotatsu* table littered with dishes, books, and cosmetics, and clothes strewn everywhere. Because she had overslept on both garbage collection days this week, a sour smell wafted from the bags by the door.

"Michael Bernard Johnson," the shorter one said, looking over her shoulder, disapproval in his voice, "is your father, correct?"

"*Hai*," she squawked out. "But—"

He continued, as if he had memorized a script for such a situation, and any deviation would mean having to start over again from zero. He offered standardized condolences and then a set of instructions. When he paused at strategic places, Naomi added *hai, hai* again, indicating she understood. Or at least, that she was listening. But her brain was processing his words as if they were Greek. Nothing made sense.

When he got to the end of his talk, he asked, "*Wakarimasu ka*?"

"Yes, I understand," she confirmed, not understanding a thing.

The cops bowed once more and left.

After shutting the door, Naomi sank down at the *kotatsu*, trying to steady her breathing. The cops were right. Mike Johnson *was* her father. That much she knew. But she hadn't seen or heard from him since she was two years old. Until five minutes ago, she didn't even know if he was dead or alive. She certainly didn't know he was in Japan.

She was just beginning to wrap her head around the fact that she needed to go to the hospital to make funeral arrangements for a man she hadn't seen in twenty-five years, but her arms and legs were incapable of propelling her into action. Coffee, she told herself. And a bath. Nothing could be done anyway until she was completely sober.

Maybe she should have let Tyler come home with her last night. Maybe she should have pretended to believe him when he said nothing was going on with Kaori. That way, she wouldn't have to be alone right now. But the smug look on Kaori's face as the two of them jumped apart last night outside the back door at Commando Shot Bar when Naomi went to throw away some empty beer bottles clearly suggested otherwise. As if Tyler was the grand prize in a competition, the jerk.

Actually, it was a good thing he *wasn't* here.

Naomi swallowed a couple of aspirin and texted Ashley, knowing that from her best friend, she'd get sympathy and understanding. She stripped out of last night's clothes that reeked of cigarettes and let them fall to the floor with the others. She connected her iPhone to the bluetooth speaker and put on Taylor Swift. In the bathroom, her favorite room in the tiny apartment, she squatted on a small plastic stool next to the tub, scrubbed her body, and rinsed down before climbing in. With her knees drawn to her chest in the steaming water and Taylor's music playing from the other room, she repeated the name the cops had told her over and over: *Michael Bernard Johnson. Michael Bernard Johnson.*

She had always known he was a *gaijin,* a foreigner. There was no hiding that fact when her mother returned to her village in disgrace with a toddler in tow—one with curly brown hair, hazel eyes, and a lightly freckled complexion. It may have been the 1990s elsewhere, but people in that village had the narrow mindsets of previous generations, and her grandfather, a tea farmer, could barely hold his head up. Egged on by his all-powerful mother, who was the real person in charge of that family, he solved the problem by finding a husband for the wayward daughter. Unfortunately, the deal the two of them had arranged with a widower and his mother did not include Naomi. So Yumi headed off to be a mother to two different little girls and Naomi stayed with her grandparents and their oldest son's family.

Because everyone thought that forgetting was the best way to move forward, Naomi hardly ever saw her mother after that. The last time had been at her great-grandmother's funeral. After the services were over and before Yumi returned to her husband, they snuck away and shared an ice cream in the park near their house. They talked about Naomi's upcoming entrance to elementary school, and her mother promised she would visit again soon.

The following week, Yumi jumped off the fifth floor of the local city office. The note said that she couldn't bear her life any longer.

At least Naomi had some memories of her mother. Her picture was on the shelf in the *butsudan*, the family altar. If no one else was around, Granny would bring out albums and tell stories about her daughter. But of her father, she knew nothing. In fact, if a small ID photo with *Mike Johnson* scrawled across the back hadn't fallen out of her mother's old English dictionary when Naomi was twelve years old, she wouldn't have even known his name. She remembered staring at his foreign face in shock, seeing herself in his eyes, nose, and chin. When Granny came into her room to put away laundry, she snapped the dictionary shut and hid the picture—the *only* thing she had ever had of her father. Because if her cousins Yusuke or Keisuke had gotten their hands on it, they would have destroyed it just for the pleasure of tormenting her.

That was the moment she understood her father was an actual person and not merely her DNA donor. With a name to go on, she searched for him on the school library's computer. Unfortunately, there were thousands of guys named Mike Johnson out there.

But now, for the first time in twenty-five years, Naomi knew exactly where Mike Johnson—that is, *Michael Bernard Johnson*—was and what he was doing. He was lying dead in the Keio Hospital morgue.

Blinking back a wave of tears, she climbed out of the bath, dried off, and dug through the pile of clothes in the corner for something clean to wear. After deciding on black slacks and a gray sweater, she checked her phone.

I'll be there as soon as I can, Ashley had texted.

CHAPTER TWO

Naomi was unsure where to go or what to do once she got to Keio Hospital. She stumbled around with her words at the reception desk so much that the woman thought she was a foreigner at first and almost called for an interpreter. Sympathy washed over her face when Naomi managed to say that her father was somewhere in the hospital, *dead*, and the woman escorted her to a private waiting room and brought her a cup of green tea. Minutes later, another hospital employee, looking like he had finished college the week before, came in to explain the necessary procedures. At least she wasn't asked to identify the body like they do in detective shows. After all, how could she know for sure it was even him?

Naomi answered, *"Wakarimasen,* I don't know," to all the questions concerning the papers to be signed and the decisions to be made. To make matters worse, she had forgotten to bring her registered seal with her.

The door opened a crack, and a wiry man with curly white hair stuck his head in. "Miss Kihara?" he said, bowing deeply. "My name is Kenji Sakaguchi. I know—I mean, I knew your father. The hospital informed the university of his... um, passing... and they called me."

Naomi bowed back, wondering how this person knew her name.

The man nodded to the hospital employee and slid into the chair next to her. When his eyes fell on her face, he gasped. "I'm sorry, but you look just like Mike."

"I- I do?"

"It's uncanny." He took a deep breath before continuing. "This must be a shock for you. I know you haven't seen your father in many years."

Naomi wasn't sure how to respond, so instead, she blurted out, "They expect me to arrange the funeral." As an afterthought, she whispered, even though the hospital employee was sitting right across from her, "But I don't have any money."

"I'll help with the arrangements. And as for money, I'm sure that can all be sorted out later."

Naomi exhaled with relief and let him take charge. The necessary documents were soon filled out, signed, and stamped. While he made a series of telephone calls in both English and Japanese, her mind was reeling. After all these years, she was in contact with her father. In a manner of speaking.

Once all the arrangements were made, the man suggested they go have coffee. Naomi texted Ashley to let her know she'd be at the Starbucks next to the hospital's entrance.

"Sakaguchi Sensei," she said after they were seated, addressing him in a formal and respectful manner. "May I ask how long you have known Mike Johnson?" She couldn't bring herself to say the word *father.*

"About twenty years. We were graduate students together at Temple University, and we ended up teaching at the same university."

"He was a professor?"

"English and American literature."

Naomi had always pictured him as an actor, a singer, or maybe even a professional baseball player. Certainly not an academic. And certainly not in Japan all this time. A bitter bile rose in her throat when she realized she could have passed him on the street.

Or maybe she had sat next to him on a train. Or worse, what if he had been a customer she had served beer to at Commando? What if she had flirted with him?

Naomi mustered up a neutral voice. "Are you aware that the last time I saw Mike Johnson was when he deserted my mother and me twenty-five years ago?"

"Miss Naomi, didn't you know your mother was the one who left him?"

That wasn't what she had been told.

"But your father always said she had been right to leave. That everything had been his fault."

Unpleasant memories of being teased for having neither a mother nor a father bubbled to the surface. She had learned at a young age what people meant when they talked about women who had babies but no husbands. Later, she discovered that when the baby was *half,* with no father in sight, it was far, far worse. And if your mother committed suicide on top of that, there was only one explanation. Everything was *your* fault for being born. Brushing a tear off her cheek, she asked, "Do you know what happened between them?"

"Not exactly. But I do know the root of the problem was your father's drinking."

Naomi wondered if her breath still smelled like last night's tequila.

"But that was back then. I've known your father for more than twenty years, and I never saw him take a drink. Not even once. He always said AA saved his life. I also know he spent years looking for you. He even hired detectives."

"Detectives?" Naomi noticed the wet spots on the table—her tears—and realized the last time she had cried this much was when she was in elementary school and her dog got hit by a car. Her grandfather smacked her hard to make her stop, but he did nothing to her cousins, who were the ones who had let her dog out of the garden in the first place.

"I-I can't believe he was looking for me all this time." She reached in her bag for another pack of tissues. What would her life have been like if he *had* found her? If he had taken her away from her grandfather, who could barely stand to look at her? From her cousins, who could get away with anything because they were boys? "How did he find me?"

Sakaguchi Sensei averted his gaze while Naomi blew her nose. "Some months back, your father saw your picture in a magazine, and he knew it was you because you looked just like him. That gave the detectives something concrete to go on."

Naomi had to think for a moment because it had been quite a long time since she had done any modeling. Then she remembered—it had to have been for that beautician in Harajuku who needed a haircut model last spring. The morning of the shoot she had been so hung over, she almost canceled. The only thing that had propelled her out of bed that day was the promise of a free haircut.

"After the detectives tracked you down, Mike visited your grandparents in Shizuoka—"

Naomi's head jerked up. "He went to see my grandparents? And they didn't tell me?"

"I gather things did not go well with your grandfather."

A searing hot anger burned away the tears. Of course, Grandfather would keep her father's visit a secret. Of course, he would decide that not telling her would be for the best. It was always better to ignore anything uncomfortable or unpredictable. Naomi wanted to kill him.

"Once Mike had your basic information, it wasn't hard to find where you live and where you work."

"Where I work?" she repeated in horror. Why couldn't it have been a bank, a brokerage firm, a department store, or even a supermarket? Anything would have been better than a bar where all the foreigners go to get drunk. "Why didn't he contact me?"

"I guess he was waiting for the right moment."

Naomi's tears reappeared, and she dabbed them away with the tissue. "All my life, I thought he had deserted us. That he didn't want us. That he had gotten married and had a whole different family. I thought he had forgotten me."

"Your father never forgot you," Sakaguchi Sensei said quietly.

"He never married?"

"He did, but he never had other children."

"Where's his wife now?"

"Nanako died of breast cancer—about ten years ago."

"Oh. I'm sorry to hear that."

Just then, Ashley burst through the door and strode to their table. Naomi sprung to her feet and let her friend's arms surround her in a hug. In a voice as rough as sandpaper, she whispered. "I'm so glad you're here." She saw Ashley's blue eyes flash toward Sakaguchi Sensei, sizing him up to determine if he was somehow responsible for Naomi's tear-stained face. "This is my father's friend," she said, introducing them.

"It's nice to meet you," Sakaguchi Sensei said, also switching into English.

"I'm sorry," Naomi said, turning to him. "This is too much for me to process all at once. Could we talk about this later? Maybe tomorrow?"

"Of course." He circled his home telephone number on his business card. "Go home and get some rest. Call me tomorrow. I'll help you with the funeral. My wife and I will help you."

Naomi nodded and put the card in her wallet. "Thank you for your kindness. I couldn't do this alone."

CHAPTER THREE

"Do you want to go home?" Ashley asked as they headed toward Shinanomachi Station, her arm around Naomi's shoulder.

Naomi shook her head. "I just had to get away from there. I couldn't take any more."

"Do you want to go get a drink?"

"Oh god, no."

Ashley leaned in to sniff her friend. "Well, some people get to party on the weekends, but others spend their Saturday nights covered in baby poop and spit-up spinach."

For the first time that day, Naomi let out a genuine laugh. "You love every moment of motherhood, and you know it."

"That's true," Ashley said, flinging her long blond hair behind her shoulder as she flagged down a taxi. She looked far more like a fashion model than a high school English teacher from Texas. "I do. But I took Emily over to Hiroshi's parents, and I'm not about to let this opportunity go to waste. You can have tea, but I'm having wine."

By the time they settled into a tiny Italian restaurant in the basement of an old building near Shinjuku's West Exit, Naomi had filled Ashley in on what she had learned from Sakaguchi Sensei. She had also changed her mind about the wine.

"I knew that would happen," said Ashley, wiping her hands on one of the hot towels the server had brought to the table.

"Yeah, me too," said Naomi.

"Okay. Talk. Tell me how you feel about all this."

Naomi took a sip of the wine. "You know that I've always wondered about my father. Now I find out he's been in Japan all this time. I guess I just didn't expect that."

"But at least now you know he didn't forget you. That he was always looking for you."

"I suppose. But I'd feel better if he wasn't dead."

"I'm sure you would."

"The thing is, I kind of feel bad that I don't feel worse about him being dead and all. I mean, I'm *sorry* he's dead, of course. I'm sorry I won't have a chance to meet him. But it's weird that I don't feel *more* emotional about it."

Ashley topped off their wine after the server had removed their antipasto plates and set down bowls of minestrone soup. "That's understandable. You didn't know him."

"But now I'll never get the chance to."

"You'll get to know about him, though. I know it's not the same as if you had met him, but it's still pretty damn good. Look at what you learned from his friend. He was a professor. He lived in Japan. He was married once. You have no siblings. You didn't know any of that stuff before, but now you do." Ashley broke off a hunk of the bread and dipped it into a bowl of garlicky olive oil. "Maybe you'll discover you have other relatives as well. Maybe even cousins."

"I didn't even think about that."

"And if you do have any, they could hardly be worse than the ones you've already got."

Naomi laughed, but after a few moments, she said with a hint of pride, "Can you believe he was a professor? At Yamanote University, of all places?"

"Well, of course I can. You got your smarts from somewhere and obviously not from those Kiharas. Look at how much you like to study and how much you like to read. And now we know why."

Naomi nodded at the server, who had come to remove their soup bowls. "It *is* good to know that my father wasn't just some random foreigner my mother hooked up with."

"Your cousins are idiots for putting that idea in your head."

Ashley had met Naomi's family only one time, not too long after they both had started working at Friendly English Conversation School—Ashley as a teacher and Naomi as a receptionist. Ashley wanted to see some Japanese countryside during the summer break, and Naomi needed to make her annual visit home to pay respects at the family grave. She invited Ashley to come, believing her family would be more bearable if she had a guest with her. But she had forgotten how her carefully cultivated Tokyo persona always disappeared around her family. Her confidence evaporated. Her posture became hunched and her voice became soft and hesitant. She scurried about like a mouse whenever her grandfather, her uncle, or her cousins demanded something. Naomi had been mortified letting Ashley see that side of herself, and she thought she had made a huge mistake by bringing her there. During that overnight visit, Ashley remained polite and quiet—an ideal guest. However, she flashed her a secret smile when Yusuke or Keisuke acted particularly idiotic. She gave Naomi the slightest of slight eye rolls when Grandfather huffed out one of his conservative pronouncements. On the way back to Tokyo, Ashley squeezed Naomi's hand and said, cementing their friendship, "You're worth a million of them. And don't you ever forget it."

Naomi sprinkled parmesan cheese on the cod roe pasta the server had set down and picked up her fork. "Can you believe my father started out as an English conversation school teacher? Sakaguchi Sensei told me he was teaching at one when he met my mother. And—oh god. Do you think the pattern is repeating itself with Tyler?"

"Are you planning on having a baby with that jerk?"

Naomi shuddered. "Of course not."

"Your father may have started out as an *eikaiwa* teacher in an English conversation school, but look at how he ended up. A professor. Tyler will still pretend to be a hotshot at Friendly when he's in dentures and diapers. He's been there now—for how long? Five years?"

"Six. At least. He was already a head teacher when I started working there."

"See? What a loser. I mean, who stays forever in *that* dump? That place is infamous for being the worst of the worst among conversation schools. You know that. One year was more than enough for me," Ashley said with a scoff. After deciding to marry a mild-mannered book editor named Hiroshi and remain in Japan, she landed a permanent position as a regular teacher in a private girls' high school.

"Well, there is Beer Belly Bob. He's been there a lot longer."

"Yeah, but everyone knows he can't do anything else because of his forged degree. Granted, Tyler's BA in television history from that fly-by-night university isn't much better. But here in Crazy Land, a degree is a degree is a degree." Ashley broke off another piece of bread. "Even *you* jumped Friendly's sinking ship."

"I didn't have any choice about that, did I?" Naomi replied wryly. To save money, the conversation school had laid off all the Japanese office staff and forced the Japanese teachers to double up on teaching and administrative work. "Pouring beer at Commando isn't any better."

"True. But you and I both know that's just temporary. Look at how many times in the past few months the convention center has called and asked you to come and work the trade shows. You aced their English test."

A smile spread across Naomi's face. "I did, didn't I?"

"And who else at Commando did that? Tell me, which one of those fools you work with passed that test?"

"No one. Just me." Considering she was also the only one who didn't go to college, that was an achievement Naomi was tremendously proud of.

"It's just a matter of time before they give you enough work you can quit Commando. I mean, look at you. No one can speak English like you do. Maybe you could even take those college classes that you've always wanted to. Or go back to Australia. Go to college there."

Naomi nodded. Any of that would be fantastic if it weren't for one minor detail: her dismal bank account.

"I just don't understand why you don't break up with Tyler once and for all. I know you don't like to hear it, but he's a creep."

"Oh, come on. He's not *that* bad."

"I guess you could say he's not as bad as a convicted felon or a terrorist. But I keep telling you, you deserve someone nicer. Someone who cares for you. And being nice one day out of three doesn't count, you know."

"I know, but—"

"You've got to stop being afraid of being alone. That's what the real problem is. There are worse things in life than that. And you've got to stop letting people walk all over you."

"I don't do that."

"Yes, you do. You're always way too nice and you never say no to anyone. Just because the men in your family treated you like dirt doesn't mean you deserve to be. Tyler's not for you, and he never was. I don't blame you for drinking too much when you're around him, because how else could he be even halfway bearable?" Ashley reached for the bottle. "More wine?"

"Well, gee, after that, no thanks," Naomi replied, laughing. "You finish it up. I'm going to order coffee. And then I'd better go home and call my grandmother. I want to know why she didn't tell me my father had visited them."

"Do you want me to be with you when you call?"

"That'd be seriously great, but I should do this on my own."

Ashley reached across the table and patted Naomi's hand. "You'll be fine."

"I'm so glad you're my friend."

. . .

Naomi pushed open the door to her apartment and wrinkled her nose at the smell emanating from the trash bags. No wonder the police had acted so persnickety that morning. And that growing pile of clothes in the corner would not march itself down to the laundromat and hop into a washer. The last thing she wanted to do today was laundry, but unless she wanted to start wearing dirty underwear, she had no choice. First, though, she needed to call home.

"Granny," Naomi said as soon as her grandmother picked up the house phone. "Why didn't you tell me that my father came to see you last month?"

There was a long moment of silence. "I guess that foreigner found you, anyway."

"That foreigner is dead, Granny. He had a heart attack." Not giving her grandmother a chance to react, she pushed on, unable to keep her voice from wobbling. "He didn't leave *us*—my mother left *him*. You knew that, didn't you? He didn't desert us like everyone made me believe. Why have you been lying to me my whole life?"

"Your grandfather…"

Naomi sighed. Whatever her grandfather thought to be best was the *only* way of doing things in the Kihara household. "Granny, did you know that my father had been living in Tokyo all these years? Did you know that he'd been looking for me the whole time?"

"I—"

Naomi choked back a sob. "If you had told me he had visited, I could've met him. I could've met my father before he died."

Granny's voice broke. "I'm sorry. I wish things could have been different. I wish your mother—"

Naomi sighed. There was no point in blaming her. "Never mind, Granny. It's in the past. Can't change it now."

"If you want, I'll come to Tokyo."

The thought of Granny replacing her old-lady farmer clothes with that outfit reserved for special occasions and heading for Tokyo's urban metropolis put a sad smile on Naomi's face. Her last trip to Tokyo for a family funeral had traumatized the old lady for weeks.

"No thanks. That's okay."

"Then why don't you come home?"

"I have a funeral to plan. I'm going to be the chief mourner."

"Chief mourner? Really? Well, I have some *hesokuri* if you need it for the funeral."

"Thanks for offering, Granny. Someone from his university said they would help with all that."

How could Naomi stay angry at the woman who had raised her like a daughter, especially when she had just offered her secret savings? Poor Granny. First under her mother-in-law's oppressive thumb and then that woman's son. Her life had been tough, that's for sure, but at the same time, she was Naomi's *only* ally in the Kihara family. In fact, if it weren't for Granny, she never would have been able to go to Australia when she was sixteen. She had been accepted for a prestigious study abroad program, but of course, Grandfather opposed, saying she would just get herself into trouble like her mother did. Her uncle, aunt, and cousins echoed his words, and no matter how much Naomi cried and pleaded, he wouldn't budge. All that work Naomi had put into learning English—watching American TV shows over and over again. Studying every grammar point in her English textbooks and repeating the example sentences a hundred times. Reading every English book in the school's tiny library. All that seemed to have been done for nothing.

But Granny put on her special outfit, went to the high school, and came back with her homeroom teacher. It was only after Yamato Sensei convinced Grandfather that Naomi's acceptance into the program would bring honor to the family that he allowed her to go. Of course, learning it wouldn't cost him a single yen—it was a fully covered scholarship—didn't hurt, either.

So, Naomi had her year abroad, living with a nice Indian family in a Sydney suburb. Even with all that English study under her belt, she could barely communicate when she arrived. The first two months were awful, but then it got easier because she began to understand what people were saying. She made friends. She joined the school's art club and went to the countryside with them to sketch the scenery. She studied hard and borrowed books from her favorite teacher.

In fact, she began to envision becoming a teacher herself.

Her dreams were squashed when she got back to Japan. As far as her grandfather was concerned, her year abroad had completed her education. The family resources needed to go toward her cousins' education and not toward a girl who would ultimately marry into a different family. Feeling hopeless, Naomi did the bare minimum to finish high school, and the day after graduation, she left home and headed to Tokyo. For a few months, she stayed with a friend from her art club who had graduated a year earlier and was attending a trade school. After working double shifts at convenience stores, restaurants, and bars—she saved up enough to move into shared housing. The conditions there were something awful, but the steady stream of foreign tenants meant her English kept improving. And simply by being in the right spot at the right time, she landed a job as the receptionist at Friendly English Conversation School. The pay was low, but she got to use English all day long. Sometimes all night long as well, because by that point, she was almost never without an American, Australian, or British boyfriend.

"Well, what about a black dress?" said Granny. "Shall I send you one?"

Naomi hadn't planned that far ahead. "That'd be great. Thanks."

Next, she called Tyler.

"What's up?" he asked cautiously. He probably thought she was going to get after him about Kaori again.

"My father died."

"Oh, Jesus," he said, sounding contrite. "I'm sorry to hear that, Naomi. Do you have to go back to Shizuoka?"

"It's not my grandfather. It's my *father*."

"What? Your biological father?"

"Yeah, crazy, huh?" Naomi inhaled and spoke evenly. "I didn't even know he was in Japan—" She lost track of her thoughts when she heard him urinating in the background. "Um, anyway, the police found my contact info in his briefcase. I had to go make arrangements this morning."

"Like next of kin?"

"Yeah."

"Shit. That's kind of cool, huh? Just like in the movies."

Naomi ignored that comment. "Get this, Tyler. He had private detectives looking for me. For years."

"Private detectives? That costs shitloads of money. They aren't cheap, you know. They charge by the hour."

Leave it to Tyler to miss the important point of all this.

"Maybe you'll get some money out of him. After all, you are the long-lost daughter. Maybe you should get a lawyer or someone to look into it."

She didn't mention her father's lawyer had already called, and she was going to meet with him after the funeral.

"So, listen, do you want to get together tomorrow afternoon? I'm off, and I know you don't have to go into Commando until late, right? There's a game, and some of the guys are going to Dubliners to watch it."

"I don't think so."

"Oh, right," he said, as if he just remembered why Naomi had called. "Do you need me to come over tonight or something? I could come and comfort you."

"Oh, god no. I mean, no, that's okay. Thanks for offering, though."

"Anyway, when's the funeral?"

"Wednesday. The wake's on Tuesday."

"Okay. I'll definitely be at the wake, but not too sure about the funeral, though."

Naomi knew Wednesdays were Tyler's day off. Of course, he wouldn't want to waste his free time on something so boring as a funeral for someone he didn't know. A wake, on the other hand, usually had plenty of free food and booze.

Ashley was right. Being with Tyler was not better than being alone.

CHAPTER FOUR

Naomi sat between Ashley and Sakaguchi Sensei during her father's funeral service at Tokyo International Church. Ashley squeezed her hand while the minister spoke about his volunteer work for a homeless shelter and while his friends and students gave moving eulogies. When a girl from his seminar class read Robert Frost's "Stopping by Woods on a Snowy Evening" aloud, sobbing echoed throughout the church. Naomi swallowed her envy towards the people who had known her father and stared down at the floor.

When the service was over, she stood next to the coffin and bowed to a long line of people paying their final respects. Her feet ached from the tight black pumps, and her pantyhose felt like they would split down the crotch at any minute. After the last mourner departed, a short, balding man approached Naomi and murmured something while handing her his business card.

"Who was that?" asked Ashley after he turned to leave.

"Mr. Matsumoto. The lawyer. I have to go to his office tomorrow and settle things."

"Tomorrow? So quick?"

"Yeah. I hope the condolence money people brought covers the cost of all this," Naomi whispered. Now that the church was empty, her mind returned to her low bank balance. She hadn't been to that many funerals before, and never to a Christian one.

She couldn't remember what her relatives had paid the temple priest when an elderly cousin passed away, but she thought it was somewhere in the neighborhood of three hundred-thousand yen. And that was just for the chanting. What this was going to come to, she had no clue. "I don't suppose you know," she said to Ashley with a wry smile, "what the going rate for a kidney is?"

. . .

The next day, Naomi tugged at the skirt of the suit she had bought when she interviewed for her receptionist job at Friendly English Conversation School. It still fit, but barely. She was ushered into Mr. Matsumoto's office and offered a seat across from his desk.

"I hope you don't think this is rude of me to ask," she said as soon as she sat down, "but will there be enough money to cover the funeral?" It was best to be upfront with the fact she was pretty much broke.

The lawyer studied her from behind his tortoise-rimmed coke-bottle lenses, and Naomi felt foolish when she realized he probably knew plenty about her financial circumstances. "Miss Kihara, you needn't worry about that."

Naomi exhaled in quiet relief. Even if she had to take on another job, she would *never* ask her grandfather for money. Figuring she would be on her way as soon as she signed some papers, it was a surprise when Mr. Matsumoto asked if she would like tea or coffee. Despite his balding head and conservatively cut suit, Naomi realized he was much younger than she had first thought.

"Oh, I don't want to be a bother," she murmured. But from the way he was looking at her, he clearly expected her to choose. "Well, coffee would be wonderful. Thank you."

A few minutes later, the secretary came in with coffee and strawberry tarts piled high with whipped cream.

"I have a terrible sweet tooth," Mr. Matsumoto said, smiling and showing a mouthful of uneven teeth. "Please, go ahead."

Naomi stirred the cream and sugar into her coffee and nearly swooned when she bit into the tart.

"Good, isn't it? It's from my favorite shop in Ginza."

Naomi nodded and took another bite. If she ever needed a lawyer, Mr. Matsumoto would be her guy, for just the cakes alone. She was wondering how much they cost and if it would be rude to ask where the bakery was. He was talking, but she was focusing on the creamy custard and buttery crust. But something he was saying got her attention, and the strawberry she'd been saving for last suspended halfway between her mouth and the plate.

"I'm sorry. Could you repeat that?"

"I said your father made you his heir, and as a result, you have inherited Mr. Michael Bernard Johnson's entire estate."

Naomi's mouth moved a few times—like a fish in an aquarium. No sounds came out.

"I see you are surprised." He watched her from above his coffee cup.

She squeaked out, "But he didn't know me at all."

"That is true. In fact, I had even suggested it might be a good idea for him to wait before making such a decision. He wanted everything to be finalized, but at least he agreed to wait until the test results were back before signing everything."

"Test results?"

"The DNA test," he continued, not noticing her shock. "The detective he had hired took a glass you had drunk from at your workplace. He had it tested, so there would be no doubt you are his daughter."

"Is that legal?" Naomi asked, feeling violated. "To test people's DNA without their knowledge? I mean, if he had these doubts, then why would he—"

"Miss Kihara, your father wanted to make sure that there would be no question if someone should decide to contest the will. He wasn't checking to see *if* you were his daughter—he didn't want anyone else to doubt it. You, and *only* you, were to be his heir."

"Oh."

"Of course, no one expected he would pass away at such a young age. Therefore, it was most fortuitous that he had made these prior arrangements. Now, are you ready? We haven't much time."

"Time for what?"

"But first, let me tell you that there is the condominium. I have not been there, but Miss Matsuda, my secretary, visited it yesterday. She said it was a little untidy but quite large and nice."

"Condominium?" Naomi repeated dumbly.

"Yes, in Shinagawa. It's one hundred and five square meters, and the estimated value is," he said, looking down at his notes again, "ninety-two million yen. Because he had mortgage insurance, it is now paid in full." He went on, not noticing that Naomi's jaw was practically dragging on the desk. "And there is the cash and an insurance policy. I estimate you will receive fifteen-million-yen cash after all the funeral expenses, taxes, and other bills are paid. Of course, this does not include the American assets." He looked up from his notes. "Oh, I see you have finished your tart. Would you like another one?"

"What? Oh no, thank you. Could you please say that again?"

The lawyer smiled kindly, as if Naomi wasn't all that bright. "I can help you with everything on this side, but your situation is complicated because of the property in the United States."

"Property in the United States?"

"Oh yes. We will have a Zoom meeting in a few minutes with Mr. Jason Perry."

"Who?"

"Your father's American lawyer, of course. He will fill you in on all those details." He wiped the corners of his mouth with his napkin and stood up. "Miss Kihara, I recommend you use the washroom now if necessary because we will talk to America soon. I must do so myself, so please excuse me. The ladies' room is just outside the door."

Before he left the room, he turned around. "I believe you speak some English. Is that correct?"

All Naomi could do was nod.

"Good. Because there is much to discuss concerning your farms."

Farms?

Even though she didn't have to go, she stumbled into the ladies' room and leaned on the sink, taking deep breaths in front of the mirror. She smoothed down the wisps of curls that had escaped from her ponytail and returned to Mr. Matsumoto's office to find him trying to get a Zoom conference going. While his secretary came in to sort out which buttons needed to be pushed, Naomi kept from fidgeting by clasping her hands together in her lap.

"Well, Naomi," boomed a voice when Mr. Matsumoto turned the computer screen toward her, "I'm Jason Perry. First, I just want to say how sorry I am about your father. I've known Mike my whole life, and well… it was so unexpected. Our whole town is still reeling in shock."

In shock herself, all Naomi could do was nod at the man.

"Okay, here it is in a nutshell. There are two farms. And your great-grandmother's house. Oh, and I'd better not forget to tell you there are also houses on the farms as well. Barns and some other buildings, too. Now, in addition, there's—" The man stopped and frowned at the screen. Then, upping his volume, he said, "Should I repeat that a bit more slowly? Do. You. Understand. Me?"

"Yes, Jason," she said, skipping any honorifics and speaking more sharply than she had intended. She was *not* hard of hearing, and nor was she mentally challenged. "I understood everything you said. It's not the English that's the problem. It's just that all this is an awful lot to take in. Until an hour ago, my biggest worry was whether I'd have sufficient funds to pay for Mike Johnson's funeral."

Mr. Matsumoto's head jerked toward her in surprise, and Naomi knew his opinion of her had shot up a dozen notches. Just because she worked in a bar and didn't go to college and major in English literature didn't mean she was stupid. Her English was just as good, better, in fact, than any of those college students she worked with. Half of them wouldn't recognize a book even if one flew up and whacked them in the face.

"Of course," Jason said. "I'm sorry."

From the way the corners of his mouth were twitching, Naomi doubted if he was sorry in the least. She was tempted to ask him if he really was a lawyer because, from what she could tell, he was sitting in a kitchen! And what kind of lawyer had such long curly hair that he kept brushing out of his eyes? They were supposed to look more like pudgy Mr. Matsumoto and not like someone who looked like they had just come in from a long hike.

"I can imagine this is all an enormous shock for you," Jason said. "I've known your father for a long time, and he told me that finding you made him the happiest man on earth. His only regret was that he couldn't tell his grandmother about you because she died just before that. She was ninety-five, so I guess it wasn't entirely unexpected."

Ashley was right. Here comes a whole new family. "I'm sorry to learn," Naomi said, returning to politeness mode, "that my great-grandmother has passed away as well."

"Excuse me, Miss Kihara," Mr. Matsumoto interjected in heavily accented English. "We must proceed now with the explanations. Taking too much of Mr. Jason's time is most wasteful."

"My time isn't a problem, but Shin-itchy's right," Jason said, leaning back in his chair and crossing his leg over his thigh. "There's an awful lot to talk about."

Naomi stifled a giggle. Shin-itchy? She'd never be able to think of Mr. Shinichi Matsumoto as anything else.

"So anyway, let me start over. There's a house in the town. That's Felix, Nebraska, in case you don't know. And there are the two farms, each 160 acres. Now, the farms have been in your family for more than a hundred years. I believe your great-grandmother's grandparents homesteaded one and the other one was bought in the early 1900s. And well, the farms belonged to your father's grandmother."

"Oh, okay." Naomi had no idea how she was supposed to respond to any of that.

A long, heavy silence filled the room. Mr. Matsumoto became antsy, as if there was some sort of computer glitch on his side, and he started jabbing at the computer.

But then Jason spoke. "I don't know if you know anything about the accident."

"What accident?"

"What's wrong with me? Of course, you wouldn't have heard about the accident. How could you? What happened was this," Jason explained in a soft voice. "About thirty years ago, your grandparents, your father's brother, and his wife and baby were killed in a head-on collision. As well as a carload of teenagers. It was one of the worst accidents the state ever had."

Ten minutes ago, Naomi didn't even know she had relatives. And now she learned they were all dead? "I don't know what to say. That's so awful."

"Evelyn, your great-grandmother, was home that day. And Mike had just gotten out of the navy and was over in Japan. They were the only two people left in the Johnson family. So when your great-grandmother died several months back, Mike inherited her estate. And now that your father is gone, everything belongs to you."

"But I don't know anything about farming."

"Miss Kihara, you grew up on a tea farm, did you not?" Mr. Matsumoto said, getting a word in.

"I did," she replied, turning to face him. "But I had little to do with that. Sometimes I helped, but I didn't do much." Her grandmother had insisted that she stay out of their fields, that it was no fit work for a young girl. Her grandfather agreed because even with the modern farming conveniences they now had, he didn't want his granddaughter ruining her body (and thus, her chances of marriage) with backbreaking work.

"Well, you won't have to worry about the day-to-day details," Jason said. "You have tenants who farm for you. My father managed both farms for Evelyn—legal matters and accounting." He took a sip from the University of Nebraska mug that was in front of him. "But I'll be doing all that for you now instead of him because he's retired."

"What exactly are my responsibilities?" Naomi asked. "I mean, if I'm the owner of these farms? I guess what I'd like to know is how this farm ownership thing works. To be honest, the only thing I know about tenant farming is…" Naomi closed her eyes to think before adding, "from *The Grapes of Wrath*." When she saw the look on both men's faces, she stuck her chin out. "I like to read."

Jason threw back his head and laughed. "You're thinking of sharecroppers. And fruit pickers. Great book, by the way, but an entirely different situation. Lots of people around here, especially retired farmers, rely on tenants. They're usually locals with farms of their own or the children of locals who want to get into farming."

"So, it's not exploiting anyone?"

"It's not exploiting anyone. Both sides benefit. There's a contract between the farm owner and the tenants to protect both of you. They do the actual farming, and you get a percentage of the profits. But you pay for the seed, and you pay the taxes."

"Miss Kihara," Mr. Matsumoto said. "Do you understand to which extent the land you own is?" When she shook her head, he wrote what 320 acres were in square meters and slid the paper across the desk.

"Holy shit!"

"Farming is always a bit of a gamble," Jason continued, unable to suppress his smile this time. "Some years you make good money, and some years you don't. But you own the land, free and clear. And that's really something."

"There is one more important issue," said Mr. Matsumoto. "Shall I tell her now?"

From the way Mr. Matsumoto was looking at her, Naomi wondered if she should prepare herself to receive some bad news. Like maybe the whole thing was a big joke, and they were going to take everything back. He cleared his throat. "Your father wished you to take his remains home. For burial."

"Oh, okay."

"And," he said, "your father requested you remain one year. In Felix—"

"The thing is," Jason said, interrupting, "your father thinks—well, I guess I should say, he *thought*—you might want to sell the farms. Of course, it would be within your rights to do that, but he wanted to give you a chance to discover your roots first. To learn more about who you are and about where you come from. Before you can sell the farms, you must come here for a year. Could you do that?"

"Yeah, sure. I guess," Naomi answered, wondering where in the world was Nebraska?

•   •   •

"Felix, Nebraska!" exclaimed Ashley. "Where in the world is that?"

"I don't even know where Nebraska is." Naomi had collapsed on a small bench next to the first-floor elevators of Mr.

Matsumoto's office building and called Ashley as soon as she could. Her legs were shaking so much they couldn't get her out the door, let alone to the station.

"Straight north of Texas and right in the middle of the United States. Oh, no! Keep talking. Emily's just spilled juice all over the table." When she returned, Ashley said, "So your father's from Nebraska? Two things come to mind: corn and football."

"What about beef?" Naomi said, remembering something that Jason had mentioned.

Ashley scoffed. "Hey, I'm from Texas. Nebraska beef is small potatoes in comparison."

"Yeah, yeah, yeah. Everything is bigger and better in Texas."

"You've got that right, darling," Ashley said with an exaggerated drawl.

Naomi also laughed, but then said, "I didn't know *anything* about my father, Ashley. A week ago, I was going about doing my own thing, and then, wham! All this." Her voice had a hysterical edge to it.

"What are you complaining about? You're like the star of your own rags-to-riches story."

"I'm not complaining. It's just weird."

"I guess you never imagined anything like this happening to you."

"You know me, I don't even buy lottery tickets." Naomi's voice caught, and she brushed away a tear that was forming in her eyes.

"So you've got to go to Nebraska?" said Ashley. "For an entire year?"

"Yeah. Go figure. It's going to be my first overseas trip since I was a teenager in Australia, and it's to some place I've never even heard of. Some place I just learned how to pronounce."

"And when is this life-changing event going to take place?"

"As soon as the paperwork's done, I guess. Apparently, there's quite a lot. Mr. Matsumoto can take care of the Japanese stuff. Or, maybe I should call him Shin-itchy Matsumoto, like my American lawyer did. Did you ever think you'd ever hear *me* talking about my two lawyers?"

"I can't say that I have. One maybe, but definitely not two."

"Ha. Ha. Ha. Anyway, after all that gets sorted out, I'll go to Nebraska." Naomi rolled the name off her tongue again. "Doesn't that sound exotic?"

Ashley snorted. "Not really."

"Anyway, my father registered my birth at the American embassy and somewhere I've got a birth certificate. So Jason said I should be able to get an American passport."

"Jason?"

"My American lawyer. Listen," Naomi said, finding strength in her legs to carry her to the station. "I'll call you tomorrow. I've got to get going, or I'll be late for work."

"What! You're going to keep on at Commando? After this?"

"I know it's crazy, but I need that job until I don't have to worry about paying the rent."

"But wait a minute. What about your father?"

"What do you mean?"

"Where is he now?"

"He's in the urn."

"Yeah, but *where*?"

"Where? In my apartment. On the table. Where else could I put him?"

CHAPTER FIVE

Several weeks later, Naomi stepped into her father's Shinagawa apartment, carrying a wooden box containing his urn.

"Jeez, it smells like someone died in here," Tyler said, leaving Naomi's two suitcases right next to the *genkan* entryway.

Ignoring his comment, she set the urn on the table, pulled back the curtains, and opened the balcony door to let in fresh air. There wasn't much of a view because of the building across the street, but sunlight from the southern exposure filtered in and brightened the room. Unfortunately, the sunlight also highlighted the tobacco-stained wallpaper and the grimy carpet.

"Holy crap! Would you look at that TV? Look at all those DVDs!" Tyler zoomed toward the shelves next to the enormous flat-screen TV attached to the wall. "There's some seriously good shit here. Did your old man like classic sci-fi or what?" After a quick examination of the shelves, he switched on the TV and loaded *Alien* into the DVD player. "Have you ever seen this? It's a real—"

"Not now, Tyler. There's just too much to do." Naomi turned around and sighed. She had only asked him to come and help because Ashley was on a trip with her in-laws that had been planned for months. She thought an extra pair of hands, even Tyler's, would come in handy. What a stupid idea that had been.

"Oh, all right," he said with a huff. "I guess at least we can have some music, right? There're lots of good oldies here. My dad used to play this all the time." Tyler put Pink Floyd's *Dark Side of the Moon* on and turned the sound way up.

Naomi glared at him and turned it way down.

"What a waste to have a sound system like this if you can't blast the roof off," he muttered loud enough for her to hear.

Naomi turned away to survey the apartment, which was surprisingly tidy. Sure, there were books and papers scattered about. Everything was covered with a fine layer of dust accumulated over the past few weeks. A pair of socks and a sweater were on the sofa and a coffee mug with a thick layer of moldy milk was on the coffee table. Still, it was pretty evident that some sort of regular cleaning took place, even if it did smell musty. She stepped into the kitchen and squealed with excitement over the built-in dishwasher and oven.

Tyler followed her and started poking around the cupboards until he found an array of imported olives, crackers, and other snacks. "I bet you anything there's some pretty fine wine stashed away to go with all this fancy shit."

Considering her father had been a recovering alcoholic, Naomi thought the chances of finding any booze in his kitchen were pretty slim.

"Why don't I pop out," Tyler said after an unsuccessful search, "and go get something? We can have it when we watch movies later."

Wine sounded good, but Ashley was right—she did drink too much when she was with him. And then, they always ended up fighting. The way things were going so far today, it probably wouldn't be any different. While he was out, his phone buzzed on the table. He must've been in such a hurry to get the booze, he forgot it. A minute later, it buzzed again. This time, she picked it up. When Kaori rang three more times over the next five minutes, Naomi had a pretty good inkling that all those rumors were probably true.

After Tyler came back, she went to put the wine in the fridge, and when she returned to the living room, he was bent over his phone.

"Say, Austin wants me to meet him in Shibuya with some of the guys. It's Matt's birthday and—"

"Well, don't let me stop you from going." His flimsy lie bothered her more than him sleeping with that twenty-year-old know-it-all.

"Jeez, Naomi. Just forget it."

In that moment, Naomi knew they were through. She was about to tell him but snapped her mouth shut. Why get into a fight now when all she wanted was to be alone in her new apartment?

He wasn't the only one who knew how to lie, so she rearranged her face and put on a tired smile. "I'm sorry for snapping at you. I've got a terrible headache. A migraine." She rubbed her temples, imagining that's what people with migraines would do. "It just came on. Maybe you *should* go. I think I need to lie down. Have an early night."

"Are you sure?" Tyler frowned cautiously, as if this was a trap.

"I'm sure."

"Because I don't mind staying and helping you." As he spoke, his arm inched toward his coat that was thrown across the chair.

"I'm sure. Say hi to Austin for me. And tell Matt happy birthday." But if he said he was taking the wine with him, she'd brain him with the bottle. Apparently, he was too eager to get going to endanger his life. Lucky for him.

After bolting the door, Naomi leaned against it and gulped down deep breaths of relief. She poured herself a glass of wine all the way to the top and looked around in disbelief.

This apartment, and everything in it, was *hers*.

• • •

"Go on. Tell me. What's the big surprise?" Ashley asked as soon as they settled into a booth at lunchtime at a crowded Denny's near Ashley's school.

"I could have told you over the phone, but I wanted to see your face."

"What? Did some other relative die making you next in line for the British throne?"

"Ha. Ha. Ha."

"Well then, what is it?"

"I broke up with Tyler."

"Seriously?"

"Seriously. I sent him a text. We're through."

Ashley raised her eyebrows. "A text? How brave."

"I did what I had to do."

"You won't call him again in two days saying you made a mistake?"

"Nope. This time it's for good."

"And what about Commando?"

"Yesterday was my last day." Naomi attempted a sad face but was failing by a mile. "He and Kaori are welcome to each other. I'm done with him. I'm done with cheating guys. And I'm done pouring drinks for them. Of course, he's running around telling everyone I dumped him because I came into money."

"What a jerk. Who cares what his friends think? Like I've always said, you deserve a lot better."

"Yeah, I know I do. But I have to admit, my father made it a lot easier for me to—what is it you always like to say? To see the light?"

"It's good to know your new lifestyle of the rich and unemployed is helping you through such a time of lonely sorrow."

Naomi snorted. "Anyway, I can't wait for you guys to come over on the weekend to see the place now. I even got a few toys to entertain Emily."

The server set their lunches in front of them, and they dug right in, knowing that Ashley only had twenty minutes before she had to get back to the high school.

"The next thing to tackle is the paperwork inside my father's desk, and Jason's going to help me with that." She reached for the Tabasco bottle and sprinkled it all over her rice-filled omelet. Ignoring Ashley's look of disgust, she added an extra layer of ketchup. "Starting from tonight."

"From tonight, huh?"

"Uh-huh. By Zoom."

"How come you're grinning like you've just told me you've got a hot date lined up?"

CHAPTER SIX

On the other side of the world, Jason was on the phone with eighty-eight-year-old Shirley Nelson. She was having cold feet about turning her farm over to her forty-year-old grandson, Allen, and this was her umpteenth phone call on that subject alone. Her family had finally gotten her to leave the farmhouse she'd been living in for the past sixty-five years and move into a smaller house in town just a stone's throw from Main Street. By the way she was carrying on about it, you would think they had sent her off to the gulag.

"No problem, Shirley," Jason said, glancing at the old grandfather clock in the corner and noticing that Sharlene had hung his Stanford Law School diploma back up on the wall again. "I'll be glad to stop by and go over the contract with you one more time. All righty. See you tomorrow."

Jason debated putting his diploma back into the file cabinet, but knowing his assistant would just get it out again, he left it for now. He gathered up some papers, slipped on his jacket, and hurried through the icy wind to his Ford Explorer parked downstairs. Laughter was coming out of Bob's Bar, the only establishment still open on Main Street. Mondays were chicken wings night, and even the churches' teetotalers made an exception to stepping across the threshold of a bar when it came to five different flavors of wings. His stomach was growling, but he needed to get to the nursing home before his father went to sleep.

At the entrance, Barney, the arthritic golden retriever that used to belong to Old Man Peterson, hoisted himself up and gave a weak bark when Jason stepped in but was appeased by a few pats on the head and scratches behind the ears. Most of the residents had already retired for the night, but Jason greeted those who were still in the common room watching TV.

"How're you doing, Dad?" Jason asked when he stepped into his father's room.

"Not too bad at all, are we?" said Kelly Jefferson, answering for Ron Perry while buttoning his pajama top. "We played bingo after dinner and Ron won a candy bar. Then we watched *Dirty Harry*. Again." Kelly rolled her eyes and smiled at Jason. All the old folks loved seeing Clint Eastwood get the bad guys.

Ron pushed Kelly's hand away. "Get away from me, you silly billy nurse. I know you stole it. It was mine and you can't have it." Then he turned to his son. "You! You're back again. Don't think I don't know why you're here. I won it fair and square, and you've got to give it back to me."

"That's okay, Dad. It's in your safe deposit box at the bank. I'll bring it for you next time."

"Well, see that you do, Mister Whateveryourface is. Otherwise, I'll get my son to sue you. He's a hotshot lawyer in a big fancy law firm in… in… somewhere. He wouldn't put up with nonsense from the likes of you. Coming in here to steal my prize. I know the two of you are in cahoots, you pair of dirty boots!"

Jason changed the subject after Ron was settled into bed and Kelly had left the room. "So, Dad, did you see the game tonight?"

"Boy oh boy, I sure did. That really was something, eh?"

"Really something," agreed Jason. Talking about an imaginary football game for the next fifteen minutes was far more pleasant than being accused of stealing his father's track and field prize. It was true Ron Perry had received such an award from Felix's mayor back in the 1960s. But he never went all the way to the White House to get it from President Nixon himself.

The sedative to keep Ron from wandering around in the dark was taking hold, and his eyes drooped. After he had drifted off, Jason leaned over the bed and kissed his father on the forehead. "I'll see you tomorrow, Dad."

"He did pretty good today," Kelly told Jason when he stopped by the nurses' station to say goodbye. "You may not think so but visiting him every day like this makes a difference. I think deep down inside, he knows it's you."

"I'd like to believe that's true."

Kelly came around the counter and looked up with a hopeful smile. "Do you want coffee or something before you go?"

"Thanks, but I've got to get home and do some work."

He felt her eyes on his back as he walked out the door. Kelly looked pretty much the same as she did when she was a cheerleader back in high school, but it was no town secret that she was on the lookout for a replacement after Brad had run off with a kindergarten teacher from Schuyler, leaving her with three kids. After overhearing two women in the Husker Market gossiping in the cake mix aisle that Jason was back on the market after his divorce, he was plenty careful. The last thing he needed was to get tangled up in another relationship he didn't want.

"Hey Jason," called Doc from the back booth in the Quik Stop on the highway where Jason had stopped in for beer and breakfast supplies. "Grab some coffee and come join us."

Jason glanced at his watch and nodded. After pouring a cup from the self-service counter, he slid in next to Todd Thompson, who, pushing eighty, was just as slim and spry as he was when he was the town vet. "Can't stay too long," Jason said. "I've got some long-distance calls to make."

"To Mike's daughter?" asked Doc, eating a chocolate ice cream bar despite the freezing weather outside.

Jason nodded. The whole town was abuzz with gossip now that word was out that the long-lost daughter everyone had forgotten Mike ever had in the first place was his sole heir. "We're getting everything sorted out before she comes to Felix."

"So, it's true then," said Doc. "She's coming here."

"Yep," answered Jason. "For a year. Mike wanted her to get to know her American roots."

"What's she like?" asked Todd.

"She's the spitting image of Mike. No doubt she's his kid, that's for sure. Regardless of what some people are saying."

Todd chuckled. "I'm real sorry Mike's gone and all, but between you and me, I'm not a bit sorry the Hardys got diddly-squat of the Johnson money. Serves that riff-raff right."

Jason nodded as he finished his coffee but said nothing. He agreed with Todd, even though six months back he had cautioned Mike about changing his will to leave everything to a Japanese girl he knew nothing about. He slid out of the booth and tossed his paper cup into the trashcan. "I'd better get going. See you tomorrow."

"I'll go out with you," said Doc, scooting his chair back and slipping his arms into his overcoat. "I want to go up to the nursing home before it gets too late and check if Fred Nelson's meds are helping with his pain. The weather report said it's going to get pretty icy, and I don't want to get called out in the middle of the night."

Todd looked like he'd be calling it quits and heading home as well, but when John Brady, a retired farmer with rheumy eyes, came in and headed for the coffee, he settled back into the booth. The old vet was recently widowed, and Jason knew he was in no hurry to get back to his empty house.

Jason, on the other hand, could hardly wait to get back to his house. During the three minutes it took to drive there, he reflected on his daily routine, which began in the morning with coffee at the Up Town Café and ended with coffee at the Quik Stop.

Maybe it wasn't the most exciting life in the world, but his father had lived like this for years, and Jason didn't mind following in his footsteps. He pulled his car into the garage, grabbed his briefcase, and connected the engine to the block heater so it would start up in the morning despite the below-freezing overnight temperature. He turned the house thermostat up a few notches, popped a frozen teriyaki dinner into the microwave, cracked open a beer, and took the latest issue of *The Nebraska Lawyer* out of his briefcase. Thumbing through the journal, he sipped the beer while sitting at the old Formica dinette set and marveled at how different his life was now compared to those seventy-hour weeks he used to put in at Sullivan and Conner. The evenings were long. Sometimes lonely. But they were his, and he was fine with that.

When Marvilla Middleton called two years ago and demanded he come do something about his father, he told Heather and her father that he'd be gone for a week. Two max. But it took all of five minutes to see his father couldn't live alone any longer. And he certainly couldn't practice law anymore, either. What was Jason supposed to do about his father's clients? They had all depended on Ron Perry, and when Jason came back to Felix, they turned to him.

He imagined that those first few weeks back in Felix were what going through rehab must be like. The "withdrawal" was something awful. He missed his San Francisco home. He missed his job. He missed his BMW convertible. He missed his closetful of Armani suits. He missed the country club. He even missed Heather. Sort of.

The second month was different. It was almost as if a blinding fog had burned away. Why was he working himself to death at an excruciatingly boring job to pay for an overpriced home that was too uncomfortable to relax in? And all those Armani suits? They made him itch. He never had time to go to the country club to make the exorbitant fees worthwhile. And Heather was—well, she was still Heather.

Jason didn't want to leave his father in Felix and go back to California. He realized he had lost sight of what he had always wanted: to be a lawyer like his father and his father before him. He liked taking care of *people*—their wills, their contracts, their divorce settlements, and their labor disputes. He liked being someone who frantic parents could count on when their teenagers got arrested for minor offenses. The turning point was when ninety-year-old Floyd Knudson stopped by the office to ask about setting up a trust for Sparky. As he drew up the papers to ensure that the tomcat would have a happy old age, which included a lifetime supply of high-end cat food, he decided. He was going to stay. Corporate law was going to have to get along without him.

"How could you do this to me?" Heather's face had contorted with anger when he told her. "To my father? After everything he's done for you?"

There wasn't anything he could say to that. It was true that marrying the boss's daughter hadn't hurt his career, but that wasn't why he married her. He had been an awkward geek his entire life, and he couldn't believe his luck when Heather chased him all the way to the altar. Ignoring his father's gentle warning that they might not be all that suited for each other, Jason went along with everything Heather wanted—from an enormous Catholic wedding presided over by the Bishop, to buying a house he never could have afforded if his father-in-law Jimmy Sullivan hadn't given most of the down payment to his daughter as a wedding present. For the Sullivans, another hundred grand or two or three wasn't such a big deal, but for Jason, his share was nearly every penny he had.

He had been blinded by Heather's beauty and sharp wit, but it didn't take long to discover how different they were. He had to tell himself that no one had forced him to marry Heather and that a vow was a vow. So he went along with whatever she wanted every single time.

Until he returned to Felix.

Once his mind was made up about that, he wouldn't budge. Heather reluctantly joined him, but four months was all she could take.

The microwave dinged, and he removed the teriyaki dinner with one of Heather's hundred-dollar potholders. He couldn't do anything about the stainless-steel refrigerator, German dishwasher, induction range, marble countertops, and solid oak cabinets she had installed after gutting his favorite room in the house. He missed how cozy the kitchen used to be, but at least he hadn't let her throw away the old dinette set. There were just too many childhood memories attached to it, so he stored it in the attic. After Heather left, he hauled it back down and gave the one she had ordered from a New York designer to a pair of teenage newlyweds.

When he finished eating, he went to brush his teeth and run a comb through his hair. Unless he wanted to be one of those guys sporting a ponytail, he had better stop in at Ralph's Barbershop one of these days. In San Francisco, his hair had been trimmed by a stylist every three weeks, but it had been almost three months since Ralph's scissors had come anywhere near his head. He studied his reflection in the mirror and decided to change into sweats after talking to Naomi.

CHAPTER SEVEN

Naomi's father's 27-inch screen iMac provided her with quite a different view of Jason than Mr. Matsumoto's 13-inch laptop had for their previous meetings in the law office. It was almost like sitting across from him in a restaurant. He wasn't what you would call handsome, at least not in a movie star kind of way, but he had a face a person couldn't forget. His blue-grey eyes, which were lined with pale lashes, shone with warmth, and when he smiled, they crinkled upwards. His dusty blond hair had a few streaks of silver, even though Naomi was pretty certain he was nowhere near forty.

She glanced down at a text message that had just come in from Ashley. *Don't forget. Or you could end up regretting it.*

All right, all right! Naomi texted back.

"Look," she said to Jason. "I'm sorry, but there's something I need to know. My friend says American lawyers charge for every ten minutes of their time, and if that's the case, I don't want to waste my father's money by chatting and—"

"Well, I suppose your friend isn't entirely wrong. That certainly would have been the case at my former firm. In fact, you'd already be out a hundred bucks for these first fifteen minutes, but—"

"Oh my god, so that means—"

"Wait! That's not how I do things. I'm sorry to laugh, but you should see the look on your face. Listen, if I billed by the minute in Felix, I'd end up bankrupt without a single client. I've worked like that before, and let me tell you, that takes all the fun out of practicing law. For me, it's not about the billable minutes, it's about developing close human relationships."

The word "relationship" brought an image to Naomi's mind that went far beyond a lawyer/client one, and she felt a blush creeping up her neck. She cleared her throat and put on a neutral expression. "Well, that's good to know. Anyway, should we start? I still don't want to waste your time."

"I bet Shin-itchy told you to say that. Am I right?"

"That's exactly what Shin-itchy did," Naomi said, imitating Jason's pronunciation. "So, shall we get down to business?"

"Not so fast. That's not how we do it in Nebraska," Jason said with a wide grin. "First, the small talk. Usually about weather or crops. And then, of course, any local gossip. Since you probably aren't very conversant about crops yet and you don't know anyone in Felix to gossip about, I suppose it's got to be about the weather."

Naomi laughed, and they chatted easily for a few minutes before Jason cleared his throat. "I suppose now we really should get down to business. First, I want to show you something."

Jason shared his screen, and Naomi stared at the numbers on a bank statement.

"Is that dollars or yen?"

"Dollars."

Naomi was silent for a moment. "That's a lot, isn't it?"

Jason nodded. "I wasn't even aware this account existed until after I found the bankbook in Mike's files. Other than yearly updating to keep the account from going dormant, Mike never touched a penny of it. Judging from the date the account was opened, I'd say it was from the insurance payout. You know. From the accident."

Naomi felt another pang of regret for losing a family she had never known. "But how come he never—"

"My guess is he felt guilty for profiting from their deaths. Guilty for being the only one who was still alive."

"Do you think that's why he drank?"

"I wouldn't be the least bit surprised."

Naomi looked down at her tee shirt and worn jeans. "I guess I can afford to get a new outfit."

"I guess you can."

"What about a new water heater? The old one doesn't work well."

Jason laughed. "There's quite a bit you can get now, Naomi." He brought a mug to his lips and took a sip. "I hope you don't take what I'm about to say the wrong way, but I've seen people run through their inheritances at a breakneck speed, buying things like boats, cars, snowmobiles. And end up with nothing."

"I know how to be careful with money, and I can give you a hundred percent guarantee I won't be buying anything crazy like that."

"Listen, why don't we figure out an amount you can use to kick start your new life? A new outfit, of course. A hot water heater. What else do you need?"

They agreed the tobacco-stained wallpaper and discolored carpet needed to go. The sofa with cigarette burns in the arm, too.

By the time Naomi's wishlist was completed, it was getting late, and they still hadn't tackled her father's desk. They agreed to meet again the following day—night for Jason and morning for Naomi.

■　■　■

They went through Mike Johnson's desk, drawer by drawer, and while they chatted, Naomi sorted the contents into four piles: to send to the university (mainly student reports and meeting agendas), to throw away (expired coupons, memos, and to-do lists), to examine more carefully later (official looking stuff in Japanese), and things related to her father's Nebraska affairs. The last drawer was on the bottom left-side, and under a stack of files was a small wooden box. She set the box on the desk and opened it.

On top was her American birth certificate. Naomi picked it up to examine closely. "My middle name is Evelyn," she said, her voice wobbling a little. "I never knew I even had a middle name, let alone my great-grandmother's."

"It's a beautiful name, Naomi. It means," he said, doing a quick search on his computer, "Wished for child."

Naomi smiled wistfully as she took that in.

Next were the reports from the detectives her father had hired. As soon as she saw the picture of her doing shots at Commando, she shut the file. Jason certainly didn't need to see that. She lifted out something bundled together in a purple silk *furoshiki* cloth. She unfolded the cloth and found a small stack of notebooks. "Journals," she said as she wrapped them back up and returned them to the box.

"Aren't you going to read them?"

"Aren't journals supposed to be private?"

"Maybe when people write them. But not when they're... not when they aren't here."

Naomi wasn't sure she wanted to delve that deeply into her father's private life. "Maybe I'll read them later."

"People generally write diaries because they want to leave a record of their lives. Maybe he wanted you to read them someday."

.   .   .

A few weeks later, Naomi walked Jason through her apartment on her new iPad. Her father's desk was cleared out and there was no more business for them to deal with, but they still talked every day. Sometimes more than once.

"From now on, smokers will just have to go out on the balcony," she said, settling down on her new cream-colored leather sofa.

"You stayed under budget. Right?"

"Yes, Mother. Absolutely."

"Remember—"

"I know, I know. I have to live within my means. Well, I know how to live like a poor person. I have no problem with that."

"You're not poor. Far from it. But—"

"Don't worry. I have no intention of plowing through the money," she said, quoting his words right back to him, amused by the cute frown on Jason's face.

She didn't say anything about last week though, when she blew her own savings—every single yen in her old bank account—in an art supply shop where she had stopped in to buy a sketchpad and some pencils. When she was filling out the forms to have everything delivered, she wondered if she had lost her mind spending 95,000 yen all in one go like that. But this, she had decided, was to be her inheritance present to *herself*. She set up an art corner in the brightest spot of her apartment and started drawing again for the first time since high school.

"Did you get your American passport yet?" Jason asked, bringing her back to the here and now.

"Not yet. But I did get that—um, you know—security number thingy."

Jason snorted. "Oh, I bet there was no problem with *that*. The IRS loves new taxpayers."

"Anyway, as soon as the passport gets here, I'll book my ticket. But I still have to go see my grandparents. Maybe tomorrow," she said with a sigh. "Or the day after."

"Why do you keep putting that off, Naomi? Don't you want them to know what your father did for you? Don't you want them to know you're going to America?"

"Of course, I do. But..." Even though Naomi had told him about her family, she was pretty sure he had no idea how awful they really were.

"I bet you haven't even read your father's journals yet, either." After a long moment of silence, he asked, "What are you afraid of?"

"I don't know. I guess there could be all kinds of things in them I don't want to know about. I don't want to have a reason to hate my father, not after all this," she said, her arm sweeping across the room.

"Listen, Naomi. I knew your father. He wasn't perfect, but he wasn't a bad person."

"I just can't understand why my mother would leave him and go back to her parents' house. Because if being with *them* was better than being with my father, he must've been pretty bad." Naomi inhaled deeply, and then sighed. "Maybe it's better not to know."

"Like not knowing anything about your American family? Were you better off not knowing about them?"

CHAPTER EIGHT

Naomi called her grandmother to tell her she'd be coming home later in the week. Then she watched a couple of episodes of *Buffy the Vampire Slayer* from her father's DVD collection. Well, ten, to be exact. After lighting some candles and incense, playing Sudoku on her phone, thumbing through a fashion magazine, and putting the finishing touches on a sketch she had made of some children playing in the park, she padded to her father's desk at 1:00 a.m. and retrieved his journals.

As she carried them back to the living room, a yellowed snapshot of her parents fell out of one. Her mother was obviously pregnant, and they were having a picnic under blossoming cherry trees, laughing like they were having the time of their lives. Naomi could have stared at the photo all night long but set it in the bookcase to be framed later.

While arranging the notebooks in chronological order, she found loose papers folded inside one—a draft of a letter to her. Much had been scratched out, but what she could read went like this:

Dear Naomi,

I know you probably don't remember me at all, but I think of you every single day. I can't believe it took me all these years to find you, and...

Tears pooled in her eyes and streamed down her face as she continued reading. Her father described his elation when he saw her photo in a hair magazine and how the private detective could track her down after having that to go on. He wrote about his visit to her grandparents and of his shock when they told him about Yumi's suicide. He apologized for having been too self-centered to recognize her mother's depression and for not getting her the help she had needed.

The letter dropped into Naomi's lap as she processed those words. All these years, no one in her family had ever even hinted that her mother had suffered from depression. Her grandfather rarely spoke of his daughter, let alone of her suicide. But her cousins, especially when they got older, made her feel that her mother killed herself because of the scandal she had brought upon the family—and Naomi was living proof of that scandal. But depression? That was *never* mentioned. Naomi felt a sharp pain lodged somewhere between her heart and her stomach when she considered the possibility that there had been a clinical reason why her mother wasn't able to stand living any longer.

Of course, depression would have been a taboo subject. Of course, it would never have been mentioned. Grandfather wouldn't have been able to stand the thought of the neighbors thinking that Yumi Kihara was crazy and that insanity might run in the family.

Rubbing her eyes with the sleeve of her shirt, she returned to the letter. Her father wrote that even though he had loved her mother, he had loved alcohol back then even more. No matter how much Yumi had begged him to give it up—because she refused to marry him unless he was sober—he couldn't. He lied. He screwed up. He promised. He screwed up again. The breaking point was when he had taken Naomi to the park. Instead of watching her like he was supposed to, he drank highballs sold from a vending machine in front of the liquor store across the street until he passed out. A concerned passerby thought two-year-old Naomi was lost and took her to the police station where a hysterical Yumi found her six hours later. The next day, they disappeared. *Your mother,* her father had written, *put you first. As any good mother would. It wasn't until after I lost you both that I pulled myself together.*

He got sober a year later and started searching for them. Unfortunately, knowing Yumi was from somewhere between Tokyo and Nagoya wasn't much help. *I couldn't believe my luck when I saw your picture while thumbing through a magazine when I was waiting to get a haircut,* he had written. *I knew immediately it was you, and an hour later, I hired another detective to track you down. That was the day my life irrevocably changed.*

Naomi yanked a handful of tissues out of the box on the coffee table and blew her nose. What if her father had brought his own book to the barbershop that day? What if a different magazine had been sitting on the table? What if she had just gone back to sleep the morning of the photo shoot like she had wanted to?

I'd give anything, the last paragraph started, *to go back in time and start all over again. I want you to know that I have always loved you. I can never make up for the lost years, but I hope you let me into your life and that we can have a future together. Your father, Michael Bernard Johnson.*

Naomi put the letter, which was now spotted with tears, back into the journal. She stood to stretch her legs by the window and looked down at the traffic below. Even though it was nearly two in the morning, the hum of taxis and cars five flights down was still audible. She considered running to the convenience store for ice cream, but that was becoming too much of a midnight habit, especially after cutting back on the booze. How long had it been since her last drink? Ten days? Two weeks? She wasn't quite sure. But after reading about her father's struggles with alcohol, it was a relief to realize she hardly thought about it now that she was away from Commando Shot Bar. And away from Tyler.

She brewed a pot of tea, picked up a tangerine from the bowl on the kitchen counter, and with her legs tucked under her, she settled back onto the sofa and opened the oldest journal. At first, the writing was practically indecipherable. Drunken nonsense. Thirty pages in, it changed.

He wrote: *I haven't had a drink for ten days.*

Ten days after that: *I haven't had a drink for twenty days.*

And then: *I haven't had a drink for six weeks.*

After being sober for several months, he described his first AA meeting. He had just gone to see what it was like, but an older man referred to as "T" began talking to him and shortly after that, became his sponsor. Her father wrote about how "T" had talked him out of going to the liquor store in the middle of the night many times that first year. He wrote about how the two of them had hiked and bowled and swam—anything to stay away from the bars, to stay away from the booze.

Naomi learned of her father's milestones—about getting his master's degree and his job at Yamanote University. About his doctoral studies. About his grandmother in Nebraska. About getting married to Nanako and how her death from breast cancer three years later almost caused him to drink again. She learned about his double life of keeping one foot in urban Tokyo and the other in rural Nebraska. She felt his sadness when his grandmother died and his disbelief when he saw Naomi's picture. He even described the details of how he had set up his will to ensure Naomi's future. Tears streamed down her cheeks when she read how he had hoped and prayed that she would allow him to come into her life.

Mike Johnson didn't write in his journal every day, week, or month. But whenever he did, it always began the same. Including his last entry, dated on January 31, a week before he died: *I haven't had a drink for twenty-six years, nine months, and five days.*

•　•　•

"I did it," Naomi said when Jason picked up her call. "I stayed up all night and read my father's journals. And there was a letter explaining what had happened. About why my mother left."

Jason watched her for a few moments, before asking in a quiet voice, "How do you feel?"

"You were right. It *is* better to know what had happened. But it's weird. I know you won't believe this, but it never occurred to me that my mother had depression. All these years, and I thought... well, I thought she just wanted to leave. To be free of everything. If I hadn't been born, she wouldn't have had to marry that old—"

"Ah, Naomi," he said, her name sliding from his lips. "None of that was your fault."

"It didn't feel that way growing up. All these years—I never once connected my mother's suicide to depression. Now, it seems so obvious. How could I have been so blind? So stupid?"

"You weren't blind or stupid. You were just a kid."

"I know. But still." Naomi's eyebrows had knitted into a deep frown when she added, "What if I'm like my parents? What if I get depression? What if I become an alcoholic? Or what if I get the best of both worlds and become a depressed alcoholic?"

"Your mother was who she was and your father was who he was. That doesn't define who you are. Or who you have to be."

The sun was high in the sky when Naomi finally climbed into bed. While drifting off to sleep, her thoughts were not of her parents or of what could have been. They were of Jason—his kind eyes, his sweet smile, and his gentle voice.

CHAPTER NINE

"*Tadaima*," Naomi called out, announcing she was home. She slid open the heavy wooden door of her grandparents' farmhouse and slipped off her shoes, stepping up onto the wooden floor, and turned around to arrange them with the toes pointing outward.

"Nao-chan! I didn't expect you so soon." Granny hurried out of the kitchen, wiping her hands on a floral apron. Her crooked grin exposed two gold teeth. "The bus from the station isn't due for another forty minutes."

Naomi dropped her bags and bent down to give her a hug, even though the Kiharas were not ones to display affection. "I took a taxi."

"Taxi," the old woman whispered in horror. "Why, that must've cost a fortune."

"Oh, I had some taxi coupons that were about to expire," Naomi lied, not wanting her to worry. There was only one bus an hour to her village, and on top of that, a ten-minute walk up the hill loaded with gifts for the family. It was worth the splurge. Besides, she wanted to spend as much time with her grandmother as possible before anyone else came home.

"I'll make tea while you pay your respects," Granny said.

Naomi put on a pair of slippers designated for guests and shuffled down the wooden hallway. She slid open the paper *shoji* doors, stepped out of the slippers, and padded across the tatami floor to the *butsudan* that housed her ancestors' spirits. She kneeled before the alter that held photos, sweets, and an Ozeki One Cup Sake (for her great-grandfather, who was reportedly fond of the stuff), lit an incense stick, placed her hands together in prayer, and bowed deeply.

"He came back, Mama," Naomi said to the youngest photograph on display. "My father came back. He was sorry for what he put you through and for how things ended up. I-I want you to know that he did right by me in the end." Naomi stood to leave, but turned around. "And another thing. He stopped drinking."

She went into the kitchen, which was the same as it always had been. The dining table dominated the room, and on it was a lacquer tray with a teapot, different-patterned teacups belonging to each family member, and a wooden bowl filled with an assortment of sweet and savory snacks. Alongside one wall was a stainless-steel sink and a two-burner gas stovetop with a small drawer-like oven under it for grilling fish. A dish cabinet took up the opposite wall, and a utility cart in the corner held a rice cooker, microwave, and hot water pot. The lingering smell of grilled fish, simmered root vegetables, pickled radish, together with the thump-thump sound from the washing machine just off the kitchen, filled Naomi with sensory nostalgia.

Instead of the usual box of sweets purchased at Tokyo Station just before getting on the train, Naomi produced several Mitsukoshi Department Store bags.

"Oh, what were you thinking? Spending all that money?" Granny always managed to grumble and smile at the same time.

"Put the sweater on. Let's see how it looks." Naomi got the scissors out of the drawer and snipped off the tags before Granny could protest. Otherwise, everything would be put away, saved for a special occasion that would never come. As she helped her grandmother into the lavender cotton sweater, she noticed how frail she was. Her frame felt like it was made from dried out chicken bones. How old *was* she now? In her eighties? "Now, try on the apron."

Seeing the delight on her grandmother's face made Naomi feel guilty for putting off her visit for so long. If only there was some way to come home without having to see anyone else.

The thumping of the old washer came to a halt, and Naomi got up to help hang what she knew to be one of the many loads of the day. They slipped their feet into clogs and stepped outside. At the clothesline, Naomi decided to order a new large-sized washing machine for Granny as soon as she got back to Tokyo. And even though she knew her grandmother would hesitate to use such a contraption, she would get her a dryer, too. That would put her over her inheritance splurge budget, but she didn't care.

The morning passed. For lunch, Granny fixed Naomi's favorite: udon noodles and vegetable tempura. But then, her grandfather came home from his meeting with the neighborhood association, and the atmosphere in the kitchen became as heavy as if it was weighted down with a thick cotton quilt.

Naomi stood and bowed. "Hello, Grandfather."

He grunted a greeting and settled into his seat. He thumbed through the mail, and Granny placed a steaming cup of tea in front of him. "I heard about that funeral business," he said, after taking a noisy sip. "I don't know why you needed to get involved with matters that shouldn't have anything to do with you."

"Grandfather's right, Nao-chan," said a voice from the doorway. Despite the diminutive attached to her name, her cousin's tone was far from friendly.

"Elder Brother," she said, standing and addressing him like she had been brought up to do. She had given up bowing to him a long time ago, but Ashley said his continuous digs about her height were only because he felt bad that he was so short. So now Naomi stood next to him every chance she got. "What a nice surprise to see you," she lied, looking down at him. "I didn't think you'd be here."

"You owe nothing to that foreigner," Yusuke pontificated as he pulled out a chair and sat at the table. With a sneer, he added, "Except, of course, your appearance."

"Yusuke," their grandfather said, frowning. "Why are you home so early?"

"I had a dentist appointment. It wasn't worth going back to work afterward." He loosened his tie, reached over for a rice cake, popped the entire thing into his mouth, and began chewing with his mouth open.

Naomi saw Grandfather glance over at the clock. It looked like marriage and a soon-to-arrive honeymoon baby hadn't yet switched on Yusuke's responsibility button.

"You're right, Elder Brother," Naomi said, returning to the topic at hand. "It's true I don't owe him anything. I wish, however, that I had gotten to know him. My father, Michael Bernard Johnson—or I should say, Dr. Michael Bernard Johnson—was a professor at Yamanote University."

Because Naomi rarely volunteered any information, they all stared at her.

"My father," she pressed on, "was a brilliant man. I guess now we now know where *my* love of books comes from."

She let that sink in. If she had been given nine years to finish college like Yusuke, she would have had her master's degree by now. Maybe even a Ph.D. She wouldn't have needed two years of cram school to get in. She would have graduated on time and not wasted the family's money on game centers and all-you-can-drink bars. At least her other cousin Keisuke got in on his first try. But since he had never graduated, three years of his tuition was also down the drain. When her uncle got transferred to Osaka, Grandfather insisted they take Keisuke with them, thinking a change of scenery would make him leave his room. It didn't. Her aunt and uncle were probably stuck with him forever. Naomi couldn't help but think it served them right for having raised mean bullies.

Grandfather grunted, stuck his wife's reading glasses on his nose, and opened the newspaper. Yusuke's wife waddled into the kitchen in a pink maternity dress covered with green and blue teddy bears. Her yellow socks looked awfully tight around her puffy ankles.

"Elder Sister," Naomi said, feeling somewhat ridiculous since Sadako was actually a year younger than her. Most people wouldn't follow such archaic manners, but Yusuke, finding another way to keep Naomi in her place, insisted. She continued with her fake smile. "It's so nice to see you. And you look *really* radiant."

"How nice you could come to visit." Sadako spoke as if Naomi were a stranger. Perhaps she was worried her husband's cousin was planning to follow in her mother's footsteps by announcing a move home with an illegitimate baby.

Yusuke waggled his fingers in Sadako's direction, and like a trained monkey, she got him a beer. Naomi might have felt sorry for her for having such a pig for a husband, but she had gotten sick and tired of her going on and on about their damn honeymoon baby during her last visit, when everyone knew the baby was the reason for the wedding in the first place.

"Grandfather," Naomi said. "There's something I need to tell you."

The old man frowned over the reading glasses. Yusuke and Sadako exchanged glances, not even attempting to hide their smirks. It looked like they couldn't wait to hear what she was about to confess.

Naomi paused. Took a few breaths. Arranged a serious expression on her face. This was one sweet moment that could never be replicated, so she was going to play for all it was worth. "The thing is…" she choked out, giving quite a performance, "m-my father made me his heir."

Yusuke and Sadako's disappointment was palpable. They had been all huffed up, ready to light right into her, and seeing that fun sucked right out of them almost made her laugh out loud. Her grandfather harrumphed like it was no big deal and returned to his newspaper. But Naomi could tell his interest was sparked.

Yusuke snorted. "That loser? He didn't look like much at all when he came sniffing around here."

Naomi felt like she had just been kicked in the stomach when she realized even Yusuke had gotten to meet her father. "Loser?" She fought to keep her voice level. "Is that what you'd call a man who owns two farms?"

That got Grandfather's attention. "Two farms?"

"Yes. In America. A total of 320 acres." While their eyes pinged around at each other in surprise, she turned her attention to Sadako. "Elder Sister, I almost forgot. I got this for *you*. After all, you're eating for two, and it's a good time to indulge, right?" It was pretty obvious that Sadako had been indulging for quite some time, but probably not on anything as outrageously expensive as this enormous box of Godiva chocolates.

She knew Grandfather was trying to work out the metric conversion of acres, so she helped him out with that. "That American system is difficult, isn't it? It was quite a shock when I learned 320 acres is almost 1.3 million square meters."

If her family's jaws had dropped any further, she could have used their mouths as dustpans to sweep up crumbs off the kitchen floor.

"Why, that's bigger than our village," her grandmother gasped.

"Yes, it is," Naomi agreed, her eyebrows furrowed in a thoughtful frown. What she wanted to do, though, was jump on the table and dance a jig. Instead, she reached over, took one of the rice cakes off the plate, and nibbled at it. Then, almost as a casual afterthought, she added, "Oh, I forgot. There's also an apartment in Tokyo. And cash, too. Quite a lot, actually." She finished the rice cake and narrowed her eyes at her cousin. "I guess you could say we have different definitions of the word *loser.*"

Naomi put her teacup in the sink and turned around. "I wish I could stay longer and catch up on all the news. But I just came to say goodbye. I'm going to America next week to take care of things. Did I forget to mention the houses? Well, there's my great-grandmother's home—which I'll live in. And there're two other houses on the farms as well. Isn't it amazing," she said with a bright smile fueled entirely by adrenaline, "how everything turned out? My American lawyer tells me I never have to work again if I don't want to."

Ashley's voice was in her head when she was mentally asking Yusuke how he liked them apples.

PART TWO

CHAPTER TEN

"Yoo-hoo!" A squarely built older woman with a set of amazingly white and uniformly sized teeth was tapping Naomi on the shoulder. "Time to wake up!"

"Have we taken off yet?"

"Oh, my goodness, you were out like a light before the doors were even shut. I thought you might have died. I was about to ring for the stewardess, but when you started to snore, I figured you were just plum tuckered out." The woman reached into her purse and handed Naomi a paper napkin. "Here you go, dear. You might want to use this." She pointed at the dribble of drool running down Naomi's chin.

"Thanks," Naomi murmured as she wiped her face. Now that the seatbelt signs were turned off, everyone was eager to retrieve their belongings out of the overhead compartments. A lanky teenager in a cowboy hat reached over Naomi's head and pulled hers out and set it in the aisle for her. Then he retrieved her seat mate's bag as well.

"Why thank you, young man," chirped the woman. "That's mighty nice of you."

The guy tipped his hat, making Naomi feel as if she were a character in a movie. She followed the passengers, wheeling her bag containing her father's urn through the airport. In the few minutes it took to get to the security doors, the butterflies that

DIANE HAWLEY NAGATOMO 63

had been living in her stomach for the past few weeks turned into concrete ping-pong balls. What was she doing this far from home? For a whole year? She turned and glanced over her shoulder, wishing there was a rewind button she could push to do this crazy trip in reverse. She would even endure that four-hour delay in Minneapolis because of tornado warnings again if she could go home to her cozy Tokyo apartment.

"Naomi! Over here!" Jason, in a simple white button-down collar shirt and a pair of black jeans, was grinning and waving at her.

She took a breath, put on a smile, and headed toward him.

"There you are!" he boomed as he pulled her into a hug. "Finally!"

She rubbed her nose where it had banged on Jason's shoulder. She had been looking forward to meeting him for the longest time. All those Zoom talks. All those emails. All those messages. She felt like she knew him. But now, standing in this strange place, she wondered how different this was from women who got swindled by men they had met on the internet. Men, they believed they'd fallen in love with. Idiot, she reminded herself. She wasn't here because of *him*. She was here because of her *father*. This thing with Jason was something different. But what it was, she didn't know.

"Um, I have to go to the restroom." She handed him the pull-along suitcase handle and made a beeline toward the door, needing some time to gather herself. Inside the bathroom, pairs of feet were visible from under the doors and the sounds of people's bladders being emptied could be heard. Clearly, there was no manner mode button in American bathrooms you could push to play waterfall music to mask those sounds. She headed to the stall furthest from the entrance and was taken aback by the gaps in the stall doors. Not wanting to catch an accidental glimpse of someone, she fixed her eyes on the wall ahead and pushed into the stall. As the pressure on her own bladder was relieved, she remembered what Ashley was always saying. Something about Kansas. Something about not being in Kansas. Well, Naomi didn't know a damn thing about Kansas, but here she was now, in Nebraska. Even the bathroom disinfectant smelled strange.

Aware that her feet (and possibly even more!) were exposed for all to see, she tapped out a brief text to Ashley to let her know she had arrived. After mustering up the courage to leave the relative security of the stall, she washed her hands, splashed water on her face, and picked off flecks of mascara from under her eyes with her fingernails. She smeared on some pink lipstick and headed back.

Jason was waiting for her at the carousel, where bags were just beginning to appear. "Um, that one," Naomi said, pointing to an enormous hard cover purple suitcase. "And the big black one."

"All righty," he said, once the two oversized bags were on the luggage cart.

"Sorry, but there's more."

Five minutes later, two duffle bags big enough to contain several squirming children came bumping down the belt. The excess baggage cost nearly as much as another ticket, but how was she to know what she would need for an entire year?

"I guess it's a good thing I brought a truck," Jason joked, loading up a second luggage cart.

Naomi stole sideways glances at him as they wheeled everything out of the airport and into the heavy, humid air. He was tall—a full head and shoulders taller than her. She had kind of thought that he might be, but a person can't come right out and say in an online call, "Hey, stand up so I can see how tall you are," can they?

As Jason hoisted her suitcases into the back of a pickup truck, she slipped off the linen jacket she had bought a few days earlier for her getting-off-the-plane outfit and fumbled in her bag for a small hand towel to mop the sweat off her forehead. She pointed at her carry-on bag and said, "My father is in that one."

"Well, let's put him here behind the seats, shall we?" Jason opened the right side of the truck for her, and she climbed in. He went around and got in on the left, slipped on a pair of Ray-Bans, cracked the window to shoo out a few flies, and turned on the ignition. "Ready?"

She nodded.

"So," he said as he exited the parking lot, "how was your trip?"

"Oh, it was great." She didn't tell him about the awkward moment at immigration in Minneapolis when a large intimidating woman barked at her to get into the line for US citizens when she had stopped, brand new US passport in her hand, in front of the lines separating the citizens from the visitors. She didn't tell him she stuttered at the immigration officer—a scary guy with wild red hair and a porous nose—when he demanded to know why, according to his computer, this was her first American passport and her first trip to America. After he stamped it and waved her through the line, two other customs officers scrutinized her bags. One even swabbed the box holding her father's urn for explosives. While waiting at the gate for her connecting flight to Lincoln, she checked her purse to make sure her Japanese passport was still there.

She felt so Japanese.

Now, in the car, Naomi feared she might have turned mute because her ability to speak seemed to have disappeared. She kept her eyes glued to the window and thought about how different everything was from Tokyo. Even the McDonalds looked odd, with a parking lot ten times its size and filled with gigantic trucks. Other fast-food places were also unfamiliar. Jason asked if she had ever had something called a *runza,* and when she shook her head, he said they'd have to rectify that unfortunate situation soon. As they passed a place with a giant King Kong on the roof and little King Kongs scattered about in the front, Naomi managed to comment, discovering she could still talk, after all.

Jason chuckled in response, and pulling into a gas station, said, "Gotta get some gas."

"Are those pigs?" She pointed at the truck full of squealing animals on the other side of the gas pumps. Her voice sounded normal.

"Well, hogs, actually. Probably heading to the slaughterhouse."

That matter-of-fact comment rendered Naomi right back into silence. While Jason filled up the car and scraped off what appeared to be squashed insects from the windshield, she recalled Ashley's advice. *Fake it till you make it.* So she turned on her smile when Jason got back in the car and tried to pepper his small talk with intelligent responses.

Jason pulled onto the expressway, which he called the Interstate. "It'll be about thirty minutes more," he said after exiting onto a two-lane highway. He slowed down behind a farmer on a tractor and let three semi-trailers whizz by before overtaking him. They passed fields of what she learned were corn, oats, and soybeans. White two-story farmhouses. Grazing cows. Not a single traffic light.

"Welcome to Felix," he said, slowing down and turning left into a cluster of trees and onto what he said was Main Street. Two blocks later, he turned left again, and pulled up in front of a large, white, two-story house that was similar, but not quite identical, to the others on the tree-lined street. "Well, here we are."

Naomi clutched the door handle and peered up at what was to be her home for the next year.

"I'll bring in your things later. Let's get you inside and settled first. Get you something nice and cold to drink."

Naomi followed him past the petunias lining the sidewalk, up the front porch steps, and into the unlocked house, shoes and all. They had barely gotten in the door when a woman with a cake on a platter and a paper bag filled with vegetables marched in. Despite her bright pink pants suit, an extraordinary amount of turquoise jewelry, manicured nails, and mascaraed eyes, she seemed to be around Granny's age.

"I told Wayne you wouldn't need an entire bag of corn," the woman said. "So, I took a couple for myself. But these tomatoes are from my garden out back. Just picked them a little while ago."

It was the first time for Naomi to hear tomatoes pronounced that way: ta-may-dahs.

Then the woman grabbed Naomi, kissed her on the lips, and hugged her tight. "Oh, my poor dear, bless your heart. You must be exhausted after coming all that way from the Orient." Still clutching Naomi, she pulled back a little and peered into her face. "Well, well, well. Let me take a look at you. You look more Oriental than I thought you would. You've got those slanty eyes."

Naomi was too shocked to respond. No one had ever said such a thing to her before. *Ever.* No stranger had ever kissed her on the lips like that before, either. At least not when she was sober.

"But I guess they look all right on you. Look at your chin! Your cheekbones! Your freckles! Exactly like your father's. He had a dimple just like that—before he put on all that weight. I always told Mike he had to watch his weight. I always said—"

"Now, Marvilla," Jason interrupted, "let the poor girl catch her breath."

"Oh, my goodness, you're right!" The curls from her tightly permed hair bounced up and down. "You, my dear, are a sight for sore eyes." She reached inside her bra, pulled out a crumpled paper napkin, and wiped away a tear before pulling Naomi into a hug again.

"Naomi," Jason said, as he extracted her from the woman's grasp. "This is Marvilla Middleton. As you can see, she knows who you are. She's been living next door to your great-grandmother for about a hundred years."

Marvilla giggled and batted her eyes at Jason. "Now, don't be such a tease. You know it's only been forty years. After Evelyn moved in from the country."

Then she turned her attention back to Naomi. "I've stocked the fridge for you, dear. I didn't know what you liked, so there's a bit of everything. And I cleaned up in here as well. Your father was going to sort through Evelyn's things in the spring, but I guess he just couldn't wait to follow his family to Jesus. The house is still pretty much the way your great-grandmother left it."

Naomi followed them past a cabinet filled with framed photos and into the kitchen. Marvilla opened the fridge to find a place for her vegetables and motioned for Naomi and Jason to sit at the kitchen table. The house was at least fifty years older than her grandparents' house, so she had expected it to be falling apart. She thought it was going to be small and rugged—something like Laura Ingalls' house in *The Little House on the Prairie*. She knew all about that because, to prepare for her trip, she had reread the books and watched the entire TV series. The gleaming kitchen with walnut cabinets, clutter-free tiled kitchen counters, and polished floors was a surprise. Unlike the piles of clutter in Granny's kitchen, this one had homey decorative touches with a sunflower theme: the sunflower pictures, sunflower dishtowels hanging above the sink, and sunflower potholders draped over the oven's handle. The fridge, stove, and dishwasher were enormous. This was an *American* kitchen.

The black rotary dial phone on the counter exploded in a ring that made Naomi jump, and Marvilla rushed over to pick it up like she owned the place. "Oh, hi, Doreen. Yes, she's here. Just got in the door... That's right... Well, she looks a lot like Mike, that's for sure. But of course," Marvilla said, smiling brightly at Naomi, "her eyes are from her mother's side of the family... That's right... Uh, huh... Well, all righty, then."

Marvilla hung up and began pulling plates out of the cupboard. "That was Doreen. You'll be meeting her over at the Presbyterian Church tomorrow."

"To make the final arrangements for your father's memorial service," clarified Jason, taking a bite of the cake. "Say, Marvilla, this is really good."

"Well, it should be. I added two packages of pudding to the cake mix. What do you think, Naomi? Tasty, huh?"

Naomi was picking at the thick layer of chocolate frosting. "Um, it's very rich."

"Yes, isn't it? Some people cut corners and use Crisco or Oleo, but not me. I believe in butter. *Real* butter."

Naomi didn't have to answer because suddenly a new subject was flung at her.

"I know you're exhausted," said Jason. "So, we won't talk too much tonight. But I wanted you to know that Roger White's got a car he's not using, and he's agreed to lend it to you for the time being. I've put it in your garage, and it'll do until you get your own."

"Get my own what?" Naomi's teeth were coated with the buttery frosting.

"A car. No sense in renting one." He reached into his pocket and slid a set of keys across the table.

Naomi stared at them. "I- I don't know how to drive."

Jason started. "Say what?"

"You know, in Tokyo, it's not... I don't... Well, the truth is, I've never driven a car. Unless driving around in circles on the racetrack at Disneyland counts."

"And here we all were," Jason said, laughing, "arguing over what kind of car you should have. We were concerned about you driving in the ice and snow next winter. It never occurred to any of us you wouldn't know how! Oh, and before I forget, you can use this if you like." He took a phone out of his pocket. "It's Evelyn's old phone, and I thought you might find it handy for making local calls. All the numbers you might need are already in it."

Naomi nodded gratefully before Jason and Marvilla moved on to discuss what they should have for dinner. Naomi watched their mouths move, but now it seemed like they were speaking from the far end of a dark tunnel. Her head felt as heavy as if she were riding the Yamanote train line after midnight, and she closed her eyes for just a second.

"Just look at this girl, Jason. She needs her beauty rest," Marvilla said, tugging on Naomi's arm and jolting her out of her daze. "Let's get you up to bed."

"But my bags—"

"Jason can put them in the green bedroom. You can worry about them later."

"But," said Jason, "shouldn't we tell her about—"

"Oh, pooh. There's plenty of time for all that. The poor dear can't keep her eyes open any longer. Now, I fixed Evelyn's bedroom up for you because that's the nicest one in the house."

The oak floorboards creaked beneath their shoes as Naomi followed Marvilla up the stairs and into one of the bedrooms. Marvilla pulled a nightgown out of a tall chest of drawers and handed it to Naomi. "Here. You can use this. I found it the other day. Your father must've sent it to Evelyn because it has some of that funny writing on the label. But she liked to keep things back, yes she did. Lord knows what she was saving them all for. Now me, I like pretty things, and I believe in using them. Because, like I always say, you can't take them with you to the pearly gates."

Naomi let herself be pushed into the bathroom. After checking the lock, she sat on the toilet and peed while staring at the enormous clawfoot tub. She had no idea where her toothbrush was, but she washed her face with the bar of soap, and in the medicine cabinet she found a bottle of Oil of Olay, which seemed to be moisturizer. Evelyn's nightgown covered her body like a tent. She cracked open the door and peeked out. Seeing she was alone, she padded barefoot to the bedroom and climbed between sheets smelling of lavender and sank into the soft mattress. As she drifted off to sleep, she wasn't sure if Marvilla had just tucked the blanket in around her and kissed her on the forehead or if she had imagined it.

CHAPTER ELEVEN

Naomi's eyes flew open, and for one panicked moment, she didn't know where she was. Fumbling in the dark, she switched on the light. It all came back to her. She was in Nebraska, in her father's family home, wearing her great-grandmother's voluminous nightgown. A whirring sound came from an electric fan in the corner and the curtains fluttered in the breeze. It was only 2:30 in the morning, but she felt like she had just downed six mugs of double espresso. She climbed out of bed—the floor creaking under her footsteps—flipped on the light switch and stepped into the hallway. Her suitcases were lined up in what was indeed a green room. The walls were pale green, and so were the curtains and bedspread. She found her cosmetic kit and brought it into the bathroom, arranging her lotions and creams in an oak cabinet. The clawfoot tub looked like a great place for a nice, long soak, but just a slow stream of water escaped from its narrow spigot. Only someone with the flexibility of an Olympic gymnast could maneuver themselves under that for hair washing, she thought as she bent over the sink to give her hair a basic shampoo. Without a shower to wash herself before bathing, she sponged off her travel grime the best she could, and then climbed into the tub while it filled up. The water was about the same temperature as the room, so she didn't stay in for long.

After changing into shorts and a tee shirt and feeling a bit more like herself, she looked into the other rooms—one was pink and the other was light blue. Each had large beds, large dressers, and large walk-in closets. The blue room had been her father's—his clothes were in the closet and papers and books were piled up on a desk. Naomi was going to pretend she never saw the four overdue library books from Yamanote University on the bedside table. She picked up a framed photo of him as a teenager that she noticed on the dresser. Marvilla was right. Except for the eyes, she looked just like him, right down to the same spray of pimples she used to get across her forehead when she was a teenager.

She perused the books in the bookcase and took out her father's high school yearbook. His picture was on practically every other page. In the sports clubs—football, basketball, baseball. Track and field. Golf. And even swimming. There was a picture of him playing Captain Von Trapp in the senior class musical production of *The Sound of Music,* decked out in a uniform and standing with his seven children. He was king of some kind of event—homecoming—it was called. The closet held boxes of memorabilia—treasures of information—that she'd look at later. Suddenly, she was hungry. Starving.

In the kitchen, she hunted in the fridge for something to eat. Pushing aside Marvilla's cake, she settled on toast and a glass of milk.

While the bread was toasting, she looked around the downstairs rooms, feeling a bit like a burglar. The laundry room behind the kitchen not only had a big washer and dryer, there was also a shower, which would make personal hygiene a lot easier compared to using the bathroom sink. Next to the kitchen was a formal dining room with a large, polished mahogany table and a dozen polished chairs. A gleaming silver tea service was on the buffet, and crystal goblets and a floral-patterned set of dishes filled the china cabinet. Every wall and surface held framed photos of people in old-fashioned clothes. Some photos appeared to be more than a hundred years old, and the people's faces seemed stern and scary. The men had scraggly beards and wild-looking eyes, and the women had severe hairstyles and blouses buttoned all the way up to their chins. Other black and white portraits were probably from the forties and the fifties. She didn't know who any of these people were, but her eyes fell on the family portrait on the upright piano. She picked it up to see better and recognized her father right away, even with his goofy 1980s hairstyle. Next to him was a young couple with a baby. That had to be her Uncle Steve and his wife Cathy. Her cousin Alison. Her grandparents, Tom and Mary Johnson. The matriarch sitting in the middle was Evelyn, widowed quite a few years before that. Seeing their faces made that awful accident seem all the more real and wrenched Naomi's heart. No wonder her father had turned to alcohol—his entire family was wiped out in an instant. She wiped the dust off the picture with the hem of her tee shirt, put it back, and stepped into the office that was right behind the dining room. Like the rest of the house, it was meticulously tidy. She pulled open a drawer in the desk to find it filled with manila folders, each one dated and going back to the 1970s. Some sort of farm records, but they could have been written in Arabic for all the sense they made to her.

The living room at the front of the house appeared casual and formal at the same time. The lemon-colored sofa had lace coverings protecting its arms and back and looked like it was never used. The threadbare brown recliner and a similar blue one in front of the TV seemed to be where all the action was taking place in this room. Between those two chairs was a metal TV tray, piled high with twenty-year-old *Reader's Digest* magazines. Eerily, considering no one had been living in the house for months, a pair of reading glasses was perched on top of them.

Naomi went back to the kitchen to check on her toast. She slathered it with jam and took it out to the front porch. While eating it on the porch swing, she watched the darkened street. An owl hooted, and way off in the distance, she heard a car. She missed the lights and noise of Tokyo, and a wave of homesickness washed over her. How would she ever be able to last a year in this strange place?

People wore shoes in the house.

They ate huge hunks of cake.

They rambled nonstop.

Naomi was feeling mighty sorry for herself. Twelve months. Three hundred and sixty-five days. Three hundred and sixty-four, if you subtracted yesterday. One day at a time, she told herself. She could do it. She would force herself to. This was, after all, the chance to reinvent herself. To *become* a new person. She had done that when she was a high school student in Australia. Away from her grandfather, her uncle, and her cousins—who had chipped away at her self-confidence as if their biggest goal in life was to mold her into a lifeless statue—she blossomed. Of course, the minute she returned to Japan to complete her senior year of high school, she saw that she had changed, but they had not. Going to college was not going to be in her future, but neither, she quickly decided, was a marriage with one of the village boys, either. Just like her mother had done, she escaped the moment she could. Unlike her mother, however, who Naomi now knew had fallen in love with her father right after arriving in Tokyo, Naomi had a stream of bad boyfriends and had gotten stuck in a dead-end job. She never dreamed that she would be given an opportunity to start all over again.

This time, she would do it right.

She stared at the church across the street and inhaled smells she couldn't identify but knew were connected to the earth, to nature. Her eyes had become adjusted to the dark, and the moon was casting silvery shadows through the elm trees onto the steeple. "A year is nothing," she whispered in a voice that sounded stronger than she felt.

Suddenly, an idea popped into her head.

She stood, the swing bouncing behind her, and went upstairs to retrieve a sketchpad and pencils from her suitcase. Back on the porch, she studied the scene in front of her and began to draw. When the sun peeked over the horizon and the birds in the trees began their chatter, her sketch of the church was half done. Tomorrow, she'd do the trees.

Back in the house, she stretched out on the sofa and fell asleep until the banging on the screen door woke her up.

"Good morning, dear." Marvilla walked into the living room carrying a tray of freshly baked cinnamon rolls. "Are you feeling okay?"

Naomi slid her sketchbook behind a sofa cushion and wondered if Marvilla was going to make a habit of appearing at 8:00 a.m. "Yes, thank you."

"No wonder you were up in the middle of the night, considering you went to bed with the chickens."

"You were watching me?" That took her mind off of Marvilla's sandals on the carpet.

Marvilla tittered and shook her curls. "Oh, my goodness, no. I always check the lights over here when I go wee-wee in the night. Regular as clockwork, I am."

Naomi wasn't sure if Marvilla was referring to her bathroom habits or her spying activities.

"Oh, look. There're my glasses. I've been looking everywhere for them." Marvilla plucked them off the TV tray and set them on her nose. Then she picked up one of the *Reader's Digests* and put it in her purse.

The telephone rang, and Marvilla looked at Naomi expectantly. Unsure exactly how a rotary dial phone worked, she picked it up carefully. The person on the other end did all the talking, and all she had to do was say *yes* or *no*.

The phone rang again as soon as she set it down. This time, it was Jason. "How did your first night go?"

"It was okay, I guess. And now Marvilla is here."

"With her famous cinnamon rolls, I bet."

"And someone named Dorothy is taking me to the church today because I don't know how to drive."

Jason chuckled. "Who needs the internet when Marvilla's around to broadcast the news? But listen, I've got to go to court in Riley today, so how about I come around and pick you up after dinner, say around 6:30? You can practice."

"Practice what?"

"Driving."

"But I already told you that I can't drive."

"It's easy enough to learn. There's a vacant lot on the south side of town. We'll start you off there. After you get your learner's permit, you can drive on the roads."

Before Naomi could protest, Jason changed the subject. "Oh, and another thing. I've arranged for Joe McElroy—he teaches agriculture over at the university—to come tomorrow. He knows all the nuts and bolts of farming like nobody else. He'll give you a crash course. And after that, we'll go out to your farms so you can meet the tenants and take a look around."

Naomi nodded into the phone. But what she wanted to do was head straight to the airport so she could go home. Where things were normal.

CHAPTER TWELVE

Marvilla stuck to Naomi like glue and talked her ear off all morning. At the post office, where she showed her how to collect her mail. At the Uptown Café, where she introduced Naomi to nearly everyone in town. At the Husker Market, where they stopped in to buy milk. So, it was surprising when Marvilla announced she had errands to run and wouldn't be going with Naomi to the church to make the memorial arrangements. Naomi felt like she had been tossed overboard without a lifeline when she got in the car with Dorothy and Doreen, but they liked to talk just as much as Marvilla. They chattered all the way to the church, which turned out to be a block from Naomi's house.

The Reverend Plank was waiting for her in what looked like a school cafeteria but was called the Fellowship Hall. She drank coffee with Dorothy (who Naomi learned was the organist) and Doreen (who Naomi learned was the head of the Women's Sunday School Society), while planning Tuesday's memorial. Jason had already taken care of most of the details, and it turned out the only thing Naomi really needed to decide was which hymns were to be sung and whether the lunch following the memorial would have egg salad sandwiches with the cake and cookies. Naomi thought it was a little strange to have lunch at three in the afternoon before understanding lunch meant *refreshments.* Filing away that information for future use, Naomi left the choice of hymns up to Dorothy and agreed that sandwiches were unnecessary at that hour of the day.

Once that was settled, Dorothy and Doreen hurried their cups to the kitchen to wash, leaving Naomi with Reverend Plank. He was a swarthy man who already had a bald patch on the back of his head, but he didn't seem that much older than Naomi. She almost told him she didn't believe in God when he asked her about her home church in Tokyo, but the large crucifix hanging on the wall behind him stopped her. "Um, Tokyo International Church," she said, remembering where her father's first funeral was held. "But I don't go so often," she added, just in case there was a god listening to her lie through her teeth.

"Our Heavenly Father expects us to worship him in his home every week to keep us from the paths of sin. You must fight the sins of the flesh and—"

"Sorry to interrupt, Reverend," said Doreen, coming back into the Fellowship Hall and placing her hand on Naomi's shoulder. "But we need our girl here up at the organ to hear the hymn selection for the service."

"Oh, that man," Doreen whispered, rolling her eyes as soon as they were out of earshot. "He thinks he knows everything there is to know and can come here from Oklahoma and boss us all around. Well, I suppose he means well, being a man of the cloth and all that."

"Oh yes, but it's a hard pill to swallow, considering the fact that he was a cashier at some gas station before he decided to go to seminary and then come here and bother us," said Dorothy as she sat down at the organ. She played a few bars of "Amazing Grace," before leaning toward Naomi and adding in a conspiratorial tone, "We certainly miss our poor Reverend Winkle."

"Oh, my goodness, yes. We certainly do," echoed Doreen. "Now, *he* was a fine man. A fine preacher. He saved up all his fire and brimstone talk for the pulpit, right where it belongs. You could meet Reverend Winkle at the Uptown Café any other day of the week and have a downright pleasant conversation with him. Why, he'd even go to the Catholic Church when they had their fish fry."

Dorothy sighed. "Reverend Winkle never took the fun out of things."

"He was a sweetheart, all right," said Doreen with a touch of nostalgia. "Even if he did lose his marbles in the end. Too bad we had to put him in the nursing home, but what else could we do? Poor man. It wouldn't have been so bad showing up and preaching in his underwear like that, but it just didn't look good in front of those Gideon Bible people who were visiting that Sunday."

"And besides," Dorothy added, "It's plain crazy for an old man to run around in his underwear when it's twenty degrees below zero."

Naomi was processing all this when the sanctuary's quiet was pierced by childish shrieks from the fellowship hall.

"Those are the little Planks," Doreen explained. "All five of them, all under the age of eight."

"That poor woman," said Dorothy.

Naomi had no trouble understanding she was referring to Mrs. Plank.

She turned down lunch at the Uptown Café with her new friends because all she wanted to do was go home, eat something light, and take a nap. Jet lag was bad enough, but smiling until her teeth hurt was even more exhausting.

It seemed like she had barely put her head down on the sofa, but when the doorbell wrenched Naomi out of sleep, she saw two hours had passed.

"I've been wanting to meet you," said the woman on her doorstep as she pushed her way into the house, clots of dried mud on her sandals making a trail across the carpet. "I'm Donna. I knew your father. Quite well, actually. My husband was his cousin, so I guess you could say you and I are related." She plopped down in the chair by the window with such a force Naomi thought its legs would snap right off.

"Um… it's very nice to meet you. Can I get you something to drink?" Naomi thought the wheezing woman, with sweat streaming down her neck through folds of fat, might drop over from heatstroke.

"Yeah, I'll have pop," she said, pushing back her stringy hair with dirty fingernails. "Diet if you've got it."

"Sorry?"

"Well, regular is fine, then. But not Pepsi. Can't stand that stuff. If it's not Coke—"

"Oh." Naomi registered another new word. "I don't think I have any soft... um, pop. But let me see what I have."

Naomi returned to the living room with a glass of ice water and a slice of Marvilla's cake to find Donna handling one of the antique figurines in the curio cabinet with a smoldering cigarette dangling from her lips. She hurried back to the kitchen, grabbed the first thing she could find, and got a coffee mug over to Donna just as the ash was about to fall onto the white carpet.

"You probably wanna know why I'm here," Donna said, dropping back into the chair. "I'm—"

"Hello, Donna."

Donna and Naomi both jumped. Neither had heard Marvilla come in.

"What are you doing here?" Marvilla's voice was icy.

"I thought you went to Riley."

"I just bet you did."

"Your car's not in your driveway."

"I'm having the oil changed." Marvilla astonished Naomi when she yanked the cigarette out of Donna's mouth and dropped it into her glass of ice water.

Donna hoisted herself up, lit another cigarette, and tossed the match onto the metal TV tray. "Never met a Jap face to face before," she said, scanning Naomi with a mean squint. "Can't understand Mike's attraction to them."

"Oh, for crying out loud," Marvilla muttered after the screen door slammed shut. "I didn't think that woman would get here so fast. It's a good thing I didn't go to Riley after all. Don't let her in the house again."

That woman had been so awful, Naomi had no intention of doing so.

Marvilla marched the untouched piece of cake into the kitchen and dumped it down the garbage disposal as if it were full of worms.

"She said she was a cousin."

"Cousin schmousin." Marvilla said as she opened the fridge and got out the cake. "She was your father's second cousin's *wife*, and that's it. That Donna was nothing but a tramp in school. First comes marriage and then comes the baby carriage, if you know what I mean. But what're you going to do when you get a bun in the oven when you are seventeen?"

Marvilla was so worked up, Naomi figured now probably wasn't the time to remind her that her own parents never actually got married.

"Here." Marvilla slid a slice of the cake toward Naomi. "Eat. You're too thin. Now," she continued after Naomi stuck her fork into the cake and ate a mouthful. "Your great-grandmother Evelyn was a Hardy. But Bruce, that's her brother, married some woman from Missouri. Well, I suppose Winnie was all right. But those children of theirs didn't even have the smarts to come in out of the rain. I tell you, Bruce and Winnie would be turning over in their graves if they knew how Eugene went and lost their farm. Can you believe that? It was free and clear. No mortgage. Well, I always say a fool and his money is soon parted. And what did that Eugene expect when he mortgaged it to the hilt to buy fancy cars and fancy tractors? You've got to pay the piper when the bank comes knocking on the door. If there's nothing else I know, I do know that."

Naomi ate another forkful of cake and nodded, as if she knew what Marvilla was going on about.

"Anyhoo, Carl—that's Eugene's son—got himself tangled up with that Donna." Marvilla frowned at some buzzing going on around their ears, got up, and retrieved a yellow fly swatter from the top of the fridge. With expert aim, she brought it down on the counter in three rapid smacks. She removed the corpses with a paper towel and sat down again. "Don't forget, dear. You've got to keep the screen door closed. Now, where was I? Oh, yes. Donna was a fast one, all right, and the boys chased after her like bees to the honey. But who could blame them? That cow was giving out all the milk for free. She swore up and down that Carl was the Daddy, and I guess he was a big enough fool to believe it. Donna was always running to far-off places like Kansas City and doing lord knows what in them. Anyway, their kids—Gary and Jeremy are your..." Marvilla had to pause for a second. "Your third cousins. More cake?"

"What? Um… no, thank you. I'm fine."

Marvilla pushed the cake platter away, but after a second, pulled it back and cut herself another sliver. "And then there was all that stuff with Gary. He—" Marvilla stopped, the fork halfway to her mouth. "I guess I'd better let Jason tell you all about that." She licked the frosting off her finger and sighed. "Like they say, you can't choose your relatives, not even the distant ones." She scooped up the plates and carried them to the sink. "Jason should've filled you in on all this, but like he said, it's not something to talk about on that computer telephone thingy."

"Fill me in on what?"

"Oh, honey, I'd better just let him tell you." She turned around and, with her hands on her hips, said, "I'm not one to speak ill of people behind their backs. But between you and me, that Eugene was a damn fool for losing his money, and his son was even a bigger one for marrying a tramp who didn't know enough to keep her knees together."

CHAPTER THIRTEEN

That evening, Naomi got behind a steering wheel in a car for the first time in her life. It didn't feel all that different at first because that was the same side the passengers sit in Japan. On the left. When Jason handed her the keys, she asked, "Are you sure it's okay? Is it *safe*?"

"How could it possibly be dangerous?" Jason waved his arms at the vast space outside the car. "What would you hit? That?" He pointed at an abandoned building several hundred feet away at the other end of the parking lot.

"Is it even legal? I mean, I don't have a driver's license." Naomi was trying to figure a way out of this. "What if I get caught and they kick me out of the country?"

"You're in a vacant lot. Not another car within a hundred feet. All you have to do is learn how to go forward, stop, and maybe back up. Believe me, you'll get the hang of it right away. But just to be safe," he winked, "let's make sure our seatbelts are on."

Jason was right. After a few jerky starts and stops, Naomi was driving. At least she was going forward. Then to the left. The right. Backing the car up was a bit more of a challenge, but after five minutes, she had mastered the art of going in all directions.

"I guess that wasn't as difficult as I thought it'd be," she said, grinning with pride. "I don't know why my grandfather said driving would be too much for a girl."

Jason grimaced. "He said that?"

Naomi laughed. "Oh, he said lots of things. He was an old-fashioned kind of guy." She thought of Ashley when she added, "Some would call him a real male chauvinist pig."

"Well, you'll show him, won't you? The next step, of course, will be the streets."

"Now?" Naomi looked as if Jason had suggested skydiving was also on tonight's agenda.

"No. For that, you'll need your learner's permit." He handed her a booklet with Nebraska driving rules in it. "You'll have to pass the test, but it's not too difficult. I'll take you to Riley next week to get the permit, and then you can practice on the streets. And maybe a week or two after that, you can get your license."

They switched spots, and Jason pulled onto the highway. "Well, I gather Marvilla took you to the Uptown Café this morning, so tonight I'll take you to another important Felix landmark. The Dairy Delight is *the* place to go to on a summer evening." Jason bought two soft-serve chocolate ice cream cones there from a teenager behind the counter named Tracy, and they sat on a bench facing the sun hovering over the cornfields in the distance. Crickets chirped in the bushes and starlings swooped overhead, making their last rounds before settling in for the night.

Naomi was hyperaware of Jason's thigh and shoulder just inches away from hers. The awkwardness she had felt with him yesterday after getting off the airplane had disappeared, and the comfortable camaraderie they had shared those months they communicated by distance returned. He looked down at her with his beautiful blue-grey crinkly eyes and smiled. She tilted her head up towards his, her heart racing.

Then Jason said, "I guess you met quite a few people today around town, didn't you?"

"Oh yes," she replied a little too quickly, shifting her body slightly so that her bottom moved away from Jason, but her knees faced him. "There were the people in the café. The post office. The church. I was probably hugged more times this morning than I've ever been hugged in my entire life. Maybe twice as much."

Jason chuckled. "Yeah, I guess we are a hugging kind of folk around here."

"Oh, and I guess I should mention, I also met Donna Hardy. Her, I didn't hug."

"I was hoping you wouldn't have to meet any of the Hardys just yet."

"Marvilla had quite a lot to say about them."

"I bet she did." The distaste in his voice made it seem like he had swallowed something nasty. "Look, it's too nice an evening to spoil talking about them. There'll be time enough for that."

They sat in silence, watching the sky as if it were a canvas where an artist was adding brush strokes of crimson and magenta. Naomi jumped when a few tiny twinkling lights appeared near her feet.

"Fireflies," said Jason. "The first I've seen this year. Some say that the first fireflies of the season bring good luck."

She stared down at them for a while, but when she looked up, she saw Jason had been watching her. Squashing her urge to lean over and kiss him, she asked about Marvilla.

"Marvilla," he replied easily, "is many things, but maybe the most important is that she was your father's peace of mind. His eyes and ears. She was why he never had to worry as Evelyn got older. Marvilla took Evelyn shopping, to the doctor, to the beauty parlor. And she looked after the house. Made sure the lawn got mowed, the sidewalks got shoveled, the roof got fixed. That kind of stuff."

"I guess he was really lucky to have someone like her right next door like that." Naomi thought about how Marvilla had hugged her as if she were her own long-lost granddaughter. "Does she have a family of her own?"

"She was married a long time ago, but depending on who's doing the talking, her husband either ran off and got himself killed in a car accident in St. Louis, or he went to find work in St. Louis and got himself killed in a car accident there. But either which way, he left her with a son to raise all by herself."

"Where's her son now?"

"John? Again, depending on who's doing the talking, you'll hear that he died of brain cancer —"

"Oh, how awful—"

"Or of AIDS."

"Marvilla's son was gay?"

"Yes. But he was good at football."

"What does that have to do with anything?"

"Things were different when John was growing up. Back then, that kind of thing was hardly ever acknowledged. Or talked about. But around here, you can be forgiven for just about anything if you're good at football. And John was so good that the Cornhuskers wanted him."

Naomi frowned. "They wanted him to farm corn?"

Jason burst out laughing. "The Cornhuskers is a football team. The University of Nebraska football team. You'll find out soon enough, but we Nebraskans take the Cornhuskers *very* seriously. Anyone recruited to play for them is accorded immediate hero status."

"Oh. Football."

"But John turned them down. He went out west to go to Berkeley. Well, that upset people a *lot* more than him being gay. He had taken away the town's chance for fame and fortune for producing a football star."

"I get that. In my hometown it would have been baseball."

"It seems laughable now. But back then, it was a town scandal. John went out west to Berkley and never came back. Other than to visit now and then. When he got brain cancer," he air quoted, "Marvilla went to California to help his partner take care of him."

"Oh, poor Marvilla. That's so sad."

"But remember. If the topic comes up, don't mention AIDS. Marvilla says it was brain cancer, and so brain cancer it was. Because either which way, John isn't coming back."

The sun had sunk behind the cornfields, and it was time to head home. "I guess," Jason said as they got in the car, "you'll figure it out soon enough, but there's another thing. Marvilla doesn't get along well with our new preacher. Well, I guess he's not *that* new. Compared to Reverend Winkle, who was our guy for nearly forty years, three years seems like nothing."

"Reverend Plank?" Naomi didn't tell him she didn't like him all that much either.

"Most people side with Marvilla on this. Namely, because they aren't about to let some outsider come in and tell them what to think. Not even a preacher. And besides, anyone who says *her* son is burning in hell will never get her seal of approval."

"He says that?" Naomi felt even more disgusted with that man.

"Well, to be honest, Peter Plank says that about everyone he disagrees with. Or anyone who disagrees with him. But people around here don't take kindly to outsiders who come in here and—"

"I guess I'd better watch my step, then."

"You're not an outsider. Go look in the cemetery. All your relatives are over there."

Clearly, he hadn't heard all those comments today at the post office and the Uptown Cafe about how exotic she looked.

"Of course," Jason said as they got out of the car and walked toward the house, "people around here don't like being treated like country bumpkins by some big city girl."

Was the word out that Naomi had asked for a soy cappuccino at the Uptown Café? Had she somehow offended the owner, who stared at her and then laughed? "Oh, I didn't mean to—"

"I wasn't talking about *you*." Jason swallowed uncomfortably. "I was talking about my ex-wife."

That caught Naomi off guard, and she almost tripped on the top step. Had she met the ex at the post office, the café, or even the ice cream stand? Trying for breezy but missing by a mile, she asked, "So, how long were you married?"

"Five years." As if he could read her mind, he added, "She's not here. She's in California. I wanted to tell you earlier," he said, as they sat down on the porch swing. "But it's not so easy to introduce an ex-wife into a conversation."

"Is she from around here?"

"Oh god, no," Jason said with a snort. "To make a long and boring story short, I went to law school in California. After I graduated, I stayed. I met Heather, and we got married. The marriage didn't work out. I hated my job. I hated my life in California. I realized what I wanted all along was to be a lawyer like my dad. Someone who takes care of people. Well, my ex hated being here, so she left. Thank god we had no kids to complicate things. The last I heard, she was seeing some optometrist."

Naomi had fixed her gaze on the church across the street while she was processing the hurt she detected in Jason's voice. They had known each other for months now, but this was the first time he mentioned a wife in the background. Even if she was an ex.

"That part of my life is over," he said. "I want to put it behind me. I want to move on."

Naomi's heart squeezed tight when she thought Jason was about to kiss her. But then, a look she didn't recognize flitted across his face, and he stood. "Well," he said. "I'd better get going."

Naomi went into the house and locked the door. Unable to curtail her curiosity, she got out her iPad. It didn't take long at all to find an extensive digital trail of Jason and his ex. Their so-called wedding of the decade was in a full-page spread in *The San Francisco Chronicle*. Pictures from restaurant openings. Charity extravaganzas. Even operas and symphonies. Naomi zoomed in on Heather Sullivan Perry and groaned. How could she ever compete with someone as movie star gorgeous as that?

Jetlag forced Naomi awake in the middle of the night. But wanting to catch the full moon's shadows on the trees in front of the church, she grabbed her sketchbook, took it out to the porch, and completed her drawing. It wasn't perfect, Naomi thought as she studied her work, but it wasn't bad at all. After adding a few finishing touches, she went inside and dozed on the sofa until the sun came up. Before Marvilla arrived with another gazillion calorie concoction for her to eat, she decided to go running. She'd better start paying attention to the number of calories going in and the number of calories going out. So she changed into her new running outfit, did a few perfunctory stretches in the living room, and set off through the side door. By the time she got to Main Street, just a block away, she was out of breath. Considering she hadn't gone running since—well, forever—that wasn't surprising. She slowed to a walk and took in the old-fashioned two-story buildings on both sides of the street. The supermarket, drugstore, and clothing store were still closed. Pretending to do some more stretches, she watched what was going on near the Uptown Café.

A rotund, middle-aged man in bib overalls and a red baseball cap left the post office, went into the café, and sat at a table by the window with a group of similarly clad men.

A car pulled into a vacant space in front of the café, and a man who looked to be at least a hundred got out of the car and hobbled toward the entrance before the woman, presumably his daughter, could give him a hand. From the way he was jerking away from her, he clearly did not want her help.

A blue-haired woman clutching the steering wheel of a beat-up beige sedan beeped her horn and waved at Naomi. Naomi waved back but hurried on. It was just too early in the morning to have to start in on a whole new round of hugging people.

A few doors down was Patty's Beauty Parlor, and next to that were some businesses that seemed to deal with farming. She saw the sign for Jason's law office above something called the Masonic

Lodge, and she paused and peered up at it. Not wanting to look like some sort of stalker, she made a left onto a residential street and cruised up and down the ten blocks that made up Felix, counting five churches along the way. The school was at the edge of the town. Some parents were dropping their children off out front, and older students were pulling into the parking lot, honking and waving at each other in cars that looked so old they'd never pass inspection in Japan. She overheard a group of girls talking about summer vacation, which was starting from tomorrow. She did a double take at one driver as he pulled into the parking lot. The car was full of children who scampered toward the elementary school entrance. The boy, who looked barely in the vicinity of puberty, joined a pack of other kids in hoodies going into the doorway marked Junior High.

Naomi peeked in the windows of the building adjoining the primary and secondary schools and saw a group of older citizens reading newspapers and using the computers. A library! She pushed open the door, and the librarian looked up in surprise.

"I'm Linda Schmidt," she said, walking toward Naomi with her hand extended and a warm smile on her face. "I'm so sorry to hear about your father. We knew each other back in high school."

A man reading the *Omaha Herald* called out, "Naomi, you're out and about early." He pointed at the headlines and said, "I see your country is considering having another election for Prime Minister. How do you feel about that?"

Naomi, who never followed politics, mumbled a neutral answer.

But before returning to his paper, he asked, "How did your driving lesson go yesterday?"

"Um, great, thanks."

"Are you here to use the library or the gym?" asked Linda.

"There's a gym?"

"Come on, I'll show you."

"Hi, Duane," Linda shouted to the sole person in there, shuffling on a treadmill. "The best time," she said to Naomi, "is in the morning around now, when the only competition for the equipment is Duane. The worst time is in the late afternoon when the football team trains. That's when the place smells like a zoo."

Naomi pointed at a sign on the wall and asked why there was an age limit for using the gym, but apparently not for driving. Linda laughed and explained that farm kids could get a special permit to drive their siblings to and from school.

"But isn't it dangerous?" Naomi hoped she didn't sound judgmental.

"Maybe, but some of those kids have been driving on their property for years—tractors, lawnmowers, and even cars. And without a farm license, the parents would have to go back and forth to town all day long."

Back in the library, Naomi asked if she could borrow a book. "Something by Willa Cather, if you have it."

Linda looked surprised. "No one's asked me for her in years."

"All I know is that she's a Nebraska writer. I thought I should give her a try."

By the time Naomi left the library with her book tucked under her arm, the morning cool was beginning to disappear. Several neighbors were out mowing their lawns, and the air smelled green with grass.

"Hello!" called out a man who was watering the roses in front of the church across from Naomi's house. He set down the hose and came over and introduced himself as Pat Mueller. After a bit of chitchat, his wife Rebecca joined them, handing a bag of zucchini to Naomi and promising more where that came from. It took a few seconds for her to realize that this kind man was the minister of the church. How different he seemed from the one yesterday, and she wondered how come they weren't having her father's memorial service across the street with these nice people instead?

Marvilla stepped out of her house wearing a canary yellow pantsuit. "I'm heading uptown for coffee, Naomi," she called out. "Do you want to come?"

"Thanks, but I've got to get ready to go to Jason's office, and I have some things to do first."

Felix was turning out to be not so bad after all, Naomi thought as she walked up the sidewalk to her house. People were pretty friendly, and so far—completely against her expectations—it *was* kind of nice here. That was what was in her head before she noticed the porch buzzing with flies. Before her brand-new sneakers came into contact with something slimy and smelly. Before her right foot shot out from under her, and she slipped and fell sideways into the shit that someone had spread all over her porch.

CHAPTER FOURTEEN

Naomi's shrieks brought the neighbors running.

"Oh, my dear lord," exclaimed Rebecca. She pulled Naomi up and got her into the garage. She wrapped a tarp that had been lying across the tool chest loosely around her and led her into the side door of the house and directly into the shower off of the kitchen.

Reverend Pat called the sheriff and Marvilla called Jason. They arrived within minutes but had to wait half an hour for Naomi to shower off what had been determined to be barnyard manure.

Jason jumped up and slung his arm around Naomi when she came into the living room in a change of clothes Marvilla had found for her upstairs. "Are you all right?"

"Of course she's not all right," Marvilla said, fuming on Naomi's behalf.

"Why would anyone do that?" demanded Naomi.

"Well, that's what I'm here to find out," said a man, offering his hand to Naomi. "I'm Tom Young. The sheriff. Did you hear anything outside in the night?"

"No. But I was on the porch in the middle of the night. Maybe around two. Everything was fine then."

Tom looked up from his notepad. "Can I ask what you were doing outside at that hour?"

"I had jet lag and couldn't sleep. So I was drawing." As if she was expected to produce evidence, she got up to retrieve her sketchbook from the top drawer in the dining room buffet.

Jason whistled, looking over Tom's shoulder as he thumbed through it. "I didn't know you were an artist."

Tom handed the sketchbook back to her, and she wished she hadn't shown it to them. "I went inside and left through the kitchen door around seven to take a walk."

Just then, one of the volunteer firefighters who had come to help clean up called from the front porch. "Hey Tom, could you come out here?"

Everyone followed the sheriff to the porch.

"It's not just manure," the man said.

"Damn," Tom muttered when he saw the dead cat. "Who'd do such a thing?"

"Who?" said Jason. "The Hardys, that's who."

"Well, I don't know. Is there a possibility that it could be..." Tom hesitated before adding, "racially motivated?"

Naomi's eyes opened wide in surprise. "Because I'm Japanese?"

Tom looked embarrassed. "I don't think we can overlook that possibility."

"Other than Larry Culp, I can't imagine who that would be." Jason turned to Naomi. "His uncle had been a POW during the war, so it's possible he'd have an axe to grind with the Japanese. I'm not sure he even remembers any of that now. Not to mention, even if they did let him out of the nursing home, he wouldn't have the strength to lift a bag of apples, let alone all that manure."

"But his sons might," said Tom. "And they aren't what you'd call model citizens, you know."

"That may be so, Tom," said Jason. "But you and I both know the Hardys were behind this."

"Well, maybe they were and maybe they weren't. I'll go have a talk with them and see what they have to say." Tom slipped his notepad into his shirt pocket and turned to Naomi. "Until we get this figured out, I'd keep my doors locked if I were you."

"What's really going on here?" demanded Naomi after she, Jason, and Marvilla went into the house.

Jason looked over at Marvilla for help, but her lips were clamped tight. He took a deep breath. "Some people might be kind of unhappy that Evelyn's estate went to you after Mike died. And not to them."

"You mean people like Donna Hardy?"

"When your father died, Donna thought one of her sons would be next in line. You see, most everyone had forgotten that Mike had ever had a daughter in the first place. And only a few people—like me and Marvilla—knew that he had found you and changed his will."

"So, to get back at me, they dump *that* all over my porch? To scare me into giving my inheritance to them? So, tell me this, if I weren't in the picture, would my father have given everything to someone else?"

"No. Everything would've gone to the zoo in Omaha."

"The zoo!" Marvilla scoffed. "That's the first I've heard of *that*."

Jason turned to her. "But it's true—"

"Well, I never heard—"

"I can't tell you everything my clients ask me to do, Marvilla. You know that. You knew about Naomi because *Mike* told you. Not me. And if he had wanted you to know about the zoo, he would've told you that, too."

"Don't wander off the topic, Jason. Tell Naomi the rest."

Naomi's eyes darted between them. "The rest of what?"

Jason raked his fingers through his hair and exhaled. "Well, a long time ago, Donna and her husband Carl went through a bad patch. And rumor has it that around that time, your dad and Donna... Well, they..." When he saw the horrified look of comprehension on Naomi's face, he added, "Donna didn't always look the way she does now."

"That may be true," threw in Marvilla, "but it doesn't change the fact she was always a hussy."

"My guess," Jason said, "is that a lot of alcohol was involved."

"These things happen," Naomi said, trying to be casual about it. "I don't understand the big deal."

Jason moved his gaze away from Naomi and down to the carpet. "The problem is Donna's son, Jeremy. His birthday falls within that window of opportunity."

"He's my *brother*?"

"I don't think so," said Jason. "Your father didn't think so. But there are those who might."

"And that's why someone covered my porch with cow poop and a dead cat?"

"Well, it could hardly be Donna," said Marvilla. "That big fat slob can barely haul herself up those steps, let alone drag fifty pounds of manure up behind her."

"I'd put my money on Jeremy's brother," said Jason. "Gary's always been a one-step forward, two-steps backward kind of guy. He's just the type to screw up when things are going well for him."

"But wouldn't Jeremy be the one to benefit?" asked Naomi.

"That's true," said Jason. "But Jeremy's never been in trouble. He's had a steady job since high school. I just can't see him stooping to petty vandalism."

"Petty?" sputtered Naomi. "You call *that* petty?"

"It could have been a lot worse."

Naomi did not want to go there.

"That Jeremy's not the sharpest tack in the box," said Marvilla. "Make no bones about that. But Jason's right. Other than all that gossip when his first wife Lynn ran off with a hired hand from the Jefferson's place—he's been decent enough. For a Hardy, that is.

He provided a roof over his daughter's head and for that fool Lisa, who agreed to marry him after all that hullabaloo—"

"But getting back to the point," Naomi said when Marvilla paused to take a breath. "Jeremy could be my brother?"

"If that really was the case," said Jason, "Donna would have said something right after Carl died. If not before."

"You're right about that," said Marvilla. "That hussy would have gone straight to Mike for money after her idiot husband went and got himself killed in that boating accident in Ogallala. The damn fool didn't leave her a pot to piss in—excuse my French—because he cashed in his life insurance policy to buy that damn boat. Oh, she went on and on at the funeral like she had lost Prince Charming. But if Donna had given a hoot about the guy, she would've kept her knees together in the first place rather than crawl in the back of a truck in a bar parking lot with any old Tom, Dick, or Harry. Who could blame your father when all cats are grey in the dark?"

Before Naomi could shake that awful image from her mind, the neighbors arrived to help with the cleanup, and Don Martin, from several houses away, was ready to eliminate all traces of it with his power hose.

At least the dead cat was determined to be roadkill. It was still creepy that someone felt it would be a good idea to scrape the poor thing off the highway, but at least a psychopath hadn't killed it to scare her. Small blessings.

"So, you think Donna saw Jeremy as her ticket to get something after my father died?" asked Naomi.

"Maybe. But of course, it's total hooey," said Marvilla with a huff. "Anyone with half a brain in their head would agree. The idea!"

"But the problem is Andrea," said Jason.

"Who?" asked Naomi.

"Jeremy's daughter with his first wife. She's—"

"If you look at those damn fool sons of Donna's," Marvilla interrupted, "you'd never think a single one of them had sprung out of anyone's loins but Carl's. But when you see Andrea, you almost can't help but think the opposite. I hate to say it, but she's as smart as they come."

"But it was only after Donna planted the idea in people's heads that Jeremy was Mike's son that they saw a connection. They didn't before, but they do now," said Jason.

"So, everyone's talking about this."

"It's a small town, Naomi," Jason said. "People talk. But to be honest—when you meet the girl, you'll see she's not like the rest of the Hardys—she's smart like Mike. But it's possible she takes after her mother's side."

"Who knows what that family's like, coming from Missouri and all that," agreed Marvilla. "But let me ask you this. If that woman had been so smart, how'd she get herself tangled up with a Hardy in the first place? That's what I'd like to know. I guess she—" The phone rang and Marvilla grabbed it. She cut the call short and set the receiver on the counter. "Now, where was I? Oh yes. About Andrea. There's no question that girl's smart. Why, she could even become a professional—like a secretary or a nurse or something like that. But she needs a lesson or two in deportment, I tell you. The oddest things just pop right out of her mouth sometimes. It's no wonder, I suppose, the way Lisa lollygags about all day long. She blames it on her health, but—"

"Who's Lisa, again?" If Naomi was going to be quizzed on the who's who of this drama later, she'd get a big fat zero.

"Jeremy's second wife. Now, she's nice enough. And more Jeremy's speed than Lynn ever was. But I never heard of any sickness that sucks the energy right out of people. And all that pain and nausea? It's pure and simple laziness if you ask me. I say she'd better lay off the Cheez-Its," Marvilla said, licking icing off her thumb. "Between you and me, I think Evelyn let Andrea study here because she wanted her to soak up some of the aristocratic Johnson manners. Book smarts will only get you just so far in life."

"The main thing is," interjected Jason, "Evelyn and Mike have always been nice to Andrea. So when Donna started spreading the rumor that Mike might be her grandfather, people read a lot into that."

Before anything else was said, Marvilla stood and announced that now was as good a time as any for Naomi to go to the cemetery.

"Huh?" Naomi wasn't sure she had heard correctly.

"You know what?" Jason said, pulling himself to his feet. "Marvilla's right. We should go to the cemetery before it gets too hot."

Marvilla put the phone receiver back on the hook, picked it up when it rang a few seconds later, and settled in for a long chat. Naomi went upstairs to get her shoes, thinking the two of them had lost their minds.

"By the time you get home," Jason said in the car. "Things should be back to normal."

"That's why we're going to the cemetery now? To get me out of the way?"

"Well, there's that. But Marvilla's right. You should go before the funeral." He turned into the cemetery, which was right next to Dairy Delight, and stopped behind a silver sedan blocking the tree-lined lane.

"Hey, Glenda," Jason called out the window to a woman making her way through the graveyard, a fistful of flowers in one hand and a cane in the other. "How're you doing this morning? Nice day, isn't it?"

The woman turned and glared as if Jason might be a New York mugger.

Jason chuckled. "Glenda Goodwin comes up here every day to see her husband, but since the city asked her to be careful after she knocked over some headstones, she parks in the middle of the drive so no one can get around her." He placed his hand on Naomi's elbow as they threaded their way through clusters of headstones. Some were recent, but others seemed ancient.

"I know you're thinking this is the last place you want to visit, but there are some things I need to tell you, and it'll be easier to do that here."

"Well, it is nice here. Peaceful," admitted Naomi. Most of the dew had evaporated, but a few lone drops sat like pearls upon individual blades of grass. The air was heavy and fragrant, and she saw two squirrels scampering off in the distance.

"We think it's one of the prettiest cemeteries in this part of the state."

"It's so different from Japan." She stopped to examine an engraved epitaph. "So personal. This one here, a hundred years ago, says 'loving wife and mother.' You'd see nothing like that in a Japanese cemetery. There'd be just one large headstone with the family's name on it. And the ashes of the oldest son and his family would go there, and—Oh! Look at this! This woman here, Martha Stagg, was born in 1798 and died in 1901. How cool is that? Living in three centuries?"

"Well done! You found one of our most important cemetery residents on your first trip here." Jason led her over the slope and to the Johnson plots. Pointing at one with a recent headstone, he said, "That's Evelyn. Your father will go right next to her."

Naomi stepped in front of her great-grandmother's headstone and bowed her head and prayed like she did for her ancestors back home. She kneeled to examine the cluster of headstones on the other side of Evelyn's grave and sighed when she saw everyone had different birthdays but the same date of death. "This is strange," she said to Jason, who had squatted next to her. "A few months ago, I didn't even know that any of these people had ever existed. And now I feel sad they aren't here."

"There's something else I want you to see."

He led her to the next plot over, and Naomi saw his mother's grave. Her heart tugged a little; they both had been so young when they lost their mothers.

"This," Jason said, drawing her attention to a different tombstone, "is my big brother."

Naomi studied the grave for a moment before a horrified look of comprehension swept across her face. "Oh my god! Was he... in that accident, too?"

Jason was unable to hide the bitterness in his voice when he began to speak. "Johnny shouldn't have even been with them that day. He wasn't a part of that crowd. But they were ditching school to go to Zorinski Lake, and he went with them. Stupid idiot. After the accident, he was airlifted to Creighton University hospital in Omaha and died a week later."

"Oh, Jason..." Naomi murmured.

"There's something else you don't know. Donna's son was the driver. Gary Hardy caused the accident. It was his car, his idea, his booze. Nine people died. But not him. Gary was the only one who survived that day." He looked off into the distance and added, "I was just five when it happened, but I remember everything as if it were yesterday. My mom was already gone by then, you see. It was hard, but we three men had somehow made a family. And Gary tore it apart."

Naomi placed her hand on Jason's arm and stumbled through some very inadequate words.

"I always have to remind myself," Jason continued, "that Gary was just a kid. Only fifteen. Fifteen-year-olds do stupid things."

"Fifteen!" Naomi remembered the conversation she had had with Linda at the library earlier that morning. "He had one of those school licenses?"

Jason nodded. "The family was living out-of-town then. Of course, Gary wasn't supposed to be driving anywhere but between home and school. And he certainly wasn't supposed to be carting a carload of teenagers around."

"What happened to him? After the accident?"

"After he got out of the hospital with a broken leg, he was in juvenile detention for about a year. They released him for good behavior, but his license was suspended for seven years."

"That was *it?*" Naomi was thinking that if that had happened in Japan, Gary would probably still be in jail.

"He was a minor," Jason said, as if that excused everything.

"I guess that's why Marvilla has nothing good to say about the Hardys."

"There's more. After the accident, Evelyn wasn't doing well. I mean, who could blame her? Most of her family was gone. Mike was so far away and having plenty of his own problems. Anyway, Eugene—that's Carl's father—persuaded Evelyn to let him manage her farms. After all, he *was* her nephew. But the contract would have given him the power of attorney over her property. Eugene had some harebrained ideas back then, and he had already mortgaged his own farm to the hilt. He ended up losing it, and it's pretty likely Evelyn would have lost her farms as well if she had gone along with him. The Hardys mismanaged everything, and now they don't even own their own homes. But getting back to the point, Evelyn showed the contract to my dad, and he got hold of Mike right away. I think that was another turning point for Mike. With the alcohol, you know. That helped him see how important family is. Evelyn was *all* he had left, and he didn't want anything bad to happen to her. So he came and straightened things out. That was when my father began managing Evelyn's affairs."

"I bet that didn't go over well with the Hardys."

"You're right about that. Eugene blamed your dad for messing up his deal. I'm pretty sure the family thinks if that hadn't happened, their lives would be entirely different."

"So, what happened this morning—was it revenge?"

"I don't know if I'd call it that, exactly."

"Am I in physical danger?"

Jason shooed away the flies that had started buzzing around their ears. "Gary Hardy is an idiot and doesn't think things through, but I doubt he'd try anything again. Especially since the whole town will be watching him. And looking out for you." Glancing down at his phone, he said, "Look, we should get going. I bet Marvilla has lunch ready for us by now. And there're still lots of things for us to go over before Joe McElroy comes at 3:00."

"Who?"

"Your farming tutor. Don't you remember? We're meeting him at my office."

CHAPTER FIFTEEN

Naomi was desperate to talk to Ashley and kept checking the time, waiting for her to get home from work. There was so much to tell, things that couldn't be condensed into a text message. She wanted to get Ashley's take on the whole poop on the porch incident. She wanted to talk about the Hardys and the car accident that killed off her family. Importantly, she wanted to talk about Jason. Girlfriend style.

Study. That's what she would do to kill the time. She cut a sliver of Marvilla's cheesecake, made a pot of tea, and took it all to Evelyn's desk. If she'd been smart enough to learn English from scratch when she was a teenager, she should be smart enough to learn about corn and oats and stuff like that now. She pulled out the notes she had made that afternoon and looked up the words Joe McElroy tossed around during her tutoring session—words that made her feel stupid. And Naomi *hated* feeling stupid. Unfortunately, translating terms like crop rotation, crop residue, soil conservation, and yield wasn't much help—it was just as incomprehensible in Japanese. Then Google led her down a rabbit hole of academic articles and even more technical terms. But after typing in the keywords "farming for dummies," books for beginners popped up. Fifteen minutes later, her Amazon cart was full.

What would her friends back in Japan think if they could see her now? The party girl who used to spend Friday nights tossing back tequila was now sitting alone in an old house, looking at farm reports and eating cheesecake. Just that afternoon, she was in knee-high rubber boots wading through an actual pigpen. Riding down rows and rows of soybeans on a tractor. And tonight, she ate fresh ears of corn that she had plucked from a stalk in her tenant's garden. You couldn't get any further away from Tokyo than that.

"My farms. My land. My house." She spoke those words aloud, savoring the feeling of ownership. She got up and walked around, admiring the knickknacks, the china, the glassware. "My house. My dishes. My furniture." She felt stronger with each declaration. "My father left all this to *me*." Naomi squared her shoulders. If those Hardys thought they could scare her away, they had another think coming. If anything, she had become even more determined to stay.

When she got out of Jason's car that afternoon and put her foot onto her ancestors' farms, it was as if her heart had sprouted vines pulling her deep into the earth. Land ownership was a miraculous thing, she was beginning to realize. She had never felt attached to her grandparents' tea farm, which was to go to the oldest male, her cousin Yusuke. But this Nebraska land was *hers.* Her ancestors had homesteaded it and built it up from nothing. They were her people. Or, as Marvilla had said earlier, her blood.

Even better, there was no end to the satisfaction of knowing that it would be pretty hard for her pain-in-the-neck cousin to lord it over her now that her land holdings were so much larger than his.

And the farm animals! Jason had made it clear the livestock belonged to the Thompsons, who took care of both of her farms. But when Mary Thompson placed a newborn piglet in her arms, Naomi couldn't help but fall in love. Jason seemed to sense she was about to slip the little guy into her bag, so he pried him away from her before they walked back to the house. But not before she snapped plenty of selfies with little Fred. That was the name she had secretly given him.

Naomi checked the time. It was still too early to call Ashley, so she'd give the house a more thorough investigation. She went to check out the attic, a finished alcove accessible by a steep staircase in her father's room. As she stood in that space, arms crossed in front of her, a seed of an idea floated out of nowhere and planted itself in her brain.

Why not use this space as an art studio? It was big enough. The windows on both ends would let in plenty of natural light. Besides, what else was she going to do here for an entire year? She already had plenty of supplies—the paints, pencils, and sketchbooks she had blown her last paycheck from Commando on.

She pushed the boxes of seasonal decorations up against the farthest wall to make space and decided that in Nebraska, she would *be* an artist. And this would be the room she would do it in.

After making a mental list of what to bring up to the attic tomorrow, she headed downstairs. She stopped in front of what she still thought of as Evelyn's room. She was supposed to decide which of Evelyn's things to donate to the upcoming church bazaar, but it hadn't felt right to be poking around in her clothes. Still, she knew she couldn't live out of her suitcases forever, so she opened the top dresser drawer. Underneath a collection of underwear, bras, and girdles was a large jewelry box. Naomi took it to the bed and examined its contents. Mixed in with safety pins, paper clips, breath mints, and a handful of buttons were costume jewelry that might have been fashionable decades earlier. But there were also some fine pieces: an old cameo broach with a delicate clasp. An amethyst ring with a band that was even too big for Naomi's thumb. A pair of 14-carat gold cufflinks. A tarnished locket containing photos of a couple with hairstyles that suggested they were taken in the 1940s.

She held a platinum chain with a small diamond pendant dangling from it for the longest time before fastening it around her neck. The diamond sparkled in the dresser's mirror, almost as if it was winking at her and saying that it had been waiting for her all this time. It felt right to wear it.

"Thank you, Evelyn," she whispered.

Her earlier hesitation about going through her great-grandmother's things disappeared, and she opened the other drawers, which smelled faintly of lavender. Tomorrow she'd get Marvilla up here to see if she wanted anything.

Naomi's thoughts turned to her dear, sweet granny. Despite never having anything this nice to wear in her life, she always had a cheerful smile on her face. Aching to hear her voice, she decided to call every day from now on. And send goodies as well. She'd do everything possible to make Granny's life easier, even if it meant kidnapping her and bringing her to Felix. Imagining Granny and Marvilla trying to talk to each other made her giggle, but something told her that they would hit it off, despite all their differences.

Thinking it would be nice to sit in the formal dining room with a cocktail, she headed to the kitchen and searched the cabinets. In the end, she made do with a wineglass full of orange juice because the only alcohol she found was a suspicious-looking decades-old bottle of crème de menthe under the sink. Swirling the juice as if it were a fine vintage, she studied the old framed photos in the dining room. Yesterday, the people seemed scary. Now, they felt like relatives.

It was weird, but the more *American* she felt, the more *Japanese* she felt. Homesick, too. It occurred to her that there was a way to fix at least part of that problem. She got back on the computer and found an Asian supermarket in Chicago that would deliver, and within minutes, an order was placed for soy sauce, sake, mirin, miso, nori seaweed, and dashi. Dried noodles. Rice. Curry roux. A dozen packets of frozen natto. All the basics.

And there was no way she could eat rice from a cereal bowl. Miso soup, either. Telling herself that she might have company, she ordered several sets of Japanese dishes in various shapes and sizes.

Then something that had been niggling at the back of her mind all day long surfaced, and from that same shop, she ordered a dozen pairs of slippers. If this was her house, like everyone kept saying it was, people were going to have to start taking off their shoes. No exceptions!

It was a good thing Ashley called her on Messenger when she did; otherwise, she could have very well gone broke before morning.

"You've got to be kidding me," Ashley said after Naomi had filled her in on the past twelve hours. "It sounds like you're living in the Nebraska version of *Dallas*."

"As long as no dead bodies pop up." Naomi laughed, remembering a typhoon weekend at Ashley's apartment where Ashley insisted they binge-watch DVDs of the entire 1980s series. "Not counting that poor dead cat, that is."

"Are you scared?"

Naomi wobbled her head. "Kind of. But Jason thinks they won't come back because everyone's watching the house now. And you can't believe how nice everyone's been. At least those who haven't been dumping poop on my porch."

"I'm glad you're still keeping your sense of humor."

"They're not going to scare *me* away."

"Ooh, you go, girl!"

"You know what? You might be the only person who can understand this, but when Jason took me to my farms today, I felt so connected to them. I never, ever felt that way toward my grandparents' farm."

"Well, I can think of a thousand reasons for that."

"Yeah, but before I got here, I just thought that I'd do my time and then—"

"Do your time? You make it sound like you're in prison. Is it *that* bad there?"

"Actually, it's not. It's different from what I had expected it to be, though, and it's nothing like Australia, that's for sure. You were certainly right about that. I guess I figured when the year was up, I'd sell everything and go back to my real life."

"And now?"

"Honestly, I didn't think about how selling the farms could affect other people's lives. Not just *my* life, but the tenants' lives as well. And if I sell, then that's that. The Johnson land would belong to someone else."

"So, what are you saying?"

"I don't know. I get the feeling that Jason would like me to keep them, though."

"Oooh, Jason. Tell me, does the reality live up to the fantasy?"

Naomi laughed while a blush crept up her neck.

"Well, is he nice?"

"He is. But I found out he was married before."

"So?"

"Shouldn't I be worried about... you know, emotional baggage and all that?"

"Does he have kids?"

"No."

"Does his wife live next door?"

"No. She's in California. He said they don't have any contact with each other."

"Well, what's the problem, then?"

Naomi sighed. "There's something about the way he talks about her. Like she's not really in the past, even though he says she is. And you should see this woman, Ashley. She looks like someone who'd be walking on the red carpet for the Academy Awards. She's drop-dead gorgeous. There's no other way to describe her."

"And exactly how do you know that?"

"The usual way," Naomi said, letting out a guilty giggle. "I googled. I don't know how I can compete with someone like that."

"You just said she's out of the picture."

"Yeah, but—"

"He's single. You're single. No problem there, as far as I can tell."

"It's not just that. Maybe I shouldn't... We have no future. He... well, he's *here.* And I'm—"

"Listen, you're there for the next twelve months. What's the harm of having a little fun?"

"But..."

Ashley leaned toward her computer screen and scrutinized Naomi's face. "Ah, I get it. You like the guy. I mean, you *really* like him."

"Maybe I do," Naomi said with another sigh. "I'm not sure. He's different from any other guy I've been with. I mean, compared to Tyler—"

"Compared to Tyler, a monkey would be a prize." A full ten seconds passed before Ashley asked, "Is he the one?"

Naomi laughed uncomfortably. "Don't you see how impossible it would be if he was? I can't let myself go down that road."

"Listen, girl. To me, it sounds like you already have."

CHAPTER SIXTEEN

As Naomi walked down the church aisle past those who had come to pay their final respects to her father, she was keenly aware she was the only one in head-to-toe black. No wonder Jason and Marvilla had looked so surprised when she walked out of the house in the funeral outfit she had purchased in Japan: a black dress, black shoes, black tights, and a black bag. She slid into the front pew of the church, realizing that everyone else had dressed much more casually. Nice clothes, but nothing as formal.

The turnout was so big chairs needed to be brought in from the fellowship hall to handle the overflow. Like at her father's funeral in Tokyo, friends gave moving eulogies for a man who would truly be missed. This time, Naomi brushed away tears as she listened to her father's friends sharing memories of being in boy scouts together, playing sports in school, and his annual trips back to Felix. Mike may have lived his life abroad, they all said, but he always came home. He was one of *them.* At this funeral, she didn't feel like they were speaking about a total stranger. But unlike the minister in Tokyo who had described her father's volunteer work for the homeless, Peter Plank coughed up a long-winded sermon, using the occasion as an attempt to scare the irregular churchgoers who were there that afternoon into changing their ways. Soft snoring from two opposite ends of the church caused snickers among some of the younger people.

Everyone was getting restless because the aroma of coffee permeated the sanctuary, bringing with it the promise of cake and cookies. After an eternity, the reverend finally asked the audience to bow their heads in prayer, and before he could utter his final *amen*, Dorothy launched into "How Great Thou Art" on the organ and the congregation stood to sing. Marvilla, sitting next to Naomi, muttered, "Dorothy sure knows how to get that man to shut up." And that caused a few more snickers from the pew behind.

After the hymn came some processional music and Peter Plank marched down the aisle, his head bowed. Naomi followed with Jason and Marvilla, and they went to the fellowship hall where she received condolences. Jason had warned her that the Hardys would be there, but she was so busy talking with people she didn't see them until they were right in front of her. Luckily, she didn't have to say much to them.

"Sorry for your loss," Donna and her son Gary said before moving on to let the next person in line speak.

Naomi eyed them as they headed toward the cake table. What could have ever attracted her father to Donna, even if it was decades and a hundred pounds ago? And her cousin Gary? The man who killed eight people with his reckless driving? His short-sleeved white shirt stretched across his protruding belly, poorly hiding tattoos running up and down his arms and neck. Naomi thought he looked exactly like the type of person who would spread poop all over her porch.

"I'm sorry for coming dressed like this," said a man in a mechanic's uniform, snapping Naomi's attention back to the receiving line. "But I didn't want to be late for the service." He stuck out a hand, so Naomi shook it. "I'm Jeremy," he said. "Your cousin. I'm real sorry about your dad. I'll miss him a lot."

"Thanks. It's really nice to meet you," Naomi said, remembering this man might be more than just a cousin. Before she could scrutinize his face for any similarity to hers, he moved on.

The last person in line was a pretty teenager in a calf-length floral dress. "I'm really sorry to hear about Mike."

"Thank you," said Naomi.

"I'd love to go to Japan someday," the girl continued breathlessly. "Maybe as a missionary or as a teacher or something. Between college and graduate school. That'd be the best, don't you think? Because I'm going to be a scientist, I think it would be cool to go to Japan for a while. I *love* Japanese culture. Do you draw *manga* too, or do you just do sketches? Could you teach me? What about flower arranging? Can you do that? I want to do that, too, someday. Oh, and by the way. I *love* your outfit. Is it for cosplay?"

Naomi blinked at her in astonishment.

"And do you—"

Reverend Plank stepped over and placed his hand on the girl's shoulder. "Andrea, my dear, would you mind taking coffee around for some of the older folks so they won't have to get up?"

"Why, sure thing, Reverend," she answered, smiling brightly in his face. "Real glad to help."

"Andrea is a model member of our youth fellowship group. The embodiment of young Christian womanhood."

Not knowing how to respond, Naomi said, "That's nice," and moved away in case he wanted to start in on the state of *her* Christian womanhood. So that was Andrea, she thought as she slid into the seat next to Marvilla. The girl flitted about the room, filling people's coffee cups and looking like a perky character from one of her old English textbooks from junior high school— the kind of American she had envisioned becoming when she was a teenager. Her heart tugged a little for her because she knew what it was like to grow up knowing your mother has left you behind. She sensed a darkness under Andrea's smile and a wave of empathy washed over her. When Andrea turned around, their eyes met. Naomi felt embarrassed for having been caught staring, but Andrea smiled and waved, so Naomi smiled and waved back.

Naomi was pulled into the conversation at the table, but thanks to Marvilla taking her to the Uptown Café, where news circulated as effectively as the *Yomiuri Newspaper*, she was remembering things about people.

"I hope your shingles are getting better," Naomi said to Judy Jacobs.

"You must be getting excited about your son's wedding in Chicago," she said to Paul Mann.

"Thanks for bringing the spam casserole yesterday," she said to Becky Grace, famous for being the worst cook in town. Although Naomi had dumped the disgusting mess down the garbage disposal, she told Becky it was delicious.

By 4:30, the fellowship hall had emptied, and the ladies of the Sunday School Society were wiping down the counters, so the youth group could meet there that evening.

Back at Naomi's house, Marvilla went through the condolence cards. "Oh my. The donations come to almost two hundred dollars. Imagine that!"

"What are we supposed to do with the money?" asked Naomi, remembering that the donations at the Tokyo funeral exceeded that amount ten times over. At least half of the value went back to the givers in the form of thank-you gifts.

"We donate it to the church, of course." Marvilla looked as if Naomi had suggested they blow it all on booze. "But don't you go handing it to that Peter Plank to do what he likes with it. You be sure to specify that it's for the church's new roof. Otherwise, there's no telling what that sourpuss would do if he got his hands on it." Her face was full of disgust when she turned to Jason. "If that man calls one more time asking for money for his so-called special projects, there's no accounting for what I might do. Like I always say, God made my John who he was, just like God made

Peter Plank the damn fool he is. He needs reprograming a lot more than my John ever did."

"Go ahead. Give him a piece of your mind. I dare you."

"You wait and see, Jason Perry. One of these days, I will."

Naomi smiled at their good-natured bantering and was wondering about dinner when Marvilla pushed back her chair and announced she needed to hurry home because she didn't want to miss her TV shows. She stepped onto the porch and frowned at the sky. "I don't like the look of that. Not one bit. I'm going to go get my upstairs windows shut, and you both had better do that, too, if you know what's good for you."

After Marvilla hurried off, Naomi turned to Jason. "Do you have to go home and shut your windows, or are you free to stay for dinner?"

"My windows are just fine the way they are. And dinner sounds great."

■   ■   ■

While Naomi and Jason were sitting in Naomi's kitchen having dinner, Reverend Peter Plank watched his teenage flock during the silent reflection in the Tuesday Night Youth Bible Study. His eyes were on Andrea, who had come in straight from cheerleading practice. He was tempted to reach over and pull her skirt down over her thighs. But her eyes were closed, her lips were softly moving, and her hands were folded demurely in her lap. So different from that other cheerleader who simply couldn't stop fidgeting. Sophie Brown was crossing her legs, yawning, and checking her watch. Her mind seemed to be more on that beefy boyfriend of hers who stocked shelves at the Quik Stop than on God. She was probably imagining what she was going to let that simpleton do to her in the back of his car later that night—about how she was going to let him pull up her shirt so he could maul her big floppy breasts. About how she was going to let his hand

(and probably even more) slide right into that sticky place under those pink panties that Peter just got a glimpse of when she crossed her legs for the umpteenth time.

Peter glowered at Sophie for stirring up such thoughts and ended the silent prayer by asking the Lord to guide his flock during the week ahead. Ah, the young, he thought, feeling indulgent toward his other charges as they jumped up to get to the free chips, dips, and pop. Andrea stood, and Peter saw she was still wearing the ring. His heart rejoiced, knowing that Lutheran football player boyfriend hadn't gotten lucky this week. Andrea was just the type of girl who *would* take off the ring if that were the case. Unlike that Sophie, who's been up to who knows what. He saw Haley McVeigh and Skylar Myers were still wearing their virginity rings, although he wouldn't have expected otherwise. But then again, you never know. Beauty isn't everything. Just look at that sixteen-year-old Methodist Amy Olson toting around a baby just as ugly as her and not even sure who the father is.

At nine o'clock, Peter locked up the church and went to his home next door. He drank decaf while Leah cleaned up the remains of dinner. He listened to her prattle on about how the boys were coming down with some kind of bug. About the upcoming church rummage sale. About how hot the kitchen got when canning the tomatoes he had gotten from one of the deacons for cheap. After she put the kids to bed, Peter, like a good husband, asked her to come watch the news with him. But as always, she was too busy to spend a little time with him at the end of the day. She said she needed to put away the toys and fold the laundry.

By the time the news was over and he finished his grooming routine, Leah was already in bed. Peter stood at the door and listened to her breathing. They had gone through a rough patch a few years earlier when Leah had told him that four children were all she could handle. But Peter reminded her that such a decision was in God's hands. They prayed together for God's guidance, and that was that. God works in mysterious ways, he thought, listening to the baby noisily sucking his thumb in the crib next to their bed. It was indeed a great thing to bring another Christian soul into the world.

Peter turned off the lights and got in bed, ignoring the sour smell emanating from sheets that hadn't seen the inside of a washing machine for several weeks. Like he did every Tuesday night after the youth group, he reached over and lifted the frayed cotton nightgown that fit Leah a lot better twenty pounds ago. Afterward, while she went to the boys' room because one of them had wet the bed, Peter prayed for forgiveness. He knew it was wrong, but he just couldn't help imagining that it had been Andrea under him, and not his lumpy, frumpy wife of nine years.

CHAPTER SEVENTEEN

It didn't take long for Naomi to establish a sort of routine. A morning run (well, walk, mostly) toward the school, where she pushed around a few weights in the gym before thumbing through the magazines in the library. Then to the Uptown Café for coffee. Back home, she'd chat with Granny on the phone for a while and then with Ashley if she was available. Joe McElroy came over for an hour of farming lessons, and after that, she escaped to her attic art studio. She spent the evenings with Jason—honing her driving skills in the vacant lot, visiting her tenants out at the farms, and maybe burgers at Bob's Bar or a hotdog and ice cream at Dairy Delight. When it got dark, they sat on her front porch, watching the stars twinkling overhead, and talked until Naomi thought she could talk no more.

"I have to admit," Ashley said to Naomi a few days later, "I think that hot Nebraska lawyer is good for you." Now that they had worked out the time differences, they talked almost as much now as they did in Japan.

"You have to stop calling him that. His name is Jason."

"All right. Jason then."

"Well, I *do* like Jason. A lot." Naomi sighed and took a bite of her breakfast bagel.

"What's the hesitation, then?"

"Can't you see that it's doomed from the start? I can't stay here in this teeny-weeny town forever."

"Why not? You're from a teeny-weeny town, aren't you?"

Naomi snorted. "I know that I used to say that. I used to think that, too. But, let me tell you, a town with 749 people isn't anything like where I came from. Oh, sorry, make that 748 because Jake Jenkins died this morning. Anyway, I'll never again think a town with 40,000 people is small."

"Well, maybe he'll move to a bigger city."

"He gave up San Francisco to come back here."

"But wasn't that just to get away from his ex?"

"Marvilla said he needed to take over his father's practice." Naomi just couldn't let go of the niggling worry that there was a lot more to it than just that. "But I'm not really sure what—"

"Look," Ashley continued in a practical tone, "if it's meant to be, it'll all work out. It'll feel right, and it'll be right. Take me and my Hiroshi. I just knew from the moment I met him that he was the one. There were plenty of people who were against us, you know, but I didn't give a rat's ass. I knew it was right, and that was all that counted. So, if it's right for you, you'll know."

Naomi smiled and nodded. From the way Ashley had been carrying on and on about Hiroshi, she thought he'd be tall and handsome, like a movie star. So, the last person she ever expected to see when she finally got to meet the guy was someone short, chubby, and bespectacled. But Hiroshi turned out to be one of the kindest, sweetest, and most lovable men she had ever met. No wonder Ashley fell for him the day after she arrived in Japan.

"And look how Jason helped you set up your studio."

Naomi's smile covered her entire face. "I've never had a guy do anything like that for me before. Ever. He just showed up with all his tools after I told him what I wanted to do and built shelves and everything."

"See? Keeper material. But changing the subject, I still can't believe you've been harboring this dream of being an artist and I never knew a thing about it."

"I guess I didn't even know myself. It sort of just came to me. But hang on. Let me show you what I did the other day." Naomi opened her sketch pad and held it up. "Isn't he cute? That's Fred."

"Fred? The pig's name is Fred?"

"Well, I call him that. I don't think people name their pigs around here."

"I'm sure you're right about that. Unless they call them bacon, sausage, or hot dog."

"Shut up! I can't bear to think about poor little Fred like *that.*"

Ashley rolled her eyes. "I just bet you can't. But hold it closer to the camera. Let me have a better look."

"So, what do you think?"

"You know, he kind of reminds me of Wilbur from *Charlotte's Web.* But different. There's a manga twist to it."

"Yeah, I guess that's what I was aiming for."

Ashley studied the picture. "I have an idea," she said after a moment. "Can you scan your sketches and send them to me?"

"What for?"

"It may be crazy, but you know Hiroshi works for a publishing company, right? His section chief wants me to come up with a proposal for a children's English book. I wasn't keen on that idea at first because I didn't want to work with some illustrator who can't string three English words together. But *you,* I could work with."

Naomi gave an uneasy laugh. "I'm not a professional—"

"It can't hurt to try. What do you think? Do you want me to show them to the editor?"

"I don't know. I don't think I'm ready."

"All they can do is say no, right? And if they do," Ashley said with a sudden burst of enthusiasm, "we'll try another publisher."

Naomi gaped at her best friend.

"Or are you planning to become famous after you're dead? Like Emily Dickinson?"

"No. I'm pretty sure I'd rather become famous while I'm still alive."

.   .   .

On the way to the county courthouse in Riley, Jason quizzed Naomi on the rules of the Nebraska roads, so when she took the written test for her learner's permit, she only got one answer wrong. After that, Jason had a few things to take care of at the courthouse, so they arranged to meet at Maisy's Pie Shop an hour later. When he got there, Naomi was settled in a booth by the window, chatting with the owner.

"Just getting acquainted here with Mike's daughter," Maisy said approvingly as she set a mug down in front of Jason and filled it with coffee before he even asked. "I like this one. *She* doesn't want no sugar-free pie and fat-free pastry." She handed him a menu and headed back behind the counter.

Jason nodded, looking uncomfortable. Then he pointed at Naomi's bags. "What'd you do? Hit every store in town?"

"Pretty much." She emptied the contents of one onto the table. "Did you know you can get salt and pepper shakers shaped just like pigs? Aren't these adorable?"

"They're pretty cute, all right," Jason handed Naomi a menu and leaned forward. "Let's hope Maisy's got some pie left. Between you and me," he said in a conspiratorial tone, "she makes the best pie around. But, if you ever tell Marvilla I said that, I'll flat out deny it."

Luckily, they could score the last two pieces of sour cream blueberry, and while they were waiting for them, Naomi said, "Can I ask you something, Jason? As my lawyer? As my financial advisor?"

Jason set down his cup.

"I don't know if you know this, but I never went to college."

"College isn't everything, you know."

"You may not think that's such a big deal, but it's a big deal to me. I'm not stupid or—"

"I'd never—"

"Because I *was* smart enough to get in. Everyone said so. My teachers said so. My friends said so. The only person who was against it was my grandfather."

"It wasn't your fault."

"But it *was*." Naomi paused while Maisy served their pie and refilled their mugs. "I should've just taken the entrance exams. Maybe my grandfather would've changed his mind if I'd gotten into a good university. But I rebelled in the stupidest way possible. I blew my chances in my last year of high school and gave up. You could say he won, and I lost." She squared her shoulders and gave him a look that dared him to argue. "So I've decided to apply for one next year."

Jason blinked in surprise. "Why, that's a super idea. There's no reason for you not to do that."

"Really?"

"Sure, if that's what you want to do. I believe your father would be really happy if you used your inheritance for that."

"That's so good to hear because I've been looking into some programs. Did you know some universities in Tokyo accept mature students?" She laughed and added, "It's kind of shocking to think of myself as a mature student. But I was also thinking—"

"Tokyo?" Jason blinked in surprise. "I see... What would you want to study?"

"Well, literature. Or maybe art history. I know they aren't career-oriented degrees. But I've always wanted to study those kinds of things. And you said that I can survive as long as I'm careful with my money. Right? I don't need to get a high-paying job."

"You're right. I did say that." After stirring some more cream into his coffee, he leaned forward. "So, back to school, huh?" After a moment, he added, "You know, they have colleges in Nebraska, too."

Naomi grinned and said sarcastically, "Oh really? I had no idea." Then she added, "That could be something I—"

Jason's phone on the table buzzed. "Sorry. I've got to answer this."

"Is everything all right?" Naomi asked, seeing the frown on Jason's face when the call ended.

"It seems my dad's upset and won't calm down. I was hoping to let you drive home now that you've got your permit, but that'll have to wait. They want me to come as soon as possible."

As Jason pulled off the highway and into Felix, he said, "I could drop you off at your house, but if you like, you could come in and meet my dad. I have to warn you, though, he's not the man he used to be."

In the community lounge in the nursing home, Ron Perry was shouting at a dazed-looking man with wispy Einstein hair. "You dirty thief! Just you wait until my son gets here from California. He'll tell you a thing or two!"

"Nice to see you, Reverend Winkle" Jason took his father's arm and led him toward the sofa on the other side of the room. "Let's go sit over there, Dad."

"That man poisoned my oatmeal this morning! I just know he did!" Ron turned and shook his fists at the Reverend. "Call the paddy wagon! Take him away!"

"This," Jason said to Naomi with a sad smile, "is my dad. And that man over there used to be his best friend. He was our minister before Peter Plank."

"Hello," Naomi said to Jason's father. His plaid bathrobe had fallen open, revealing a pair of scrawny legs.

"Well, hello to you, young lady." Ron pulled himself up and squared his shoulders. "Are you the new athletic director?"

"No, sir. I'm not. I'm Naomi Kihara. But it's very nice to meet you."

"You've come to see my prize, haven't you?"

"I'd love to see your prize," she replied evenly.

"Well, I'd love to show it to you, my dear, but it's in storage right now for safekeeping." Ron patted the sofa next to him, and Naomi sat down. "Too many people around here want to steal it. Him, for example." He jerked his head toward Jason. "You'd better watch out for that guy."

"Okay," she said, a smile cracking her lips. "I'll try to remember that."

"Are you single?"

"Oh, Dad. Let's not—"

"Yes," Naomi cut in. "I'm single."

"You should meet my son. He's really—oh, dammit. I forgot. He's married to some fancy-pantsy woman out in San Francisco named Heather-Feather and living a phony-baloney kind of life. Do you know her?"

"No, I'm afraid I don't."

"Well, thank your lucky star-bars for that. Looks like an angel, but she's a snake. What my son needs is a nice girl like you. You're a nice girl, aren't you?"

"Um, I like to think I am." Naomi's cheeks were turning pink.

"So, who are your people?"

After her short time in Felix, Naomi knew the right answer to that. "The Johnsons. Mike Johnson was my father."

"Well, well, well. What do you know? I'm Mike Johnson's lawyer. I was his parents' lawyer too, but they died. In an accident." Ron's voice faded, and then he added sadly, "My Johnny died in that accident, too." Ron turned his head toward Jason, and he blinked several times as if he couldn't believe his eyes. "Jason!" he exclaimed, recognition washing over his face. "When did *you* get here? Why didn't you call? Aren't you a sight for sore eyes? Give your old man a hug."

When they pulled apart, Jason's eyes were brimming with tears.

"Where's Heather?" Ron asked, looking over Jason's shoulder.

"She's in San Francisco, Dad. We're divorced."

"You are? Really?"

"About a year now."

"Why, that's the best news I've heard since Nixon resigned. So, is this charming young lady your girlfriend, then?"

"We're friends," Naomi said, filling Jason's silence. "I just moved here. I'm living in Evelyn's house."

An uproar at the far end of the lounge got everyone's attention. Ann Mayer had knocked over the card table and was accusing Doris Springer of cheating at poker again. The nurse on duty charged over to separate them before they could come to blows like they did the last time that had happened.

But the disturbance was all it took to make Ron's moment of lucidity disappear. His face changed and anger returned to his voice. "Where's my prize, you damn fool?"

"It's in storage, Dad," Jason sighed. "I'll bring it next time."

"I'm so sorry I made your father remember all those things," Naomi said when they got back to her house.

"Are you kidding? That was the best he's been in months. It was wonderful to see him like his old self, even just for a couple of minutes. Tonight was a real gift."

Naomi nodded and paused. "Would you like to come in? I've got some nice wine in the fridge."

"Sure! How could I say no to that?"

"Make yourself comfortable in the living room," she said as they stepped into the house, "and I'll throw something together."

A few minutes later, Naomi called him into the dining room. An attractive platter of cheese, crackers, dried figs, smoked ham, and green and black olives was on the dining room table, which had been set with plates and crystal wine glasses from the china cabinet and silver cutlery and cloth napkins from the sideboard. A chilled bottle of Chardonnay was in an ice bucket.

Jason blinked in surprise. "Is there some special occasion I don't know about?"

"I guess I wanted to say thanks for everything. You know, my farming lessons, my driving lessons, my studio, and, well, everything."

"You didn't have to go to all this trouble," Jason said, obviously pleased.

"But I wanted to." She leaned across the table and lit a pair of white taper candles placed in ornately carved silver candlesticks. "I love this room, and I love Evelyn's beautiful things. So I'm going to use everything as often as I can. Starting from tonight."

"Why do I get the feeling that none of this came from the Husker's Market?"

Naomi laughed. "Thank goodness for the internet."

They clinked their glasses together and settled in for an evening of laughter as they sipped their wine and nibbled at the food. As if by mutual agreement, they steered clear of topics that would involve their pasts or their futures, and instead, they shared humorous stories—Jason's funniest legal cases and Naomi's cross-cultural mishaps dealing with foreigners in Japan. The flickering candlelight cast a soft glow on Jason's face, and Naomi had the strongest urge to reach across the table and brush his hair away from his forehead.

"I don't remember when I've laughed this much," he said when it got toward midnight. "When I've had such a nice time."

"Me, either," murmured Naomi.

Jason sighed as he scooted back his chair. "Well, it's getting late. I'd better head back."

That wasn't what Naomi had hoped he would say. "Do you have an early day in court?" she asked as she walked him to her door.

Jason acted as if he hadn't heard her question. Instead, he turned to face her, and his eyes locked in on hers. Their blue-grey color had deepened, becoming more vivid in the soft hallway light. Mesmerized, Naomi couldn't look away. Time seemed to suspend as Jason leaned down and lowered his lips to hers. Such a gentle kiss, but Naomi felt like her heart had collided with a meteor.

Jason's warm breath feathered over her jaw. "Naomi, I-I…" Whatever it was he was going to say was lost when he pulled her to him. Her arms surrounded his neck and their lips fastened together in a long, hard kiss. Naomi would have stripped naked right then and there if Jason's hands were to begin wandering any further south on her body. He pulled away, and Naomi thought he was about to suggest going upstairs.

"I'll see you tomorrow," he whispered.

Naomi's voice felt unnatural when she replied, "Yeah, see you tomorrow."

And then he left.

He left!

CHAPTER EIGHTEEN

"How come you didn't think I'd like it here?" Naomi asked Jason as she bit into a California roll at Samurai Sushi in Lincoln. Their lunch was to celebrate Naomi acing her driving test the day before.

Jason shifted in his chair. "Um... Well, it's the only Japanese restaurant within reasonable driving distance. I've only been here once... um, with my... ex. And she didn't think it was authentic and..."

"Oh." Naomi maintained what she hoped was a neutral expression. "Well, I think it's pretty good here. It's not quite the same as what you'd get in Japan, of course. But still, I think it's pretty good."

It was better to stick to the topic of food rather than think about Jason being here before with Ms. Perfect. He looked so uncomfortable Naomi couldn't help but wonder if that woman was the reason why he had made such a hasty departure the other night. She hadn't known him for very long, but she could see he wasn't the type to start a relationship if he was still in love with someone else.

"I'm pretty sure there are others you might like to try, so maybe we..." Jason stopped speaking when a Japanese man in his forties with a buzz cut and wearing a navy kimono-type chef coat stepped out of the kitchen and approached their table.

"*Konnichiwa,*" he said to Naomi, wiping his hands on his apron. "I'm Kazuo Mori, the owner of this restaurant. I was pretty sure I spotted a Japanese person out here, so I thought I'd come out and say hello."

Speaking Japanese for the first time since she had arrived in Nebraska made Naomi forget all about the fact that Jason had been here with his wife. In fact, she almost forgot about Jason as well, even though he was sitting right across from her.

"Are you just passing through?" Kazuo asked.

"Actually, I'll be living in Felix for the next year."

His eyebrows shot up in surprise. "Felix? Way over there?"

"Yeah. That's where my family's from. It's my hometown." Naomi was surprised how natural it felt to say that. "Are there many other Japanese people around?"

"At the university, yes. But not so many outside of that. At least, not in Lincoln. Say, would you like to talk to my wife? Kyoko doesn't speak much English, and I'm pretty sure she'd be delighted to talk to you."

Naomi's face lit up. "*Honto ni?* Really? Oh my god, yes! I'd love that!"

Kazuo pulled out his phone, and after a rapid exchange with his wife, he handed it to Naomi and headed back into the kitchen.

"Do you have a pen?" Naomi asked Jason, switching into English.

Naomi was laughing and nodding as she scribbled notes on a napkin. When she got off the phone, she said breathlessly to him, "Mrs. Mori invited me for lunch next week. Do you think I could drive myself to her house? She said she doesn't live far from here."

"I don't see why not. You've got your license now, and it's pretty much a straight shot here from Felix. It'll be good for you to have a new friend. I say, go for it!"

The next morning, Jason called. "I'm going to Riley this afternoon. Do you want to come? You could do the driving and hit the shops on Main Street again."

"Sorry, I can't." Naomi stuck the phone between her chin and shoulder, biting into one of Reverend Pat's plums from the tree in his backyard. "I'm playing bridge with Marvilla, Dorothy, and Doreen."

"I didn't know you played bridge."

"I don't. But they insist I learn. They say I'll be good at it because Evelyn was a whale."

"A what? Oh. You mean *shark*."

"And before that, I'm going to the library to show the third graders how to fold origami cranes."

"And weren't you at the Lutheran church yesterday helping with their bake sale?"

"Uh-huh."

"You've only been here a short while and look at your social calendar! I guess I'll have to book with you in advance if I want to see you."

"To think I was worried I'd be bored with nothing to do here. That phone of Evelyn's you gave me has been ringing all day long. Sometimes I wonder if people are beginning to think I'm her."

Jason chuckled. "Well then, how about dinner at my place tonight? I make a mean TV dinner."

"TV dinner? You're inviting me over for a TV dinner?"

"Well, for you, I'm sure I could rustle up something a little better."

The way he spoke seemed like he was promising more than just dinner, and her heart skipped a half-dozen beats.

"Let's go into the kitchen," Jason said that evening when he opened the front door. "I've got to take dinner out of the oven."

Naomi followed him through the living room, struck by how similar his house was to hers—probably because it was built around the same time and was filled with similar mementos from previous generations. Not only were there plenty of photos here and there of people, but someone in the family had also been a cross stitcher, and their framed works were prominently displayed in the hallway.

"It smells great, and—oh my god!" Naomi exclaimed when she stepped into the kitchen. "What are you? Some sort of secret gourmet cook?"

Jason turned the color of a ripe tomato. "Um, my ex…"

Of course, that woman would have to be a gourmet chef on top of everything else. "I guess she must've really loved cooking," Naomi said.

"That couldn't be further from the truth. She didn't know how to make anything beyond a scrambled egg or a boiled chicken breast."

"Then why—"

"This kitchen was just another one of her projects." He took a bottle of wine from the fridge and poured it into pink-tinged goblets and downed several quick sips.

Naomi did the same with her wine, giving her courage. "I know it's none of my business, but are you sorry she's gone?"

"What?"

"You seem upset every time her name comes up." Before she could control her mouth, she found herself asking if he was still in love with her.

Jason set his glass down. "To be perfectly honest, I don't think I ever was. Our marriage was—"

"I don't expect you to tell me everything that went on in your marriage. Or about your ex-wife. It's just that she was so perfect and…" If only she could rewind back to the moment when she stepped into the kitchen. If only she could start this evening all over again. The humming of the electric clock on top of the refrigerator reverberated through the kitchen, and she wished the floor would swallow her up.

"Perfect?" Jason finally said. "You think she was perfect?"

She might as well be honest. "I know it was none of my business, but I googled her. I saw your wedding. And other stuff, too. She's so beautiful, and I understand if you don't want to talk about her. If it's painful for you…"

Jason reached across the table and covered her hands with his. "I don't like to talk about her because I'd rather forget every single thing about her. It's true she's beautiful, but she isn't nice."

The oven timer dinged. He removed the roast chicken from the oven, set it on the counter, and sat across from Naomi. He began to speak about Heather. About how they had met at one of his firm's charity functions. How they had started dating. How she had convinced her father she wanted to marry him, even though he had no money, no background, and no power. "I joined her world. I admit it was thrilling at first. But when I came home to take care of my dad, I felt like I had been released from a cult. I wanted *this* life, and not hers."

"So she came here and—"

"She came because her father told her to. They both thought I'd come to my senses and go back to San Francisco. When she finally left, I was glad to see her go. We weren't right for each other, and we never were."

He got up to carve the chicken, and Naomi sipped at her wine, unsure if this discussion had ended or if it was just on pause.

"Honestly speaking," he said, turning around, "I have many regrets. The biggest is the mess I made by pretending to be someone I'm not. I should've listened to my father. He warned me that Heather might not be the person for me, and he was right. I don't want to go into detail because it'd be just my side of the story, and Heather would have an entirely different one. But trust me. I'm *not* sorry she's gone, and I'm *not* pining for her in the least."

"I'm sorry I snooped and—"

"There's nothing for you to apologize for. I should have told you everything upfront." He pulled Naomi up out of her chair, and wrapping his strong, ropey arms around her, he murmured into her hair, "This is the point where *everything* begins."

She turned her face toward his and saw the longing in his eyes. But then, the doorbell buzzed, and they sprang apart as if they were teenagers whose parents had come home earlier than expected. Jason put his finger on his lips and peeked out the window.

"Dammit. That's Shirley Nelson's car. She'll never leave."

Considering the way the doorbell was relentlessly buzzing, Naomi thought he was probably right about that. Jason went to shoo the unwelcome visitor away but a minute later he came back into the kitchen, followed by a woman wielding a purple cane that matched her hair.

"I'm sorry," he mouthed at Naomi as he pulled out a chair for Shirley.

He introduced the two women and then said, "Well, let me take a look at that contract for you." Shirley fished it out of her bag and handed it over. "Hmm," Jason said after studying it. "It looks pretty straightforward to me. It's just the renewal notice for your cable TV subscription. They are raising the price, though."

"Why, that's just highway robbery!"

"Isn't it? They've got us over a barrel, that's for sure. Because you and I both know, without cable, we can't get any of those good shows on the oldies network here."

After Shirley agreed she'd rather pay the fee than do without her favorite programs, she started shooting hungry eyes at the chicken on the counter. Jason glanced over at Naomi, and she nodded.

"Would you like to stay for dinner, Shirley?"

It was after ten by the time Shirley was ready to go home, and since the older woman was giddy from a glass and a half of wine, Jason figured he had better take her home and see her to her door.

"How about a drive tomorrow afternoon?" he whispered to Naomi after he settled Shirley into the passenger side of her car. "We could go to Branched Oaks—one of the Salt Valley Lakes near Omaha. We can swim, have dinner afterward... like," he added in a husky voice, "a real date."

"A real date," repeated Naomi, feeling dizzy at the prospect. "Yeah, I'd like that."

Chapter Nineteen

Jason and Naomi sat in the shade on a faded blue beach towel and sipped iced tea from a thermos after having spent an hour splashing around in the lake. The cold water should have cooled him down, but heat radiated through every part of Jason's body. He watched Naomi's mouth move as she spoke and her damp, dark hair seemed to sparkle in the sunshine. How could he concentrate on anything when she was mere inches away from him in a tiny black bikini adorned with a few yellow butterflies? She was telling him about her visit to the Thompson farm that morning, but all he could think about was last night. About what would have happened if Shirley Nelson hadn't picked the worst time in the world to pay a visit. In fact, that had been the only thing he could think about all day long. His mind kept returning to the landscape of Naomi's lips, and even the judge at the traffic court had to ask what was wrong with him when he failed to respond to one of his questions.

He planned to revisit those lips soon. And then he planned to move down to her neck and on to her shoulder, where he learned today there was a most distracting and alluring diamond-shaped birthmark. He reached for the thermos and refilled their cups before his thoughts got him into serious trouble. The debate that had been raging in his brain for the past few weeks was completely over. It didn't matter that Naomi would go back to

Japan. Why worry about that now, when anything could happen? The here and now was the only thing that mattered.

Naomi leaned into him, tilted her face upwards, and kissed him. Just a peck, but a shiver raced up between his shoulder blades. She pulled back and smiled. Her eyes made it clear they were both on the same page.

He bent down and caught her lips in much more than a peck. "Maybe we should go." He didn't want those teenagers over by the barbecue pits to start hollering at them to go get a room, although that was exactly what he was planning to do. After some wining and dining, of course. It was, after all, a *date.*

Naomi emerged from the dressing room in a simple cotton sundress the color of crushed strawberries. Jason pressed his lips to her cheek. But what he really wanted to do was to take her in his arms and kiss her until neither of them could stand up. Instead, he asked if she was ready to go have the best steak this side of the Mississippi.

At the Nebraska Grill, they held hands across the table, ignoring their glasses of wine.

"Here you go. Anything else? Some A-1 sauce?"

Having forgotten that they had ordered food, they looked up at the server with surprise and shook their heads.

"Jason—"

"I want you." Date protocol be damned. Jason's mouth felt like it had been stuffed with cotton.

"I want you, too. So much I can't think straight."

"Do you want to go somewhere?"

"Yes. Now."

Jason pulled some twenties from his wallet and laid them on the table. They were about to walk away when he paused, picked up their untouched plates, and set the steaks down in front of the family that was squeezed into the booth next to theirs. Their two husky kids had been whining about having to order hamburgers from the children's menu ever since they came in. Because Grandma, it seemed, was paying.

"A family emergency," Jason told them. "You'd be doing us a huge favor if you'd eat these for us."

They were out the door before the parents could even blink. The way Naomi's entire face smiled, he knew he had done the right thing. She wasn't the type to grumble about violating health codes, overstepping parental boundaries, or being sued if something was wrong with the food. In the car, he pulled her to him for a hungry kiss. And another.

Two hours later, they were between the tangled sheets in a room at the first motel they had come to on the outskirts of Omaha. The Best Western wasn't the greatest hotel in town, but at least it wasn't the worst.

Naomi's head was settled into the space under the curve of his arm, and his lips brushed her temple. They had already made love twice—the first time, they barely had gotten the door shut before they fell onto the bed with an urgency he hadn't imagined existed in him. The second time, they stretched out between the sheets and explored each other's bodies as thoroughly as if they were taking the scenic route of a long, leisurely vacation.

Several strands of Naomi's hair floated up into his face, and he brushed them down with tenderness and kissed her temples again. His fingertips trailed lightly over Naomi's back. She was so quiet he thought she had fallen asleep. He exhaled a satisfied sigh and shut his eyes. Just then, Naomi pushed herself up on her elbows, kissed him gently, and they made love a third time.

•   •   •

"Did you have a nice time, dear?" Marvilla called out from her petunia bed in her front yard when Naomi got out of Jason's car the following afternoon.

"Uh-huh," Naomi answered, her cheeks burning as she hurried into the house. She was pretty sure that Marvilla knew that she hadn't been home for twenty-four hours and that she and Jason had been *up to no good,* as the old lady liked to put it. Was it possible that she somehow even knew about that quickie in the back of the truck behind an oak grove road on the way home?

"Just like teenagers," Jason had laughed.

They decided that, for now, they'd keep their relationship quiet.

Their secret lasted about a dozen hours.

The next morning in the Husker Market, Kelly Jefferson from the nursing home stopped hissing at her kids in the checkout line just long enough to say in a voice that fell short of good-natured teasing, "What's this I hear about you and Jason?"

The heads of the people ahead of Kelly, one of which belonged to that awful minister from the church, spun around.

"But doesn't he still have a thing for his wife?" Kelly added.

"I… Uh… Oh! I forgot to get milk." Naomi hid in the dairy section until she was certain Kelly and everyone else were out the door. When the coast was clear, she swallowed her embarrassment and went to pay for her groceries.

"Forget Kelly," Gina McNeil said at the cash register. "She's just jealous because she's been trying to snag Jason ever since his snobby wife, a witch with a capital B, went back to California. Jason's a real nice guy. Of course, he's not as nice as my Lenny." Gina waved a pretty little ring under Naomi's nose and then started to bag the groceries.

Just outside the Husker Market, Naomi nearly collided with Donna. "You don't waste much time at all, do you? Latching on to the first guy you meet here. I guess you know which side your rice is buttered on." Without waiting for a reply, Donna dropped her cigarette, ground it out with her heel, and headed inside.

Naomi was momentarily paralyzed by her rudeness and didn't notice when Jeremy's daughter Andrea came and stood right next to her.

"Sorry about that," the girl said. "My grandmother's a bit narrow-minded."

Well, that was the understatement of the century. "Don't worry about it," said Naomi.

Andrea giggled as if Naomi had made a joke. "You know, I *loved* talking to Cousin Mike about Japan. His stories were so fascinating. But you know what? He never told me anything about *you*. I was kind of surprised because he told me all kinds of stuff, but he never said anything about you. So, what a big surprise you are. You're almost like an alien that dropped in from outer space. But instead of it being outer space, it's Japan. Japan must be the coolest place in the world. I really, really, really want to go there someday, you know. Mike told me all about it. I want to see cosplay and a maid café and all that really cool stuff. Are there any geisha where you live? Or do they only live by Mount Fujiyama?"

Well, that certainly took Naomi's mind off the matter at hand—that the whole town seemed to know about her and Jason. "You could come over sometime. We could talk about Japan if you like."

"Really? That's great! When?"

"What?"

"When? I'm free all the time except for when I have cheerleading practice or Bible study. So, how about either Tuesday, Wednesday, or Friday? Which one is best for you?"

Thrown off balance by the girl's hectic enthusiasm, Naomi said, "Um, sure. Okay. Well, how about Tuesday, then?"

"Fantastic," Andrea said as she headed into the store. "I'll be there right after school."

"Great." Naomi felt dazed.

That night, Naomi learned how the system worked. Apparently, Doug Peter's cousin had seen them kissing at the lake. The server at the restaurant had told her friend Sandy Smith (whose mother runs the Uptown Café in Felix) about the couple who gave away their expensive steaks. But the clincher was Al Fraser, who had been on his way to visit his brother, who was having cancer treatments at Creighton University Hospital. Al pulled off the Interstate to use the facilities at the filling station next to the Best Western. Even though he was over eighty, it didn't take long for him to put two and two together when he saw Jason and Naomi drive up and get out of the car.

"Those two could barely keep their hands off each other," Al reported to his wife over breakfast.

It was only logical that by lunchtime, the whole town knew that they were a thing.

"I guess it's not a secret anymore," Naomi said.

"Do you mind?" Jason asked.

"I don't if you don't."

And that was how their relationship went public.

CHAPTER TWENTY

"Cool," Andrea said when Naomi asked her to remove her shoes and wear slippers as she stepped into her house on Tuesday afternoon.

"Would you like some, um… pop?" Naomi was now fully stocked for guests.

"Can I just have water? I read somewhere that stuff is really bad for you."

"How about Japanese tea, then?"

"Oh, wow! Can I?"

Naomi put the kettle on in the kitchen and measured tea into the pot. Reaching into the cupboard for cookies, she asked, "Would you like to stay for dinner? It'd just be something simple."

"Thanks, but Lisa and my dad are waiting for me." After a moment, she added, "Lisa's my stepmom, you know. My *real* mom ran away when I was a baby. Of course, I love Lisa and all that, but I still can't help but wonder about my birth mom."

Naomi's eyes softened in understanding. "I know what you mean. I didn't know anything about my father, either."

"Yeah, weird, huh? You didn't know anything about any of us here in Felix, and we didn't know anything about you, either. We were all pretty surprised to hear that Mike had a… a… Eurasian love child."

Naomi smiled a tight little smile and told herself that Andrea didn't know better. "Yeah, well, it was a big surprise to me, too. I didn't even know his name until I was about twelve. I searched for him, but do you know how many Mike Johnsons are out there?"

"Well," said Andrea, "my mom was Lynn Smith. Just try Googling *Smith*!"

Naomi wanted to show support for this clueless but well-meaning teenager, so she asked, "Do you know anything about your mother?"

"Not really. My dad doesn't like to talk about her. Who can blame him since he was the one who got dumped? I don't like to upset Lisa, either. Especially not now that she's always sick."

"I heard about that. I hope the doctors can find out what's wrong with her soon."

"Me, too. But I suppose it's mental like the doctors say. She can't do much, so she just watches a lot of TV." Andrea popped a whole cookie into her mouth, and while chewing, she picked up another one. "I hate TV. Our house is so small, and Lisa has the volume turned all the way up. I can't concentrate on my homework."

"You could study here if you like," offered Naomi, remembering that the girl used to do that.

Andrea broke into a smile. "Really?"

"Sure. I don't mind. There's plenty of space."

"Because I'm trying to get a scholarship for college, you know. That's why I'm taking all these summer school classes. But I need a quiet place to study."

"A scholarship! Wouldn't that be wonderful?"

"Yeah. My teachers are pretty sure I'll get one. It's a win-win situation, being the smartest *and* the poorest. I'm going to major in science. I'm good at English, too, so I thought of becoming a journalist or something like that. But Mr. Jenkins—he's my science teacher—says that there're lots of opportunities for women in science. So I've been working as his TA. I help him prepare for his classes and order supplies and stuff like that. And he lets me do independent research in the lab. That's really fun. I can learn all kinds of cool things, and I can do stuff that we don't get to do in class. You'd be surprised how much there is. But the main thing is, he'll write a good letter of recommendation for me."

"I bet your parents are so proud of you." Naomi pushed back feelings of envy for Andrea getting the support she never had.

"Maybe. I don't know. Lisa thinks I should go get a union job in the chicken plant after graduation. Can you see *me* gutting chickens? I'd hate that. Wouldn't you?"

Naomi couldn't imagine anything worse.

"My dad's okay with me going to college. If someone else pays, of course. Because he sure doesn't have the money. He knows I want to do something with my life. Something that does not involve blood or feathers," Andrea said with a shudder. "Unless it's in a lab. I guess I wouldn't mind blood, guts, or gore if it was for science. And maybe someday I could win the Nobel Prize."

Naomi smiled at Andrea's big dreams. "Wouldn't that be something?"

"Yeah, it sure would." Andrea reached for another cookie. "I'll be the first person in my family to go to college. Most of them are kind of losers. Like my Uncle Gary. You know what *he* did, right? When he was a teenager?"

Naomi nodded uncomfortably.

"Well, my dad's kind of dumb, but at least he's not as bad as *that*."

At a loss for words, Naomi merely nodded again.

"That's why everyone tries to help me out, you know? Because I'm smarter than all the Hardys put together. That's why Evelyn used to let me study here. And that's why Reverend Plank gave me a job."

"Oh, you got a job?"

"Yeah. Just a temporary one—digitalizing the old church records. You know, obituaries, birth notices—that kind of thing. They have boxes and boxes of newspaper clippings, and the Sunday School Society decided they needed to get that all organized before all their precious history gets eaten by termites. But between you and me, it's the same old thing week after week, year after year. I don't care because I get paid for doing it, and I bet you anything I can get another good letter of recommendation out of it."

"Well, that sounds great."

"I mean, I don't mind volunteering at our church. I like helping out. But it's real nice to get paid."

"Of course it is."

Andrea brought the teacup to her lips. "Reverend Plank likes *me* a lot. He's always asking me to come in to do things, and that's good, I suppose. But I'm super glad I don't have to use his office when I'm working, because don't you think that'd be a little creepy?"

"Mmm," said Naomi.

"There's a small room next to his office, and I work there. I don't like it when the Reverend gets a bit handsy and—" Andrea stopped and put her hands over her mouth. "Don't tell anyone I said that, okay? I don't want people to get the wrong impression. I didn't mean that the way it sounded."

Naomi barely had a chance to process that information before Andrea changed the subject to manga and anime. After the entire plate of cookies disappeared, Naomi stood to get more, but Andrea said she had to hurry home for dinner.

"Oh, that's too bad," Naomi said, thinking the exact opposite. The last time she had spent time with a teenager was when she was one, and it was a lot more exhausting than she had thought it would be.

Naomi walked Andrea to her old, dented Ford parked out front and waved goodbye as she drove off. If she had a better sense of the town's layout, she would have wondered why the girl had turned down Allen Street and headed toward the park rather than Arbor Street, which would've taken her home. She would have wondered why Andrea had decided to use the dirty park bathroom rather than the one at her house. But if she had seen Andrea with her fingers down her throat there, she would have understood how the girl could devour all those cookies in one sitting and still maintain her cheerleader figure.

CHAPTER TWENTY-ONE

It was Friday, and Friday meant fish fry. Winston's over in South Peak was having a two-for-one special. Naomi and Jason were taking Marvilla out for dinner for no reason other than Winston's was Marvilla's favorite place to eat, and Naomi hadn't been there yet.

Jason's phone rang just as he was putting the key in the ignition. "I wonder what Peter Plank wants."

"Well, he's not getting any money out of *me*," muttered Marvilla, all dolled up in her going-out-to-eat outfit, sunlight bouncing off of a sequined peacock on the turquoise blouse hugging the hips of her satiny slacks.

"Hi, Peter." Jason winked at Marvilla. "What's up?" But by the time he got off the phone, his buoyant mood was significantly toned down.

"What's wrong?" Naomi asked. "Did something happen?"

Jason frowned and shook his head in a way that meant neither yes nor no. "Peter said a new will was found in one of the church library books."

"What will? Whose will?" Marvilla asked.

"Evelyn's."

"Oh, now that's plain crazy," said Marvilla. "Why on earth would you put her will in a library book?"

"Of course, I didn't do that. It wasn't me. Apparently, Evelyn did. And it was written in September."

"September? What does that have to—oh. September."

"Before we get too concerned over that, Marvilla, I'll just go have a look. It's probably nothing, but you two go back inside the house and wait. You know what Peter's like. For all we know, it could be Evelyn's shopping list. I'll be back as soon as I can."

"That Peter Plank's middle name must be Stirring-up-Trouble," grumbled Marvilla as they headed back inside. This time she remembered to take off her shoes and put on the slippers. She plopped into the recliner and turned the TV on. "But don't you worry about a thing, dear. Jason will sort it all out and we'll be on our way. I just hope that man's shenanigans don't make me miss out on the fried shrimp and scallops. You've got to get there plenty early on Fridays for that."

Naomi had seen Jason's face as he drove off, and she couldn't help but wonder if it might be more serious than he had let on. Naomi reached for the remote and turned the sound down about ten notches on the canned laughter from the sitcom rerun. "What's so important about September? Why were you both surprised when Peter Plank said that the will, or whatever it is, was written in September?"

Marvilla sighed and leaned forward. "Well, dear, that was when Evelyn fell down the cellar steps, which was entirely my fault."

"What?"

"I still feel terrible because if I hadn't gone away, she could still be alive. I had a bad feeling about leaving her here on her own to go see *Shepherd of the Hills* in Branson, but it was something that I had wanted to see my whole life. And there was that nice bus—with a toilet and *everything*—that Eastern Star had rented for thirty people. I hemmed and hawed about going, but the show included an all-you-can-eat dinner. How could I turn down a once-in-a-lifetime opportunity like that?"

That was enough of a verbal detour. "Marvilla, tell me what happened."

"The plain and simple fact is, Evelyn fell down the cellar stairs after she had gone to get some of that rhubarb jam I'd put up last summer. But we can't figure out why she took it in her head to do that because she always avoided stairs. That's why she had that fool Jeremy Hardy haul down a twin bed from the attic and put it in the den. She never went up and down stairs if she could help it, and certainly not when she was alone."

"But how could that be your fault? She could've fallen down the steps even if you were next door. You weren't here *all* the time."

"If I hadn't been off gallivanting throughout the country, I would've gone down there and gotten the jam for her. If the poor old dear had just told me she was having a hankering for rhubarb in the first place, I would've left some upstairs for her. She was never the same again. And to tell the truth, after that, I lost my appetite for rhubarb."

. . .

Jason found Peter Plank sitting in his office behind an old oak desk scuffed and scratched from generations of preachers.

Peter stood. "I know you're in a hurry to see that will. But let's wait for Tom. I want to make sure that everything is above board. I know how close you are to the Johnsons, so I wouldn't want there to be any doubt—"

"You called the sheriff? Are you insinuating that I'd do anything illegal or improper?"

Before Peter could answer, Tom stuck his head in the door. "What's so urgent, Peter? My kids are out in the car, and we're heading to the movies in Lincoln."

"Sorry about that, but I found something you both need to see. Come on in and have a seat." Peter pulled a book out of his drawer and slid it across the desk toward them.

Tom picked it up. "*The Robe*? You called me over here to look at this old book?"

"It's what was *in* the book that's important," Peter said impatiently. "Look inside the envelope."

Tom shook a few receipts out of the envelope and removed the letter. After studying it for a moment, he handed it to Jason. To Peter, he said, "Maybe you should tell us how you came by this."

"Lois Lundt found it in this book that she borrowed from our church library and brought it back a little while ago. I called you both right away."

"What do you think of this?" Tom said to Jason.

"It's not as detailed as what a lawyer would draw up. But—"

"But is it legal?" Tom asked.

"Give me a second, would you?" Jason read it again before saying, "If this proves genuine, it very well could be."

Tom examined the borrowing card in the holder pasted into the front of the book. "It says here that Evelyn returned it on September 12th. She must've forgotten that she had stuck her will in the book."

"That was the day she fell," said Jason slowly. "Maybe just hours earlier."

"But the will was written *before* that," Tom said, looking at the paper again. "On September 9th and she was fine then." His eyes moved out the window, and he groaned seeing his wife waving and pointing at her watch. "Look, I'll have to check into this tomorrow. I've got a carload of family waiting for me and can't do much about this now since it doesn't qualify as a police emergency." He put his hand on the doorknob, and before leaving, he turned to Jason. "This is going to open up a whole can of worms, isn't it?"

"Probably so."

"But why in the world would Evelyn suddenly decide to make Jeremy Hardy her heir?" Tom asked. "Everyone knew she always intended to leave everything to Mike."

. . .

Marvilla switched off the TV and hurried out the door and down the steps as soon as she saw Jason pulling into the driveway. "Okay, Jason. Let's go. Tell us what that man's up to in the car. It's getting late, and I want to be home before my programs start."

When Naomi saw Jason's face, she realized that the chances of Marvilla getting her seafood dinner that night were pretty much on the slim side.

Jason caught Marvilla by the elbow, spun her around, and pointed her back in the direction of the house. "Let's go inside."

In the living room, Naomi and Marvilla watched Jason pace back and forth until Naomi asked, "What is it? You're scaring us."

"It's bad," he said.

"Is it bad enough to have some of that wine Naomi's got stashed in the back cupboard?"

Before Naomi could ask how Marvilla knew about that, Jason said that yes, it was bad enough for that. Marvilla retrieved a bottle, pulled a corkscrew out from the dining room buffet that Naomi hadn't even known was there, and opened it as if she had had a previous career as a sommelier.

"What?" Marvilla asked when she caught Naomi staring at her.

Fifteen minutes later, Naomi was wrapping and unwrapping the chain holding the diamond pendant at her throat around her index finger, ordering herself to inhale and exhale.

"I can't believe it," said Marvilla. "I simply *don't* believe it. I refuse to believe it. Evelyn would never do such a thing to Mike. It can't be legal, can it, coming off the computer and all that without a lawyer?"

"It doesn't matter if it was from the internet or not, Marvilla," said Jason. "Those kinds of wills can be perfectly valid."

"And you're sure it was written before she fell?" asked Marvilla.

"Why would that make any difference?" Naomi looked at the bottle of wine with longing, wanting to pick it up and swig down the rest of its contents. "Obviously, Evelyn wanted someone else to inherit. And that someone else wasn't my father."

"But it would matter," said Jason, "because if it was written after the fall, we could say that she wasn't in her right mind and didn't know what she was doing. But that's not the case because it was written two days before."

"So, it's all gone. My fairy tale dream is over." Naomi's eyes were as dry as a desert. In a monotone voice, she said, "It's okay. I'm okay. I was poor before. I can be poor again."

"Listen to me," said Jason. "No matter what happens, you aren't poor. Evelyn's will doesn't affect what your father left you. Your apartment in Tokyo. The cash in his accounts."

"But I lose the farms, right? And this house? Everything in it." Naomi unclasped the diamond necklace and dropped it on the table.

"Don't be so hasty." He stood and put it back around her neck. "We are not going to panic. Do you hear me?"

Did she look like she was going to panic? She felt as calm as a corpse when she said, "But I'll have to give the house back."

Naomi closed her eyes and thought she wouldn't be feeling such pain if the past two months hadn't happened. If she had never come to Nebraska, she never would have slept in her great-grandmother's bed, held her lovely things in her hand, or heard all the family stories from Marvilla. She never would have seen the farms or become close to the people who were taking such good care of them. She never would have started thinking about what it might be like to stay in Nebraska beyond the one-year agreement.

"I love this house," she said, "and the farms. But I guess Evelyn wanted someone else to have them."

"I tell you, Jason, those computer things are dangerous. I've seen on Oprah how people get themselves into all kinds of trouble with that internet nonsense."

Jason stared at Marvilla for a moment. "You've given me an idea." Turning to Naomi, he said, "Let me check Evelyn's computer. You haven't deleted her search history, have you?"

"I don't think so. I don't even know what that is."

They followed him into the den and watched over his shoulder. With each click of the mouse, Jason swore under his breath. Not only had Evelyn been visiting will-writing tutorial websites, but she had also been researching how to disinherit someone.

"This makes things a lot worse, doesn't it?" said Naomi.

Jason turned to Marvilla. "Did Evelyn ever say anything to you about changing her will? About leaving her estate to Jeremy? About disinheriting Mike?"

Marvilla shook her head.

"Think. Are you sure?"

"Never," she answered.

"It's okay," Naomi said, hugging the older woman after she began to sob. "If she didn't tell you, she didn't tell you."

Chapter Twenty-Two

Sharlene Roberts always tried to get to work as close to nine as possible, which wasn't easy considering she had to get all her children off to school and then swing by and help her seventy-year-old mother, who was something of a hypochondriac, get settled for the day. When she unlocked the office door at 9:08, the last thing she expected to see was her boss sprawled out on the old leather sofa and his desk littered with papers, snack wrappers, and three empty Coke cans. She made coffee and wondered what to do about Jason's ten o'clock appointment with Al Fraser. In the nine years she had been working there—seven for Ron Perry and two for Jason—she had never witnessed an all-nighter unless it involved a poker game with the Masons downstairs.

At 9:10, the phone rang.

"Jason," she said, shaking his shoulder. "It's someone from Stanley and Silo."

He jerked awake and stumbled to the desk. "Jason Perry, here."

Myron Silo got straight to the point. "I'm representing the interests of the Hardy family of Felix, and it has come to our attention that a more recent will of Mrs. Evelyn Johnson has been discovered naming my client as sole heir."

Damn that Peter Plank, thought Jason. Even though Tom asked him not to say anything, he'd do whatever he pleased, believing he was receiving instructions from Jesus H. Christ himself. "Actually, Myron, I was heading over to the county courthouse this morning to see about—"

"We will petition the court to reopen probate," Myron interrupted. "But my client is concerned about the illegal occupancy of the current resident of Evelyn Johnson's home. As a courtesy, I wanted to let you know that I'll be filing an eviction notice—"

"Come on, Myron. Is that necessary? Probate will have to be reopened, but surely there's no reason to evict Evelyn Johnson's great-granddaughter."

"I'm sorry, Jason, but my client disagrees."

"Excuse me, but who exactly is your client?" Jason nodded to Sharlene for handing him a large mug of coffee.

"Donna Hardy has retained me on behalf of her son."

That figures. He could just see her reaching for the phone to call that ambulance-chasing law firm that advertises on late-night television the moment she got the news.

"And there is no proof that this woman," Myron continued, "a Naomi Kihara, won't abscond with the valuables left in the house. The jewelry, the china, the silver. All of which, Mrs. Hardy points out, are Johnson family heirlooms and must remain in the family. She believes this woman may remove valuables from the home to sell in Japan."

Jason would have laughed at that ridiculous statement if he hadn't been so annoyed. Instead, he said cooly, "My client is the great-granddaughter of Evelyn Johnson."

"But do you have proof? Mrs. Hardy believes she is part of an elaborate scam."

"I would advise you to inform your client that if she makes any such statements in public, I will sue her for defamation of character." Thank god Mike had had the foresight to do those DNA tests.

Myron coughed a little laugh. "No sense in stirring up bad feelings. I'll advise my client to take that into consideration, Jason. But as I said, I'm petitioning the court to have your client vacate the premises within twenty-four hours. This is a courtesy call so that she can make alternative living arrangements."

Jason was out the door heading to the courthouse in Lincoln before Sharlene could ask him what was going on and whether she should reschedule Al Fraser's appointment.

■ ■ ■

Sleep was impossible, considering it was Naomi's last night in Evelyn's house. From the way Jason held her with such a sad face, she knew she might never be able to return if things went the way the Hardys and their creepy lawyer hoped. She didn't want to waste the night by sleeping, so after Jason dozed off, she slipped out of bed and went downstairs.

At least the judge had given her seventy-two hours, not the twenty-four that awful lawyer had demanded. She had time to say goodbye to George, Matthew, Winnie, Elizabeth, Kenneth, Mabel, and Pauline—her ancestors in the photos. No longer scary and stern—she had come to think of them as good company, and she was going to miss them. She stood in front of the framed wedding photos on the dining room wall. Her grandmother Elizabeth, her great-grandmother Evelyn, and her great-great-grandmother Mabel wore the same dress, the one that Naomi had found wrapped in tissue paper and scented with dried lavender and bay leaves in a cedar box in the back of one of the closets. She wished she had taken the time to try it on when it was hers.

"Goodbye," she whispered, running her fingers over the china and silver. She said goodbye to the Dresden figurines. To the Depression glass. To the hundred-year-old cast iron skillets in the kitchen.

Her eyes fell on a cameo brooch when she returned the diamond necklace to the jewelry box she had brought downstairs with her. Realizing it was the same one worn by all the brides in the wedding photos, she dropped it into her pocket. She deserved at least one small memento.

Just before dawn, Jason came into the kitchen and found Naomi looking through an album filled with black and white photos from the 1930s and 1940s. He was barefoot and bare-chested, wearing jeans that were snug in all the right places. He stood behind her chair, draped his arms around her, and nuzzled her neck. If she hadn't been so distraught by everything, she would have led him straight back to the bedroom. Instead, she sighed and leaned into him.

"I wish you'd come and stay with me."

"It's too soon for that, Jason. Besides, you know how much of a city girl I am. Being right on Main Street will almost be like being back in Tokyo. And if I want to go to the beauty parlor, all I have to do is run downstairs."

Jason smiled at her attempt at humor. "At least you'll come over every day, right?"

"Absolutely." The first thing he did when it became clear she would have to move was to make sure she had a place to work. He tidied up the shed in his backyard that his father had used as a workshop and carried everything over from Naomi's attic studio.

Jason tried to think of something to say that would make her feel better. He couldn't come up with anything, so they sat in silence. At least the judge had agreed that the house would remain empty until a final ruling could be made, and Jason would continue managing the farms with the Thompsons as the tenants. Their contracts were valid for another year, and there was nothing the Hardys could do about that. But unless a miracle happened, everything could belong to Jeremy Hardy within a month.

There was no question that it was Evelyn's signature on the new will. And while she didn't come right out and say Jeremy Hardy was her grandson, she alluded to it by writing she wanted to do right by him. She said she wanted her farms to go to a local family with local ties. Mike had plenty of his own money, and his life was permanently centered in Japan. Everything she wrote *was* true, but Jason had trouble believing she would actually leave her estate to Jeremy Hardy. So did half the town. The probate hearing would happen in three weeks, and that was all the time he had to come up with something, *anything*, to prove that the will was invalid.

So far, he had zilch.

After the kitchen was brightened by the rising sun, Jason started making breakfast. While the bacon was sizzling and the eggs were frying, Marvilla came in with warm blueberry muffins. If she was surprised to see Jason there at that early hour, she didn't say anything except to inform him that Mike never would have sat down for a meal without his shirt on. Trashy behavior like that was something the Hardys could be expected to do. Certainly not a Johnson.

"But Marvilla, I'm a Perry."

"And did your father ever eat half-naked a single day in his life?"

Jason went upstairs to put on a shirt.

By mid-morning, almost all of Naomi's things had been moved to the furnished apartment on Main Street. Jason was making the last run with her Japanese kitchen supplies, and Naomi was in the bathroom packing her cosmetics.

"Naomi!" called a voice from downstairs. "Can I come up? I want to see you!"

Naomi peered down the staircase to see Marvilla standing in front of Andrea with her arms crossed like a bar bouncer.

"It's okay." Naomi called down, wishing she had never started what had turned into a very pesky friendship.

The girl bounded up the stairs two at a time and flung herself at Naomi. "This must be so terrible for you. I'm so so so so so so sorry."

"It's not *your* fault." Naomi stepped back to disentangle herself.

"You must feel so awful!" Andrea threw her arms around Naomi again before asking if she could do anything to help her move.

Naomi shook her head. "Thanks. I'm just about finished."

"Oh, Naomi—"

"I told you it's not your fault. I'm sad for me but happy for you."

"Really? So, everything's okay between us?"

Of course, it's not okay, Naomi was thinking, but she forced her lips into a smile and moved her head up and down.

"Because I would hate to have you hate me, Naomi."

"I don't hate you." That part was true.

"I'm so glad we can still be friends."

Naomi took a step back, just in case Andrea was planning to hug her again and went into the bathroom, hoping the girl wouldn't follow. From the vanity mirror, she caught sight of Andrea's huge grin and sighed. She had been just as excited to move into her father's Tokyo apartment, but she probably wouldn't have acted so happy if someone else had been living in it. At least, not in front of them.

Naomi returned to the bedroom to find Andrea handling one of the antique perfume bottles at the vanity table, and she wanted to smack her.

"At least we still have each other," Andrea said brightly. "Right, cousin?"

"Uh-huh. Right, cousin."

"I *need* you in my life. Because who else do I have? After all—" Andrea was interrupted by Donna's shrill voice that had carried itself up from the porch. "Oh, darn! I don't want my grandmother to know I'm here. Can I sneak out through the kitchen?"

They hurried down the staircase and through the hallway. At least, Andrea probably wouldn't be showing up at all hours any more, wanting to do homework and use her internet. Not at that little one-bedroom apartment she was going to lease by the week. Seeing Andrea's eyes on Marvilla's sugar cookies, she wrapped a paper napkin around a handful and gave them to her. Anything to get rid of the kid.

Chapter Twenty-Three

Jason wanted Naomi to spend that first night with him, but she said no. Then he offered to stay with her, but she insisted she wanted to be on her own. The minute he left for the nursing home to go see his father, she showered and put on her pajamas. She got out the wine and junk food she had bought at the Husker Market earlier and began her pity party for one.

She poured the Frontera chardonnay into one of the plastic glasses from the cabinet, carried all the snacks into the living room, and began watching a TV program where professional dancers performed with celebrities.

Halfway through the wine and halfway through a jumbo bag of chips, the tears began to fall with a vengeance. She tried to feel grateful for how much her life had changed but choked back a sob. Unsure of how sound carried through the walls, she began to weep quietly, not wanting the old man next door telling everyone in town she was a certifiable nut case.

The stark contrast of Evelyn's beautiful things with the functional and cheap furniture of the rental made her cry even more. While reaching for an Oreo, she knocked over the bottle. After wiping up the linoleum with a fistful of paper towels, she remembered Jason's beer in the fridge. That Sam Adams went pretty well with the Oreos. The first couple of sips, anyway.

Her phone buzzed, and it was Ashley calling for the tenth time. It was almost as if her best friend had the uncanny ability to know that Naomi was sitting alone, trying to gain five pounds before sunrise. She stared at the snack wrappers on the coffee table, the empty wine bottle, and the half-drunk can of beer. She wasn't ready to talk to Ashley yet, but she would be tomorrow. Queasy from all that junk food and exhausted from having barely slept the past few days, suddenly all Naomi wanted was to lose herself in a deep and dreamless sleep. She crawled into bed without brushing her teeth, and her last thought before falling into unconsciousness was that the bed was surprisingly comfortable.

Naomi woke up a little after eight, feeling better than she thought she would, with an overwhelming urge to talk to Granny. As soon as she heard her warm and cheerful voice, a strong sense of comfort mingled with a splash of guilt for not calling the past few days washed over her. She laughed when Granny told her the neighbors thought Sadako's baby was awfully big for a premature honeymoon baby. She kept her opinions to herself when Granny spoke about Yusuke's problems at work. She even felt concern when she learned that Grandfather's last health check had shown dangerously high blood pressure and cholesterol. When Granny asked how things were in America, Naomi said everything was fine.

After disconnecting, she decided things *would* be fine. She would not let those Hardys (or even her Japanese cousins) have the fun of thinking that she had hit rock bottom. She was *not* going to give the town anything to talk about, either. She would hold her head high and pretend. With or without her great-grandmother's property, she was who she was, and that was that. Those Hardys may get to keep the stuff she had become attached to—things that made her feel connected to her newfound family—but her father had wanted her to stay in Felix for a year, so she would. She wouldn't run away. She was a Johnson, after all.

A voice in her head reminded her that she was also a Kihara. And somehow, that made her feel even stronger.

"Are you sitting down?" Ashley asked when Naomi finally answered her phone.

"Of course not. I'm standing on my head," grumbled Naomi. "What do you think I'm doing?"

"Well, it's hard to tell. All I can see is your face. Anyway, make sure you're sitting because otherwise, you'll fall over when you hear what I've got to say."

"What? Are you pregnant again?" Naomi asked.

"Huh? No, not that." Ashley paused. "But would that be such astonishing news that you'd fall over?"

"Maybe not. So, what is it, then?"

"It's about our book."

"What book?"

"The book I'm writing and the one you're illustrating." Ashley paused to let Naomi process that information.

"Oh my god, *that* book! Are you serious?"

"Hiroshi showed your sketches to the chief editor of children's books in his company, and he loved them. They're thinking of asking us to do two books to start with. If it goes well, it could become a series. A series!" Ashley laughed. "Look at you with your mouth dangling so far open you could catch flies in there. I bet you're glad you're sitting down now."

"But how... I mean, who... um... wow!"

"I guess it's pretty handy that you have that hot lawyer of yours."

"Huh?"

"You'll need info on tax deductions and stuff like that once our royalties come flooding in."

"Royalties?"

"You know that money they pay you when they sell your books?"

"They're going to pay us? Like real money?"

"What? Did you think this is volunteer work? Of course, they're going to pay us. So now you'll be able to sit and draw in that fancy attic studio of yours to your heart's content."

The elation of thirty seconds earlier turned to tears as Naomi filled Ashley in on the past few days.

"Oh, sweetie." Ashley's voice cracked with love and concern. "Was that why you haven't been answering your phone? Why didn't you call me?"

"I needed time to work this out in my head. To try to figure out what to do. Without the farm income, I needed to come up with something. I don't want to use up my dad's money. But I don't want to go back to working at a place like Commando, either."

"I certainly hope not. You've got tons of other things you could do. Like, be an illustrator."

"That was an option that hadn't occurred to me, but I do like the sound of that. Naomi Kihara: illustrator." For the first time since Evelyn's other will had surfaced, she felt a ray of hope. "Is it really going to happen?"

"It looks like it will. And the company's got some kind of connection with one of the big convenience store chains, so they're trying to get them placed there. They're hoping that when moms drop in to buy fashion magazines or whatnot, they'll pick up a few English books at the same time for their kids."

"Maybe we'll be as rich as J. K. Rowling!"

Ashley let out a hoot. "Don't hold your breath on that. But who knows? Miracles can happen."

Naomi's mind bounced back to the upcoming probate hearing. "Well, I'm in need of a miracle, that's for sure."

"What about Jason?" Ashley asked, filling in the silence that followed. "How are things going with him?"

"Well, he's working hard to find any loophole that will—"

"What I meant was, how are things going with *him*?"

"I have to say that he's been just fabulous through this whole thing. He's my rock. My knight in shining armor. My hero. All the cliches rolled into one. I don't know what I'd do without him. And—"

"Okay, okay. I get the picture. Stop before I get sick."

Naomi smiled. "Hey, you asked! And besides, I had to listen to you go on and on about your 'my Hiroshi' until the cows came home. Now you have to suck it up and listen to me talk about 'my Jason.'"

Ashley raised her eyebrows. "Till the cows came home?"

"What can I say? I'm in the heartland. I must be dreaming about cows. But back to the point, this book deal will give us something to celebrate in Denver."

"Denver?"

"Yeah, we're going to take a little trip. We decided that it'd be better than sitting around here worrying. And I guess there's some big law library Jason wants to check out. But listen. There's something else. You have to promise not to laugh—because you always do. But I'm beginning to think he's really the *one*."

"Does that mean you're planning to stay in Felix, Nebraska, population 748?"

"Oh, I forgot to tell you that Amanda Schmit had a baby."

Ashley stared at her blankly.

"So the population is back up to 749."

"Oh," Ashley said. "So anyway, are we talking about *love*?"

"Maybe. I don't know exactly how I feel, but everything's so different from—"

"Those jerks you used to hook up with? Like I always said, you just needed to wait for the right person to come along. And when he did, you'd know. Like me and my Hiroshi."

"Yeah, yeah, yeah. Just like you and your Hiroshi," said Naomi. "You know, before all that stuff with Evelyn's will happened, I drove to Lincoln. All by myself to go see my new Japanese friend whose husband runs that restaurant I told you about. And while I was there, I stopped by the university and found out how to apply to their literature department. Believe it or not, I'm thinking of starting college. Maybe from the winter semester. I was kind of thinking that I could become a teacher."

"That's a fantastic idea!"

"Because of what's been happening, I basically forgot about it. But when I woke up this morning, I realized I could still do that. Well, at least I can take a few classes to see if I like it or not. It's worth giving it a try, don't you think?"

"Absolutely. But—"

"But what?"

"It's just that I'll miss you if you don't come home."

Chapter Twenty-Four

Meanwhile, out in California, Jason's ex-wife Heather was cooking up plenty of trouble.

A few weeks earlier, her father had dropped a bombshell, changing her from a pampered socialite without a care in the world to a woman who had good reason to be concerned about her future.

On the day Naomi and Jason had their first real date, amazing sex and all, Heather was enjoying a typical afternoon at her favorite spa, being massaged, wrapped, steamed, peeled, painted, and waxed. Her hair had been blow-dried to perfection, her French manicure and pedicure matched her outfit, and she was looking forward to being seen at that popular new French restaurant.

When her father, Jimmy Sullivan, came banging on her door at seven-thirty that evening, Heather was annoyed by his timing.

"I can't talk to you now, Daddy," she said, pecking his cheek. "I have a date." She paused to admire her reflection in the hallway mirror. The five hundred dollars she had spent was a small price to pay to look this perfect.

"Cancel it."

Heather laughed. "I'm going to Sparks, and you know how hard it is to get a reservation there. If you need a date for some function at the firm tonight, you'll have to get someone else to go with you, Daddy, because I just can't."

Jimmy grabbed her arm, steered her into the living room, and pushed her onto the sofa.

"What in the world has gotten into you?" Heather exclaimed, rubbing her elbow where it smarted. She was used to her father getting upset, but he usually didn't get physical. "If you're here to scold me about going over my allowance again, I promise I'll do better next month."

"Pay attention, you little fool! Grandma Anna is writing you out of her will!"

Heather's serene face, cultivated as her trademark because she thought it would lead to fewer wrinkles, cracked, and from under its surface appeared a hard and angry one only a few people had ever witnessed. "What are you talking about?"

"You heard me. She's cutting you out of her will."

"Oh, Daddy," she sighed, recomposing her features. "You must be mistaken. I'm her only grandchild."

"That crazy old woman doesn't believe in divorce and you're divorced. Now, if you had just gone and had a civil wedding, like you should have in the first place, you wouldn't be in this fix. But *you*," he said, shaking his finger right in her face, "were the one who insisted on a church wedding that set me back more than a hundred grand. *You* were the one who insisted that the bishop preside over your wedding vows. Well, missy, you know what that all boils down to? It means you're good and married in her eyes."

"But Daddy, Jason was—"

"Doesn't matter. As far as your grandmother's concerned, marriage is for better or for worse and all that crap. And if moving out to the boondocks with your hayseed husband was the *for worse* part, then that's that. Let me tell you, she is one real pissed-off old bat who hates the fact you deserted your husband to live in sin with that bug-eyed optometrist. So, she's decided to leave the whole fuckin' lot to the church."

"But Daddy, Timothy and I aren't living together. You know that. And besides, you've no idea how awful it was in Nebraska—"

"I don't give a shit. As far as she's concerned, you're living in sin, and she's not about to leave her fortune to an adulteress. And that means *you.*"

"But she can't do that, right? I mean, the will was written a long time ago. She can't go and change it now, can she?"

"She can do anything she wants with her money. It's *hers,* not *yours.* No matter how much you've been acting as if it's already in your hot little hands." He marched to the liquor cabinet, poured a generous shot of Johnny Walker Blue Label, and downed it in one gulp. "Don't think I don't know all about that."

"Well, she must be going senile," Heather said, ignoring the nerves in her stomach jumping around as if they were exploding popcorn kernels. "There's no other explanation for it. You and your lawyers can prove that."

"No, we can't, you silly goose. She went and had her mental health checked out by two doctors. Non-Catholics, mind you, and one of them a Jew. And you know how she feels about *that.* She wanted there to be no question of her sanity. If it weren't for my contact at Bernstein and Silverman giving me the heads up, you wouldn't have gotten wind of a thing until she was cold in her grave. You'd be sitting in the lawyer's office with your finger up your ass while the bishop does a happy dance on the altar."

"Oh, Daddy. Do you have to be so crass about everything?"

"So," he said, leaning dangerously close to her face, "what you're going to do is this. First, you're going to get on the phone and cancel your date. Then you're going to break it off with that optometrist. Now, I'm sure he's nice enough to screw, but he's not five million dollars nice enough."

"Now really—" Heather hated it when her father's working-class roots surfaced.

"If you want to get your pretty little hands on that money," Jimmy said, heading back to the bar to throw another shot of whiskey down his throat, "I suggest you get that hayseed husband of yours back. And you'd better do it quick because if she loses just one of her marbles now, you'll have the church to deal with. The church would do anything to hang onto a donation that size. It'd freeze over in hell before you'd see a single penny of it."

After her father stormed out, Heather canceled her date, slipped into her new Araks Shelby pajamas, opened a bottle of Moët Chandon, and spent the evening thinking. It had never occurred to her that her grandmother would even consider cutting her out of her will. Of course, there was her father's money—quite a bit for a self-made man. But he could go on for another twenty or thirty years, and she didn't want to wait until she was an old woman in her fifties or sixties before having any fun.

She wanted her money now. Or *soon*, at least. Considering Grandma Anna was almost ninety, Heather had figured she wouldn't have to wait that much longer. It was getting pretty hard to make the interest payments on her credit cards, but she thought it was just a matter of time before she could get everything squared away. But now, Heather offered a quick little prayer that Grandma Anna's departure from the earthly world would be delayed. At least until after she could fix things.

By morning, Heather had worked out a plan. First, she broke up with Timothy by leaving a text message on his phone. Then, telling no one, not even her father, she caught an early flight to Acapulco. There, she was going to spend a few solo days getting rejuvenated at a spa she had never been to but was well known for making certain things happen.

Once she explained what she needed to Pedro the masseur, Doctor Garcia paid her a visit the next day. With his help, she'd get Jason back in just a few weeks.

•   •   •

"I'm really looking forward to going to Denver," Naomi said to Jason after an early dinner at Bob's Bar. "It'll take my mind off of being in this awful state of limbo."

"And no matter what happens," Jason said, finishing his coke, "There *is* something to celebrate, right?"

"I have to admit that book contract really does take some of the sting out of everything else."

He pushed back his chair and said, "I've got some things to do at the office. Things that can't be put off until we get back. But why don't you come spend the night so we can get an early start?"

"Early start? You and I both know we'd be up half the night—" She cut herself off when Joanna Schmidt plopped down at the next table and waved at them. "Talking. And you and I both know that all that talking would make any early start pretty difficult."

Jason's voice turned husky. "I certainly do like talking."

Naomi giggled. "So I say we save some of that talking for Denver. I've still got to pack. You aren't the only one with things to do tonight. But don't worry, I'll be ready and waiting at seven sharp."

Outside of Bob's Bar, they parted and turned toward the opposite ends of Main Street—Naomi to her apartment and Jason to his office.

Jason settled in at his desk, determined to get through everything as quickly as possible. A petition for an early release from the Community Correctional Center for good behavior. A simple transfer of ownership contract for a house over on Elm Street. And of course, Shirley Nelson wanted to sue the family living behind her (again!) for the noise their three kids make in the afternoon while jumping on the trampoline in their backyard.

The grandfather clock struck seven, and he was about ready to call it quits. A call came in on Messenger, and expecting it to be Naomi, he answered automatically.

"Hello, Jason."

He nearly fell off his chair. "Heather?"

For more than a year now, all communication had been through her divorce lawyer. At first, he thought she was calling to say she was terminally ill because she was *never* without make-up. She never wore tee-shirts, let alone one of his old University of Nebraska ones. "Is everything OK?"

"No, Jason. It isn't. I want to get back together."

Was that a choked sob that had just escaped from Heather's mouth? "That's not going to happen. We're divorced."

"But not in the eyes of the church. Our marriage was never annulled. So we aren't really divorced."

Jason leaned back and laughed. "That's a good one, Heather. You really had me there for a minute."

"I'm serious. We were married in the church and—"

"The only reason I went along with that circus wedding was to please your family—"

"But we could start over again. Have a family. A baby. Wouldn't you want a baby? *Our* baby?"

Jason closed his eyes and gave his head a vigorous shake. Had he fallen asleep? Was he having some sort of bizarre nightmare? He opened his eyes, but Heather was still there, staring straight at him. Her eyes were actually pooling with tears. "Are babies now the rage in San Francisco? Are Beth and Gabriella pregnant? Is that it?" Heather would hate lagging behind her friends—she never liked coming in second to anyone.

"The thing is, I still love you."

Jason snorted.

"I'm serious. I *do* love you. I miss you. I'll go live in Felix with you. I'll go to all those little places you like in that town. I'll even attend your church, even though your priest is kind of icky."

Jason couldn't help but smile. Heather's observation of Peter Plank was about the only thing she got right the whole time she was in Felix.

"So," she continued, "I'll be there in the morning. I was going to surprise you, but I just couldn't wait to talk to you. Things will be different. I promise. And—"

"Where *are* you?"

"Lincoln. I just got in."

Jason felt as if a bucket of cold water had been dumped over his head. "What are you doing in Nebraska?"

"I told you. I've come to get you back. And I want a baby. Our baby. Can you imagine? It would be the cutest—"

"There's never going to be any baby. We're over, Heather. You know that."

"But I could make you happy again. I know I could. We could go back to the way things were."

"Are you crazy? We were a disaster from the get-go."

"But there *were* lots of good times. Remember when we—"

"I'm in love with someone else."

Heather's face was unreadable for a full ten seconds before she said, "Well, shit. That's embarrassing."

"What's really going on?"

Heather sighed as she glanced away from her screen. "I don't know. I guess it's because I'm not getting any younger. Biological clock and all. And I do kind of miss you. I haven't been able to meet anyone half as decent as you."

Considering the awful things she'd said when she packed her bags and headed back to California, Jason found that hard to believe. Keeping his tone diplomatic, he said, "You're young and beautiful, and you have everything going for you. You'll find the right guy. But it's not me. It never was."

"This is so humiliating. I don't want anyone to know about this. Especially not my father. So, I'll just come and get your signature right now and take the morning flight back."

"My signature for what?"

"Our house sold. That's the real reason why I'm here. I convinced one of Daddy's couriers to let me bring the papers out instead." Shrugging, she added, "And I figured it wouldn't hurt to give us one last shot."

The only thing registering in Jason's brain was the fact that their house had sold. Because of their prenuptial agreement,

Heather got to keep her money and he got to keep his. Unfortunately, his every penny had gone into the house. But now, he had a chance to get it back.

"Look, I'll come to Lincoln right now instead." Things were bad enough for Naomi in town without Heather showing up. The gossips would have a real field day with that. "I'll be there in an hour."

Jason locked up and headed out. As he pulled onto the highway, he considered calling Naomi to let her know where he was going, but he didn't want to cast a shadow on their vacation before it even got started. He'd go sign the papers and be back by ten. Tomorrow he'd tell her everything. There would be no secrets between them.

While driving toward Lincoln into the setting sun, he thought about the money he'd be getting from the sale of that monstrosity of a house. He made a decent enough living, but there wasn't much left over at the end of the month. Now he'd finally be able to fix the leaky plumbing in his office and replace the fifty-year-old toilet. Maybe even get a new furnace.

At the hotel's reception desk, a shiny-faced woman handed Jason a note from Heather saying she was waiting for him in the bar. He spotted her immediately by the window. With the Lincoln skyline behind her, she looked like a million dollars—she always did in public. Perfect hair and makeup, and her little black dress probably cost more than the annual food budget for a lot of families. She was talking to the bartender, and her voice sparkled throughout the room. The women were eyeing her with admiration and jealousy and the men with admiration and lust—just the way Heather liked it to be.

He took a breath, headed for the table, and slid into the chair across from hers, knowing the people in the bar were wondering who the lucky guy was. At one time, being with Heather did make him feel lucky. After all, out of all the men in San Francisco, she had chosen *him.* But the black widow spider's mate must have felt pretty lucky at first, too.

"I see you are feeling much better than you did an hour ago."

"I thought you might want to see what you'll be missing."

"So, where are the papers?"

She retrieved them from her Prada bag and slid them across the table. Jason took them to the hallway to read in better light. Simple and straightforward—they should have just been mailed to his office. He glanced inside the bar and saw Heather leaning across the counter, talking to the bartender again. The two men on barstools were ogling her like mongrels in cartoons who lose control when a fancy poodle struts by. Don't get your hopes up, boys, he was thinking. She's way out of your league. But then, who knows? Maybe Heather was planning on slumming it tonight.

He smiled as he scribbled his last signature—knowing he'd never have to deal with Heather ever again. It was all he could do to not dance his way back to the table.

She was holding up two glasses of California sparkling wine. "Here's to a fine ending."

"No thanks."

"Oh, I know it's not the real deal, but it's the best they have here."

"I don't have time. I'm leaving."

"Oh, come on. Let's at least have a toast. This *is* goodbye forever, you know."

Jason glanced at his watch. If he left in fifteen minutes, he'd be home by the ten o'clock news.

CHAPTER TWENTY-FIVE

The alarm went off and Naomi shot out of bed and showered, dressed, and finished packing. Just before seven, she lugged her suitcase downstairs and waited for Jason. The Uptown Café was already bustling because it was Pancake Saturday, where the first twenty orders were ninety-nine cents. After that, the price went all the way up to three bucks.

Naomi chuckled to herself. She was definitely going to give Jason a hard time for being late since he was the one who had insisted on leaving at seven sharp. But then ten minutes passed. Twenty. That's when she got a little worried and called.

"Oh, I'm sorry," Naomi said when a woman's voice answered. "I've got the wrong number."

"If you're trying to contact Jason Perry, he's sleeping."

"What?"

"Do you have any idea what time it is?"

"Excuse me, but who is this?"

"This is his wife. And I don't know who you are, but I suggest you call my husband during regular office hours and make an appointment. It's unacceptable for clients to call him this early on the weekend. He needs his rest."

The woman ended the call, and Naomi's body felt like it had been glued to the sidewalk. As if they were being operated by remote control, her legs finally got her back into the building and her arms were able to drag her suitcase back up the stairs. She dropped the key twice before she got it to unlock the door and stumbled into the apartment. Once inside, she sank to the floor and stayed there until sweat poured down her back. When she finally got up to switch on the air conditioner, she told herself there had to be some explanation. There just *had* to be. She called Jason again, but now his phone was turned off. She checked her email. Messenger. Nothing.

She opened Instagram, and there, in photo after photo, was Jason, having the time of his life. With his ex-wife, Heather.

■ ■ ■

Jason's head felt as heavy as a bowling ball. He commanded one pair of eyelids to separate into a torturous slit, but the light from the window corkscrewed itself into his head, registering sharp pain. His breathing was ragged, and he drifted in and out of consciousness. A few minutes passed, or maybe it was an hour, when he felt strong enough to give opening his eyes another go. His head still hurt, but the dull throb was manageable. He twisted his neck and realized he wasn't alone. Where was he? In Denver with Naomi? Had he had a stroke? Some sort of amnesia?

He forced himself up onto his elbows, and the body next to him stirred. The sheet slipped down, and despite the pain, he shot right out of bed.

"What the hell happened last night?" he barked hoarsely at Heather, grabbing the bedspread to cover himself when he saw he was naked.

"Darling," she said, a languid smile spreading across her face.

"What did you do to me?"

"Do to *you*?" Heather stretched her arms over her head. "Don't you mean what *you* did to *me*? Three times, in fact."

Jason staggered to the dresser and retrieved his jeans from the lampshade. Sitting in the chair next to the television, he got one leg in. And then the other. "Did you drug me?"

Heather laughed. "Oh, dear god, no. But I had no idea you had developed such a taste for that nasty swill they call champagne here."

Jason's stomach roiled, and acid rose in his throat. He lurched to the bathroom and vomited, getting most of whatever was in his stomach into the toilet. His brain felt like it had been replaced with a rabid porcupine, but he could still reason that if Heather *had* drugged him, there would be proof. So he peed into the water glass, splashing some urine on the floor in the process. He grabbed a $5 bottle of water out of the room's mini fridge and headed straight back into the bathroom. After gulping it down, he poured his urine into the empty bottle and left the glass on the counter. Heather could use it to gargle with, for all he cared.

"Honey, why don't you come back to bed?"

He put on his shirt and picked up his wallet and phone. The battery was dead. "Where're my keys?"

"Don't you remember? The manager asked you to give them to him for safekeeping. You were having way too much fun last night to be driving anywhere."

He spotted his boxer shorts by the window and stuffed them into his pocket. With the bottle of urine in his hand, he slammed the door on the way out.

In the lobby, a middle-aged man with a ponytail and looking like he was hiding a pumpkin under his t-shirt hurried over. "Last night was such a hoot!" he said, clapping Jason on the back and breathing boozy morning-after breath into his face. "I hope your second honeymoon went well. Wink, wink, wink."

The man actually said that: *wink, wink, wink.*

Jason turned away, ignoring him. He got his keys from the clerk and stared at the bar bill he was given. Four hundred dollars? Eight bottles of sparkling wine? Seven plates of nachos? No wonder that guy thought last night was such fun.

Jason was in no shape to drive. He rested his head on the steering wheel, and when a pickup with three teenagers sitting in the front pulled in next to him, he called out hoarsely, "Hey, where are you all from?"

When he learned they were from Lincoln, he offered them fifty bucks to drive him and his car back to Felix.

"How do we know you ain't a crazy person?" The burly one with an angry spray of pimples across his forehead asked.

Jason handed him his business card. "I may look crazy now, but I've just had a rough night. I'd appreciate it if you could help me get home. And—" Stopping mid-sentence, he pushed opened his car door, leaned out, and spewed all over the parking lot. The kid, looking like he was planning to get as far away as possible, started up his truck. After Jason offered to fill up his gas tank, he agreed to help him out, saying he was running on empty and wouldn't get paid from Burger King until next week. The others got on board with the idea after Jason pointed out that it might be handy for them to have a friendly lawyer on their side someday.

Heading back to Felix, with a sixteen-year-old stranger at the wheel and another sixteen-year-old following behind in his pickup, Jason stared out the window. Bits and pieces of a jumbled slideshow of last night played through his head.

CHAPTER TWENTY-SIX

"Hello Jason," Naomi said when she opened the door, her voice as cold as a Nebraska February. "Did you have a nice time last night?"

"I—"

"I don't want to hear your excuses." She whirled around, stomped into the bedroom, and came back with an armful of clothes to dump into the open suitcase on the floor. "I trusted you. I believed you when you told me how much you cared for me." She brushed past him and yanked a duffle bag from the closet.

"Please, *please* stop."

Naomi turned to face him. "I told myself that the next time a guy cheated on me would be the last time I'd have anything to do with him. I'm not going to start making an exception for you. We're done."

"No, please. I couldn't stand the pain if—"

She cut him off with a flaming look. "Well, good. I want to hurt you. Actually, I want to *kill* you. I guess it's lucky for you that I also don't want to go to jail."

"Wait! I can explain."

"Oh really? Well, by all means, go ahead."

Jason's shoulders slumped. "Actually... I'm not sure what happened."

"So, you got magically beamed to Lincoln? Minutes after you told me you had to go to your office to do some work? Oh, what a busy, busy boy you've been, Jason. Sneaking off with your wife just before our trip to Denver. No wonder you look like hell."

Jason flinched at her vehemence. The throbbing in his temples accelerated as he tried to think of how to respond.

A bitter smile flashed across Naomi's face. "When I left Japan, I promised myself I'd never let a guy treat me badly again. I have my father to thank because I don't need you. I don't need some lying, cheating son of a bitch just because I'm afraid of being alone. In fact, being alone would be a hell of a lot better than being with *you*."

She grabbed more clothes out of the closet and stuffed them into the duffle bag, hangers and all. "I should've followed my instincts on this. You *aren't* over her. I can't believe how stupid I've been."

"No, that's not..." Jason tried to put his arms around Naomi.

"Get your hands off me right this second. Or I'll call Tom."

He stumbled backward. "You'd call the sheriff?"

"You touch me again, and I will. In fact, I want you to leave. Right this minute."

"But—"

"Get out!" Naomi's voice bounced off the walls and out the window and was probably heard at the Uptown Café.

Jason backed out the door and trudged home, feeling like a dog caught killing the family's pet kitten. After spilling his guts for the third time that day, he shook a couple of expired Tylenol into his palm, swallowed them dry, and fell across his bed. If only there was some way to go back and redo last night.

An hour later, Jason woke with a start. His head still throbbed and his stomach still felt like it had swallowed battery acid, but on a scale from one to ten, it was no longer at a gazillion. More like a fifteen.

Maybe Naomi had calmed down by now. Maybe she would listen. He plugged his phone into the charger, and as soon as it was up to 10%, he called her. But she wouldn't pick up. He saw her messages—at first teasing him for being late after he had insisted on getting such an early start. Then they showed concern. Then worry. The last message was a long string of curse words. When he saw his Instagram account, he understood her rage. Facebook was even worse.

Bile rose in his throat, but nothing left to expel had him dry heaving over the toilet. He stumbled back to bed, where he deleted the selfies with Heather, unfriended the people from the bar, unfriended Heather, and changed his relationship status back to single. After resetting his passwords, he curled into a ball. His life was ruined.

.   .   .

Heather lounged on the bed and nibbled at her room service breakfast while reviewing the instructions from the package that had been delivered from Mexico yesterday morning. Last night hadn't gone too badly, she was thinking. Those stupid hicks in the bar thought it was hilarious that she and Jason had gotten so plastered from celebrating getting back together after a minor misunderstanding. Every time Jason tried to speak, she smothered him with a pretend drunken kiss. They loved it when she got the whole bar dancing and ordered more of that awful fake champagne and nachos for the house. Two of those yahoos even helped her get Jason back to the room when she said it was time to get their second honeymoon rolling. Unfortunately, that Gamma 10 she got from Pedro in Acapulco must have been stronger than she thought it would be, and he passed out the moment he hit the bed. Not willing to waste the opportunity, she got him out of his clothes and tried to stimulate a little action, but his cock was just as limp as the rest of him. She ended up watching a ridiculously old movie on TV and snooping around on his phone. He really should have changed his passwords. She zoomed in on Naomi's face and frowned. *This* was the woman Jason had chosen to move on with? Well, that little nobody wasn't going to get away with tagging *her* husband at those pathetic town events. She updated his relationship status and uploaded the pictures she had taken earlier.

It was a good thing she had Plan B all ready to go since Jason had fucked up Plan A. Or, she thought with a mean chuckle, *not* fucked. But that didn't matter because she had everything she needed, thanks to that Dr. Garcia in Acapulco. "Ovulation just needs a little chemical boost," he'd told her when she paid him for his services in cash. "And as long as the sperm hits the target during the right time frame, pregnancy is assured."

Well, according to his calculations, *this* was the weekend to make a baby.

Heather finished eating, took a shower, and slathered herself with her prize stash of Crème de la Mer. She felt like a bride getting ready for her wedding night, but why not? Why not be beautiful when one was about to bring life into the world?

Sitting on the edge of the bed, she prepared the syringe the doctor had given her and pulled out the vial of semen. The donor was supposedly a blond, six-foot-tall, pre-law student from UC San Diego, but he could have been a high school dropout for all she cared. As long as it did the trick. She drew in as much semen as the syringe would hold, tapped the air bubbles out, and lay back on the bed. With two pillows propping her hips up, she inserted it into her vagina and injected herself with the sperm. Then she closed her eyes and began stroking herself. According to the directions, the cervix's ability to suck up the sperm was enhanced when accompanied by an orgasm.

A little while later, feeling quite satisfied, she flicked through the TV channels, confident one of those little swimmers would hit the goal. Jason's failure to perform last night was just a minor inconvenience, although it would have been nice to have had that extra bit of fun. The important thing was for him to think he did, because when she announces her pregnancy in a few weeks, Jason will have to do the right thing and marry her again. And if he ever wised up and took a paternity test, Grandma Anna would be with Jesus, and she'd have her five million dollars in the bank.

Chapter Twenty-Seven

She'd be fine, Naomi told herself as she lugged her suitcase out to the car. She was fine before she had ever heard of Jason Perry or Felix, Nebraska, and she would be fine again. She just needed to get home. Back to Japan.

But what about her farms? Evelyn's house? Shouldn't she stay and fight for them? She shook her head to clear away those thoughts. They were as good as gone anyway, and her anger was aimed at Jason. She would have expected Tyler to pull something like this because he had been a total jerk from day one. But Jason? She had trusted him. And that's what made this so much worse.

Forgetting her fear of oncoming traffic, she passed not one, but five cars on the two-lane highway before getting on the Interstate. By the time she got to the airport, she remembered her passports were still in the top drawer of the desk in the apartment, and unless she went back to Felix to get them, going to Japan wasn't going to be on today's agenda after all. She pulled into a MacDonald's parking lot, and halfway through her second Big Mac, she came up with an idea.

Two hours later, Naomi was drinking green tea in Kyoko Mori's kitchen.

"I'm very happy that you thought to come here," Kyoko said warmly in Japanese. "My husband is always at our restaurant, and I have so few friends. You are welcome to stay as long as you like."

"Thank you so much. Just a day or so until I decide what to do," Naomi said, stroking an obese cat named Shiro that had settled on her lap.

"You must be careful with foreigners. They are so different from us."

"Kyoko-san," Naomi murmured, not wanting to offend her hostess. "Maybe you have forgotten, but I am half American."

"I'm terribly sorry. Your Japanese is so good. I think of you as Japanese."

"Well, I *am* Japanese. But I'm American as well."

That evening, while Naomi shredded cabbage for the salad to go along with curry and rice, she tucked her emotions in the back of her head. After dinner, she feigned brightness while playing Othello with the Mori children at a table piled high with a familiar assortment of Japanese clutter and Japanese snacks. Every once in a while, she fingered away the wetness in the corner of her eyes, but when it came time to go to sleep, there was no stopping the tears soaking her pillow.

It was already roasting hot the next morning when Naomi went out to the backyard to call Ashley.

"So, you're going to just give up? Give *everything* up? You're just going to walk away?"

"But Ashley," Naomi said defensively, "that's what I thought you'd tell me to do. I was sure you'd support me on this. I thought you'd be the first to say I have to break the pattern of letting loser guys walk all over me."

"I know I said that, but you didn't even give Jason a chance to explain."

"Yeah, but—"

"Don't you think you'll always wonder if you did the right thing? Now, I'm not suggesting any stand-by-your-man crap. But you assumed he was guilty without even—"

"Wouldn't you? He was in bed with Heather when I called! His Ms. Perfect ex-wife!"

"Something's not right. You were together for dinner. And then he went back to his office to do paperwork. How come he suddenly decided to go party it up with his ex in Lincoln, just a few hours before your trip?"

"Right? You can see why I want to kill him. I'm just so angry and—"

"Shut up and pay attention. Does this sound like something Jason would do to you?"

"I wouldn't have thought so before. But—"

"Has he ever done anything to make you suspect that he's a cheating son of a bitch?"

Naomi closed her eyes and thought about how he had helped her fix up her art studio. Twice. How he was always doing little things for her. How he watched her out of the corner of his eyes when he didn't think she would notice. How tenderly he made love to her. "No," she mumbled. "No, he hasn't."

"And do you trust that ex-wife of his? I know you've never met her, but from what you've heard, would you trust her?"

Naomi remembered what Jason's father had said about her that time in the nursing home.

"Listen to me. If Jason's a two-timer, I'll be the first to whack him on the side of his head with a baseball bat. I promise you that. But sweetie, something isn't right."

"What do you suggest I do, then?"

"Go back and talk to him."

"I can't do that."

"Oh, yes, you can. And, oh yes, you will. I'm not going to let you run away from this. You'll be sad if he is a two-timer, but you'd get over it. At least you'd know the truth."

Naomi hated the fact that Ashley was right.

"Because what if you're wrong?"

Naomi felt a tiny spark of hope for the first time since yesterday. What if she *was* wrong?

"Ask yourself, who do you trust more—Jason or Heather?"

Before Naomi could answer, the backyard exploded with chatter as the Mori kids raced outside to splash in their inflatable pool.

"And another thing. Are you willing to give up your house, your farms, and your inheritance without a fight? Because of a *guy*?"

Moisture filled Naomi's eyes and throat. "I could hardly sleep thinking about all that."

"See? You've got to go back to Felix. If for no other reason than your inheritance."

"But—"

"And you've got to talk to Jason. You've got to find out what really happened with that woman."

CHAPTER TWENTY-EIGHT

Jason spent the day in his father's old recliner chair, staring at the TV. Episodes of NCIS blended into each other as the hours passed. The pain in his head had subsided, but not the one in his heart. He knew he should go to the nursing home, but he couldn't face anyone. Those who had missed seeing the photos of him and Heather plastered all over the internet would have certainly heard about them by now. They would know Naomi was gone and exactly why.

He was drumming up the energy to go check the freezer to see how long he could survive without leaving the house when the doorbell buzzed. Peeking out the window, he saw Naomi's car. She came back!

Putting up her hand to silence him as he opened the door, she strode into the living room and perched on the edge of the chair next to the television. "I was going to go home, but I forgot my passports. So I spent the night with the Mori family."

"Naomi, I—"

"It's not *my* idea to come here." Her voice was flat and devoid of emotion. "But Ashley insisted I talk to you to find out what happened."

Jason swore to himself that if he ever got to meet Naomi's friend, he was going to give her the biggest hug ever.

"So here I am. Talk."

Jason had little trial experience, but for the past twenty-four hours, hoping he would have the chance to set things right, he had been working on his defense. He knew there'd be only one chance. If he was that lucky. But all he could muster up after rubbing his forehead was a tortured, "I'm not sure what'd happened."

"So, in a nutshell, you drove to Lincoln, drank yourself silly with your ex-wife, and then you slept with her. Thanks a lot, Jason. That explains it so well." Naomi stood and headed toward the door.

"It wasn't like that," Jason begged. "Please don't go."

With a loud sigh, she turned around and faced him.

Jason tried again. "You know I went back to my office after dinner, right? I was about to go home when Heather called out of the blue. She told me she was heading to Felix for me to sign some papers about the sale of our house in San Francisco. I told her I'd go see her instead because I didn't want her coming here. I didn't want people to gossip. You know how they are here. I was going to go and come right back."

"Why didn't you tell me you were going? I could have gone with you."

"I should have. I'll regret not telling you until my dying day. To be honest, I was thinking about the money from the sale of the house. And besides, I didn't want you to meet her. She has a way of hurting people, and she's good at it." He looked into Naomi's face, but her eyes were unreadable. "Anyway, when I got to the hotel, Heather was waiting in the bar."

"And that's when you decided to get drunk with her."

"No. I signed the papers. I was about to go home, but then she ordered wine for a goodbye toast. The last thing I remember was thinking I'd be home before the ten o'clock news."

"Are you saying she drugged you?"

"There's no other explanation. All I know is this: I woke up in Heather's room feeling as sick as a dog." When he couldn't think of what else to say, he added, "My bar bill was almost four hundred dollars."

"Four hundred dollars!"

"I guess you saw all those pictures Heather uploaded to Instagram. It seems I bought rounds of nachos for everyone at the bar."

Naomi raised her eyebrows, and a chuckle escaped from her mouth. "It's not funny, but the thought of all those people, all your *new* friends, having such a good time over—"

"I've deleted the pictures and unfriended those people."

"Not before it became the talk of the town, Jason. I've only been in Felix just a little while, but I'm pretty sure people are talking about nothing else."

"I know."

"Did you have sex with her?"

"Honestly, I don't remember."

"At least you don't deny it. But why didn't you tell me this yesterday?"

"I wanted to. But you didn't give me a chance."

"Why didn't you make me give you a chance? Why didn't you fight for my attention? Why didn't you make me listen?"

"If it had been *today,* I could have. But yesterday? I was brain damaged."

"I'm pretty sure drugging is against the law. Are you going to do anything about that?"

"I got a urine sample, and I asked Doc to have it tested. But unless I'm willing to press charges, it'll take time to get the results."

"So, you're not going to press charges?"

"I could try, but you have to understand Heather's got limitless legal resources. And money, too. A court case like that could take years and suck me dry."

Naomi's eyes, locked into his, were still unreadable. "I should have asked what happened yesterday. I should have given you a chance to explain. And for that, I apologize."

Jason felt a flash of hope. "Does that mean we're okay?"

"I need time."

"You're going to stay in Felix, then?"

"For now." She got up to leave, and with her hand on the doorknob, she turned around. "At least until after the judge decides about Evelyn's estate. After that, Jason, I really don't know."

CHAPTER TWENTY-NINE

Naomi and Jason came to a cautious truce. Despite the stir they were causing in town, they had coffee together at the Uptown Café. They ate ice cream on the highway in the evening. And they had wings at Bob's Bar on Monday nights. But Naomi couldn't put what had happened behind her easily, so at the end of the day, they went back to their own places.

Meanwhile, Jason reviewed as many probate cases as he could, looking for anything that could sway the judgment in Naomi's favor. His main argument was that Evelyn didn't know what she was doing when she wrote that last will. But after Myron subpoenaed Evelyn's computer, showing that she had multiple drafts of wills similar to the one found in the church's library book, he knew that argument wouldn't hold.

To make matters worse, there were the people from the town who had gone with Evelyn on that Sunday school outing to their sister church in Silver City on September 11th. Their affidavits stated Evelyn had been as right as rain that day. She was fine on the bus going, fine during the bingo games, fine while having refreshments, and fine on the bus going home. As much as Evelyn's friends disliked the Hardys, they couldn't lie, not under oath. The fact of the matter was Evelyn had been in full possession of her faculties that day. It was after September 12 when her mental state changed. The day she fell.

So, Evelyn's will made on September 9th was ruled to be valid, and Evelyn's property was to be turned over to Jeremy Hardy on the first of the month. When Jason saw Naomi's face, he realized she had been counting on a one-in-a-million chance things would be okay. While the Hardy's were jumping up and down in excitement, he steered her out of the courtroom.

Unfortunately, they weren't fast enough to avoid Donna, who had blocked the courtroom exit. Stabbing an unlit cigarette towards Naomi's face as if it was her finger, she said, "So, how do you like it now that the shoe is on the other foot? I guess you're not the favored *Japanese* daughter, after all."

Jason, still clasping Naomi's elbow, moved her past without a word. They were halfway down the hall when they heard Naomi's name called out.

Naomi sighed, turned, and without even a trace of a smile, waited for Andrea to gallop over and wrap herself around her like an octopus. "I'll call you soon," the girl said breathlessly. Then she charged back to be with her parents, who, to be honest, looked perfectly stunned by their good fortune.

Marvilla had cooked as if she had expected the church choir to drop by later for a sing-along, but all Naomi could do was push the meatloaf and mashed potatoes around on her plate. Finally, she set her fork down. "I'm sorry, Marvilla. I just can't eat anymore."

"Sorry," echoed Jason. "I can't either."

"Well, I know exactly how you two feel," said Marvilla. "I barely have an appetite myself. Let me tell you, it's a darned good thing Mike never knew about this." She reached over for another spoonful of lime jello with cottage cheese and pineapple and added, "This would have simply broken his poor heart. He loved Evelyn. And we all thought she loved him, too."

"No one will ever convince me Evelyn had changed her mind about Mike," said Jason. "Or convince me she knew what she was doing when she changed her will. I just couldn't prove it. We all know how much she loved Mike."

"Well, at least the waiting is over," said Naomi. "I just have to get on with things."

Marvilla began to sob, and Naomi reached over and patted her hand. "I'll be okay. Really." As if to prove a point, she picked up her fork and popped another piece of meatloaf into her mouth and chewed thoughtfully. "Maybe Evelyn *was* right. My father didn't *need* her house or her farms. He had his own money. His own apartment. He was fine without them. But Evelyn's money can actually change Jeremy's life. And Andrea's, too. Maybe that was her goal. Maybe she wanted to help Andrea, and she knew Mike didn't need her help."

"But—"

Naomi held her hand up to stop Marvilla. "I don't *need* Evelyn's estate, either. I'll be fine without it." Her voice was confident, even though a solitary tear slid down her cheek. "I'm just glad I had the chance to live in her house. Otherwise, I never would've learned so much about my family. And I'm glad I owned the farms, even for just a short while. Because they helped me understand who I *really* am. I guess what I'm trying to say is this: I don't *need* those things to be a Johnson. I don't *need* them to be a part of this community. Because no matter what, I *do* belong here."

"Does that mean you're staying?" asked Marvilla.

"I think so. I said I'd help at the harvest fair next month. In October, I'm supposed to teach a class on Japanese culture at the junior high, and I've already ordered the supplies. I'm also caught up on the next three books for the book club."

"And don't forget. There's also the bridge club," added Marvilla.

"How could I leave now that I'm just getting the hang of that?"

"So you're staying," confirmed Jason, holding his breath.

"At least for the rest of the year. Like my father wanted me to."

An hour later, Naomi and Jason left Marvilla's house. "I was thinking," Naomi said, "we could go to your place."

Jason nodded. They walked side by side in silence, and after Jason unlocked the door, Naomi moved to the sofa. "Let's talk about what happened."

"I never meant to hurt you," Jason said as he sat down next to her, but not too close. "Please believe me."

"I don't think you'd hurt me on purpose. But you have to understand, all my life, I've let guys walk all over me. Take advantage of me. Treat me badly." Naomi stood and went over to the piano. She picked up a figurine of a shepherd boy, and with her back to him, she added, "My friend Ashley is right. I can't keep letting guys do that to me just because I'm afraid of being alone." She set the figurine down and turned to face Jason. "So, I've come to an important conclusion. I decided that I don't need you."

He looked as if his heart had fallen out of his chest, through the floor, and straight down to the tornado shelter in the cellar.

"I don't *need* you," she repeated softly, sitting back down and placing her hand on his arm. "But I *want* you. And that's the difference."

"What are you saying?"

"I'm saying I'm here with you because I choose to be. You're the person I want."

"Naomi—"

"But please, Jason. No more heartbreak."

Jason pressed Naomi's hands to his lips, and his voice hitched a little when he said, "I promise I'll do whatever it takes to make you happy again. You are everything to me, and I love you."

"And I love you, Jason Perry."

"So, what's next?"

"Let's go upstairs."

CHAPTER THIRTY

Jason and Sharlene were tying up loose ends in his office before he and Naomi finally took that trip to Denver. With Jeremy taking possession of the house that weekend, it seemed as good a time as any to leave town.

Sharlene assured him that the gossip surrounding him and Naomi would die down—someday. But the fact of the matter was that nobody liked that hoity-toity Heather and everybody liked Naomi. In fact, she told him that she had even overheard some high school girls compare them to Romeo and Juliet.

He exploded with laughter. "I guess they don't know how that story begins or ends or anything in the middle."

Someone was coming up the steps, and Sharlene whispered, "I told you that you should've headed out earlier. If that's Shirley Nelson, you'll *never* get going."

If only it had been Shirley Nelson.

"W-what are you doing here?" Jason sputtered when he recovered from the shock of seeing Heather.

"It's lovely to see you too, darling." Heather, wearing a white linen dress and carrying a Louis Vuitton bag, clicked toward him in four-inch heels.

Jason shot out of his chair as if she was delivering a hefty dose of the plague.

"Um, I- I think I'll run out to the store for a bit," said Sharlene. For all her bluster, she was actually terrified of Heather.

"Sit back down," Jason ordered. The last time he was alone with his ex-wife had almost ruined his life, and he wasn't about to take any chances. He turned to Heather. "You've got a lot of nerve coming here."

"I'm here about our baby." Heather reached into her bag and slid an ultrasound picture and a copy of a blood test across his desk.

Jason's eyes traveled to the papers, and he gasped. "That's impossible."

Heather produced a poisonously sweet laugh. "You certainly didn't act like it was impossible at the time."

"I don't want to have a baby with you."

"Oh, you foolish man." Heather settled into the client's chair, crossed her legs, and let her skirt ride up her toned thighs. "You can't decide that now that the horse is out of the barn. Isn't that the kind of quaint thing they say around here? Remember how much you used to want a baby? I wasn't ready back then. But now I am. And now we have one."

How was Jason ever going to explain *this* to Naomi?

"Now, about my bags. I've already dropped them off at the house and asked the maid to unpack them. I simply adore what you've done with the master bedroom upstairs. And the study will be perfect for the baby's room."

"You went to my house?"

"You mean *our* house, don't you?"

Heather's smug expression told him she knew exactly what she had done—she had gotten rid of the competition. He grabbed the phone. "Tom? Jason here. I need a favor. My former wife has trespassed in my house and left some things there. Could you go and get rid of them for me? I don't care what you do with them as long as they're gone as quickly as possible."

"But what about our baby?" yelled Heather, as Jason dashed out the door.

"Have your lawyer contact me," Jason yelled back. "I never want to see you again."

. . .

Heather retrieved her suitcases from Jason's front yard where the sheriff had put them and loaded them into the trunk of her rented Cadillac CTS. She was beginning to think that maybe she should have run her plan of how she was going to get Jason back by her father first. But she had been so certain she had everything covered. Not only was there Dr. Garcia's Plan B, she had also hatched up a Plan C while killing time by the hotel pool before flying back to California. Her target, who hadn't been in the bar the night before, wasn't as tall or handsome as Jason, but close enough. She thought the guy was going to have a heart attack when she propositioned him by the soft drink vending machine. But all it took was a couple of words to get him up to her room. Too bad he acted like a total clodhopper afterwards by bursting into tears and going on and on about some silly wife. As if she cared.

In the end, it didn't matter if it was Dr. Garcia's Plan B or the Guy From Mississippi Plan C. Because one of them did the trick. She was pregnant. And a good thing that was because Grandma Anna had just gone into the hospital again. Considering this was her third bout of pneumonia since January, the deal with Jason needed to be signed, sealed, and delivered as quickly as possible.

It never occurred to her that Jason wouldn't come running back if she gave the signal. After all, she was Heather Sullivan, the daughter of Jimmy Sullivan. Jason Perry was nothing but a country bumpkin lawyer. She figured a baby would hasten the process, because didn't he always say he wanted kids? Well, he's got one now, and he's going to have to step up to the plate and take responsibility for it. That's all there was to it.

Sensing the neighbors were watching her from behind their curtains, she drove to the edge of town, and under the shade of an elm tree, she came up with Plan D. What she needed was an ally, one who wouldn't take Jason's side just because his family had dug their heels into this godawful town back in the olden days. One who would see *her* side of the story. She touched up her makeup, dabbed on some perfume, and headed over to the church. Hopefully, that Reverend Plank wouldn't remember her calling him the most long-winded blowhard she had ever heard speak from behind a pulpit.

Although he looked surprised when she knocked on his office door, he invited her in.

"Reverend, you and I didn't always see things eye to eye when I lived here." Heather spoke in a honeyed and low-toned voice she had cultivated specifically for men like him. "But I need your advice about my husband."

"I thought you two were divorced."

"We're still married in the eyes of God, aren't we?"

Heather saw him doing his damnedest to keep his eyes north of her neck, so she leaned forward in the chair to give him a better look. Catching a whiff of her expensive perfume, she knew he was going to be putty in her hands. "I've changed, Reverend. I now know that God has a plan for my life. And that plan includes being reunited with my husband."

"You've been saved?" he asked skeptically. "In San Francisco?"

Heather knew what his views were about San Francisco. As far as he was concerned, it was Sodom and Gomorrah all over the place out there. She dabbed away a tear with a tissue. "Yes. It was an amazing moment when I saw the light. And now I truly understand. My husband and I were married in the church, and that makes us married for life, doesn't it?"

"Yes, my dear. It does."

"God has mysterious ways of guiding us away from the evils of Satan. But we have to do the best we can." Idiot, she thought, watching his head bob up and down in agreement. She was just regurgitating his own boring sermons back to him. "And that's why I've come to *you*. You're the *only* person who can understand." She placed a manicured hand on her belly, which was as flat and toned as an Olympian athlete. She squeezed out a tear and let out a little sob. "God has blessed me with a baby."

"But why are you crying when you have such joyous news?"

"Jason said he didn't want it. He told me to get rid of it." Heather knew that the two things that got Peter Plank going more than anything else were abortions and gay people. Or anything related to abortions or anything related to gay people. And she was right. His face turned purple.

"He told you to get an abortion?"

"He says that he's in love with some Japanese girl. He says that he doesn't want me—his wife. His helpmate. He wants that home wrecker instead." She warned herself to tone it down before she got the giggles. "A few weeks ago, I came to Lincoln with a paper that my husband needed to sign. He came to my hotel and begged for a second chance. He kept pouring glass after glass of wine and got me back to my room. And well, then he…" Heather leaned forward and put her head in her hands.

"He forced you?"

He sounded shocked, but when Heather looked up at him through her tears, she could've sworn she saw him lick his lips. Giving the tiniest of tiny nods, she added, "But we're married, right? And so I… Even though it was against my better judgment." Jesus Christ, she should get an Academy Award out of this performance. "And as a result, God made another Christian soul. But now Jason wants me to abort our baby." By that point, Heather had turned on the waterworks and wailed, "He even called the sheriff and had me kicked out of our home."

Peter stood, walked around his desk and placed his hands on her shoulders. "I'll speak to Jason. I'll talk sense into him. You'll get your husband back. I promise you."

"How can I ever thank you?"

Before leaving, Peter Plank pulled Heather to him for a hug, and when he placed his damp lips on her cheek, she felt bile rise in her throat. She made it to the curb before she vomited, and in the car, she rested her head on the steering wheel, waiting for the waves of nausea to subside.

Maybe getting pregnant wasn't such a good idea after all.

.   .   .

Andrea heard everything through the furnace vents in the tiny office where she was digitalizing the church's records. Which was the bigger scoop? Heather getting pregnant with Jason's baby? Or that she went and got religion?

Poor Naomi. Even after her own family ended up with all of Evelyn's stuff, Naomi had been nothing but nice to her. She was going to feel just awful when Jason got back together with Heather. Because no matter what, you can't ignore a baby. The Reverend was right—Jason *would* do the right thing—that's just the kind of guy he was. He may sleep around behind his girlfriend's back, but he'd *never* abandon his baby.

How Naomi managed to hold her head up after those pictures of Jason and his ex were plastered all over the place was beyond comprehension. If a guy ever did anything like that to her, she'd *never* give him another chance. But Naomi was going around acting like it was no big deal. Probably because she was getting kind of old and it must be pretty hard to hang on to a man when you're pushing thirty.

Even so, Naomi deserved to know the truth before any more excuses could be cooked up and before the town blabbermouths stuck their big old noses in Naomi's business. Choosing her words carefully, Andrea tapped out a message. It was the right thing to do.

After pushing the send button, she saw that her three hours at the church were up. She slipped the files back in the cabinet and decided to head over to the post office to see if the comforter set she had ordered from Bed Bath & Beyond had arrived. It would go perfectly with the pillows she had gotten at the new novelty store in Riley. Now the only things left were some decorative touches. Maybe she'd drive to Target tomorrow and look for some candles. She couldn't wait to move into her new bedroom.

PART THREE

Chapter Thirty-One

"Open up! I know you're in there!" After a count of ten, the banging on the door started up again.

"Go away!" Naomi shouted.

"I'm staying put until you open the door. And if you don't open up right this minute, I'm going to sing." True to her word, Ashley belted out the first few lines of "The Yellow Rose of Texas."

"Are you crazy?" Naomi hissed as she pulled Ashley inside.

"Jeez, you look terrible." Ashley kicked off her shoes and marched into the living room. "And smell terrible, too." She pulled back the drapes and opened all the windows.

"How did you know I was back in Japan?"

"Jason called me."

"He *called* you? After what he did?" Then Naomi burst into tears.

Ashley pushed her into the shower, gathered up all the empty snack wrappers, and took the empty wine bottles down to the garbage. She sat Naomi down in front of an innocuous DVD from her father's collection and started fixing dinner.

When they began to eat, Ashley said, "Talk."

"There's nothing to talk about."

"All right. Let's just eat then."

After a period of silence, Naomi said, "So he called you."

"He was worried."

"If he was so damned worried, why did he have to sleep with his ex-wife and get her pregnant?"

Ashley continued eating.

"I really thought I could move on after what had happened in Lincoln. I really, really thought I could."

Ashley leaned forward, and in a soft voice, she said, "Tell me everything."

"I was never so humiliated in my entire life! Heather showed up at Jason's house and thought I was the maid! The maid! She came in and told me to put her things away. Can you believe that?"

"Oh, Naomi. She knew exactly who you were. She knew you were the competition and got rid of you the quickest way possible. By insulting you."

"But I *was* insulted. You should've heard all the awful things she said to me. It was so humiliating."

"I'm sure it was, but would you have run away if she had come in and said something like, 'What are you doing with my man, you hussy? I want him back!'"

Naomi let out a giggle. No matter what, Ashley could always make her laugh. "Probably not. I would've said, 'Back off, he's mine.'"

"Oh yeah, that sounds exactly like something you'd say to someone's face."

"Well, maybe I'd say that later," Naomi conceded with a smile. "Like ten hours later and when I'm alone. But get this: Heather's *pregnant* and she's getting back together with Jason."

"And exactly how do you know that?"

Naomi showed her Andrea's text.

Ashley ran her eyes over the message. "For a smart woman, you can be so stupid sometimes. You let yourself be chased away by a woman who knew how to push your buttons and by a seventeen-year-old who probably feels a lot better about herself now that you aren't in town reminding her that her family snatched your inheritance right out from under you."

Naomi felt sick. Every word Ashley said was true.

"But what's done is done." Ashley stood and carried the dishes to the sink. "You're home now. You can make a clean break with Jason and get your life back on track."

"Yeah, I guess so."

"You don't need that guy, right? And you don't need that house in Nebraska or any of that other stuff. It's been nothing but heartache for you. You've got a good thing going here, you know. You've got this fantastic apartment, and your life is just beginning. Now that you're back, we'll go sign that contract."

"What contract?"

"The book contract, of course. Since you're here, there's no need to Fed Ex it to you. We'll go to the company tomorrow and sign it."

"Oh, okay." Naomi looked like she had just been informed they were going out to buy drain cleaner.

"And Jason can just stay in Nebraska with his baby mama, and that silly teenager can have your great-grandmother's house and those farms. What did you need all that for, anyway? You're fine without them, right?"

"Yeah, but…"

"But what? What's done is done. Right?"

"B-but Ashley," Naomi sobbed, "I love Jason."

Ashley pushed a box of tissues toward Naomi and waited for her to blow her nose. Then, in a voice as practical as ever, she said, "Well, if that's the case, here's what you're going to do. First, you're going to go to bed and sleep. And when you wake up in the morning, we'll have coffee and cinnamon rolls. Tonight, you sleep. Tomorrow we'll talk some more."

"Are you staying over?"

"I am indeed. I told Hiroshi I'd be back tomorrow night. Emily will be fine with his parents."

Nine hours later, Naomi stumbled out of her bedroom and followed her nose into the kitchen. "When you said cinnamon rolls, I thought you meant Starbucks."

"That's not the way I do it." Ashley placed the platter of warm, sticky buns on the table. "What is wrong with you now?" she asked when she saw Naomi's eyes welling up.

"I'm sorry. I'm being stupid. Marvilla makes them, too. The best in Felix."

"Well, forgive me if I can't compete with *that*. But you can still eat these. They aren't all that shabby."

Naomi gave her friend a hug. "Thank you for being here. I love you."

"I love you, too," Ashley replied. "And after you get all hyped up on sugar, the next thing you're going to do is take a shower, put on makeup, and call Jason."

Naomi licked the frosting off her knife and set it down. "But—"

"Absolutely no ifs, ands, or buts. You're going to show that man what he's missing—the beautiful and talented Tokyo illustrator. If nothing else, you want to at least make the man regret he ever thought twice about another woman."

Chapter Thirty-Two

After signing the contracts at the publishing company, Naomi and Ashley stood outside the building on the busy sidewalk, jumping up and down in excitement like girls on a playground.

"I can't believe it!" Naomi said. "Even if it never goes to second or third printings like they hinted at, a first run with ten thousand copies is still pretty good, right?"

"Good? It's incredible! Hiroshi said now that 7-Eleven is on board, they might even sell more. He said we'd better get busy and have our next book ready, just in case. So, I'm thinking about your idea about the squirrel family that lives in Jason's tree. Those sketches are really—Sorry," she said when she saw the look on Naomi's face. "I shouldn't bring him up when it's still raw."

"That's not it. I-I just remembered. I left all my sketches in Nebraska."

Ashley stared at Naomi. "What do you mean, you left them in Nebraska? What kind of artist runs off half-cocked without her work?"

"I guess I wasn't thinking straight."

"Well, do you think he's the kind of guy who'd destroy your stuff if he got dumped?"

That question took Naomi by surprise. "Of course not. He's not like that. He's *nice*."

"I guess you'll just have to figure out a way to get them back. That's all there is to it."

"I don't know. I've been trying to get hold of him all day, but he isn't picking up. What if he went to Las Vegas? What if he's getting married to Heather right this very minute?"

"Is that what you really think he'd do? Go off and marry that awful woman in just a day or two?"

Naomi took a deep, shuddering breath. "I don't know, but I do know that he's the kind of guy who'd want to be the father of his child, even if he hated the mother. He's decent that way." She shook her head like a dog with water in its ears. "I've got to stop thinking about that. It's making me crazy." Aware they were blocking the sidewalk, she said, "Let's go get something to eat. I'm dying for sushi."

"Oh sweetie, I can't. Emily and Hiroshi can only stand to be without me for just so long."

Naomi's face flushed in embarrassment. "Of course, you should go home to your family. You're the best friend ever for seeing me through my crisis."

"Damn right I am. But why don't you come with me? Hiroshi's always glad to see you."

"I know he is. Maybe I'll come over next week. I think I'll just wander around a bit before going home."

Naomi considered going to Commando to see what was happening there, but squashed that idea when she remembered those people weren't her friends, and they never had been. With her luck, some fresh-off-the-boat gaijin would try to pick her up. Or worse, what if she bumped into Tyler? She went to Shibuya instead and ate twelve plates of sushi, including double helpings of raw octopus and salmon roe, at a conveyer belt sushi shop. In a

Starbucks, she sat by the window with her coffee, watching the crowds go by, thinking she never once went to the Uptown Café, the Ice Cream Palace, or Bob's Bar without someone coming over to talk to her. At first, that had felt strange, but now *this* did. She supposed she'd get used to the anonymity of Tokyo again. She'd have to.

She walked to Harajuku, browsed in trendy boutiques catering to teenagers, and bought a chocolate crepe from a stand, eating it while heading toward the station. With the jet lag, the book contract, and all that walking, she was dead tired and looking forward to a long, dreamless sleep. Tomorrow she'd have to start figuring out what to do with the mess her life had become.

Because Naomi was checking her phone as she got out of the elevator, she almost stepped on Jason, sprawled out in a deep sleep by her front door. If it hadn't been for the neighbors leaving their apartment, she might have stared at him in shock until morning.

"Are you all right?" the husband asked, looking alarmed by the bedraggled gaijin passed out in the hallway.

"Oh yes. It's my friend from America. I-I forgot he was coming."

The couple gave a brief nod and hurried into the elevator as if contagious spores were floating about. Naomi bent down and shook Jason's shoulder. "What are you doing here?"

He sat up and rubbed his eyes. "I came to see you."

"How did you find my apartment?"

"Google maps. But if you want me to leave, I will."

Naomi leaned over him and unlocked the door. "I suppose since you're here, you might as well come inside. Too many mosquitoes out here."

As soon as she said that, he started scratching.

Jason took off his shoes in the entryway without any prompting and went over to the window. Looking down, he shook his head and said, "I've never seen anything like this in my whole life. Not even when I lived in San Francisco. It's practically the middle of the night, but just look at all those cars."

"Did you come here to study Japanese traffic?"

"No," he said, turning around. "I came to get you back."

"You shouldn't have come then. You've wasted your time. Go home to your ex-wife and your baby." That wasn't what she wanted to say—those words just escaped her mouth as if someone else had turned them loose. "I didn't mean—"

Jason opened his bag and handed Naomi a document in a clear file. "I got this the day you left. It's the toxicology report. Doc says I had so much rivotril in my system, it would've been impossible for me to… you know. That night, I wouldn't have been able to do anything."

"How did Heather get pregnant, then?"

"If she's pregnant, I'm not the father. The drug test proves that. So would any paternity test."

"I shouldn't have run away," admitted Naomi. "I should've stayed and talked to you. I was hurt by all those things Heather said, but I never should've let her get to me like that. I—"

"I'm sure she said terrible things. That's Heather." Jason slid his arm around Naomi and pulled her close. For a while, the only sound was a distant ambulance siren down on the street.

"I drove to the airport. I almost turned around because I realized coming back to Japan on the first airplane was crazy. But then Andrea sent a message saying that you were getting back together with Heather for the baby's sake."

"How would that kid know anything about that?"

"I guess she overheard Peter Plank telling Heather that at the church."

"Why would you think that man has any influence over me?"

"I don't know what I was thinking. I guess I just panicked."

"As soon as I knew Heather had been at the house, I went home. But you were already gone. I drove to the Mori's, but you weren't there. I went to the airport, just in case. And I saw your car and—"

"Jason, I—"

He put his fingers on her lips. "I wasn't about to give up. I went home and got my passport. The only flight I could get on was through San Francisco and Seoul, and that's why it took two days to get here. Otherwise, I would've been right behind you."

"I can't believe you came all the way to Tokyo. For *me*." Naomi felt nothing but relief.

"I'd go to the end of the earth and back for you," Jason said.

CHAPTER THIRTY-THREE

For the next ten days, Jason played the tourist. He saw all the traditional sights, but Naomi made sure he saw the wild and wacky ones as well—like an owl café one day and a cat café the next. Naomi hadn't told him that their dinner with Ashley and Hiroshi was going to be at a theme restaurant, and once he got over the surprise of being arrested at the door and treated like a prisoner in a horror movie, he went along with the fun and drank the cocktails served by mad scientist waiters.

A few days later, when Jason and Hiroshi took Emily on It's a Small World at Disneyland for the fifth time, Ashley and Naomi browsed in a gift shop.

"He's the *one,*" Ashley said. "Definitely the one."

"Yeah, I know," Naomi agreed.

■   ■   ■

The next day, Naomi and Jason took the bullet train to Kyoto and stayed in a traditional inn.

"What's all this?" Jason asked, pointing at the items on a lacquered tray of food a kimono-clad woman had brought into their private *tatami* room for their private dinner. His legs were sticking awkwardly out of the indigo-patterned cotton *yukata* robe provided by the hotel.

Naomi thought he looked just as delicious as the dinner in front of them. "Raw squid."

"And this?"

"Raw sea urchin."

He slid the delicacies back across the table toward her. When the server came in with the *sukiyaki* course, she let him have her share of the rich marbled Kobe beef.

While Jason wasn't entirely against trying weird food, he drew the line at getting naked in the hot springs with other men. So Naomi reserved a family room for just the two of them. There, *she* drew the line at getting too friendly.

"Jason," she said, shocked. "We can't do that in here. It's unthinkable. Unsanitary."

He was a good sport and saved his energy until they got back to their room.

.　.　.

Naomi didn't want to take Jason to meet her family, but he insisted. She agreed on the condition he'd keep quiet about the fact that she had lost her farms. "Call me shallow," she said, "but their opinion of me shot up after I became a landowner, and I don't want to reverse that."

"Your secret's safe with me," he promised.

Naomi saw the sour look on her cousin Yusuke's face when her grandparents fussed over the tall and handsome gaijin. She saw it get downright ugly when his wife became flustered when the gaijin helped her with the dishes. And Naomi wasn't the only one who noticed Sadako had given the gaijin slightly larger slices of the pears they had for dessert. Naomi could see all that rankled her cousin, but not as much as when Grandfather invited the gaijin into his study to sample his precious Hennessy Martin. His face turned black with rage when the door was shut, leaving him out.

Naomi and her grandmother spent that evening across from each other in the kitchen, shaking their heads in amazement at the explosions of laughter coming from the study. When Jason finally staggered into their room toward midnight, she asked him what they had talked about.

"I have no idea," he mumbled, tumbling headfirst into the futon.

The next morning, while Jason was nursing his hangover, Naomi overheard Grandfather telling Granny that Naomi would be lucky to marry that foreigner. And even though he put a damper on the moment by saying he had thought Naomi would never be able to find a husband, she couldn't help but be pleased by how things were turning out.

After the evidence of the night's debauchery had been cleared away, Grandfather asked her to come to his room. She stepped in and was struck by how frail he had become.

"Your grandmother wants me to talk about Yumi."

Naomi gave a hesitant nod. It was the first time she had ever heard him mention her mother's name.

"I am an old man now, but when I was young, I was weak. I let my mother make decisions about my family I never should have. I have carried guilt about that my entire life. I did not do right by my daughter," he said, his bushy eyebrows furling together. "And I admit that I did not do right by you."

Naomi kept her eyes on the table in front of her.

"I knew something was wrong with Yumi. I should have taken her to a doctor. I did not understand the help she needed." He pushed his glasses back up on his nose and said, "Maybe if I had been a different man, Yumi could have gotten better. Maybe she would still be alive. My actions have always been my deepest regret."

When Naomi looked up and saw sadness in her grandfather's eyes, she realized she was no longer afraid of him.

"I have been wrong all these years. I have three grandchildren. And of those three, you are the one I am proud of. You are a woman that any man could be proud to claim as his granddaughter."

Then he motioned for her to come closer, and he handed her a large envelope. "Your grandmother never told me that Yumi had brought this with her. She never told me she had saved it. Her judgment was wise then because mine might not have been."

He hobbled out of the room, leaving her alone. She opened the envelope and found photos documenting her parents' history and the first two years of her life: her parents holding her when she was a newborn, taking her for a walk through Ginza in a stroller, and holding her hand while she took her first steps. Naomi never imagined she would possess such a treasure.

Her grandfather said little else to her during the rest of her visit, but he didn't have to.

.   .   .

Two days before Jason was due to fly back to America, they discussed their futures. Naomi said she couldn't leave Japan forever, and Jason said he couldn't leave Nebraska forever. They compromised and decided to make a home in both worlds. It wasn't a perfect solution—it would be expensive and time-consuming. But it would be worth it if they could be together.

So Naomi bought an airplane ticket and packed her bags to go back to Nebraska with Jason.

.   .   .

Naomi figured it was bad news from how Jason's voice changed when he answered his phone on their last night in Tokyo. The way he shot off the sofa where they had been lounging over a bottle of Shiraz to stand by the window with his back to her made her think that perhaps she should give him some privacy. But when she heard Heather's name mentioned, wild horses wouldn't have been able to drag her out of the room. She couldn't even pretend not to listen to his side of the conversation.

Ten minutes later, he turned around, his face unreadable. A million worst-case scenarios flashed through Naomi's mind.

"You have no idea how much I love you," Jason said, sitting next to Naomi and pressing his lips to her palms. He exhaled one long breath after another, almost as if expelling a toxic substance from his body. "That was the investigator I asked to look into... well, look into what Heather had done. We used to work at the same law firm, and since he was unfairly let go, he didn't mind sticking his nose into all this. Well, it seems..."

Naomi shook her head in disbelief after Jason finished explaining what he'd just learned. "How could Heather ever think such a crazy plan would work?"

"I don't know, but the church is going to be pretty happy with the five million dollars they're getting from Grandma Anna since she passed away last week."

Naomi almost choked on her wine over the amount. "She disinherited her granddaughter because of your divorce? She was *that* strongly against divorce?"

"To be honest, I think that was just an excuse. I'm pretty sure it was because she didn't like the way Heather went through money. She was the type who helped her husband build his fortune the old-fashioned way—you know, through hard work and frugal living. In fact, the old gal reminded me of a lot of people I know in Felix. Practical to a fault and full of substance."

"So, what's going to happen to Heather now?"

"I don't know, and I don't care. I imagine the hundred grand she's getting won't even begin to put a dent in her debt. I suppose her father will bail her out like he always does, but who cares? That's not *our* problem."

"I can't believe she went to Mexico to buy sperm. That's so gross. Didn't she think you'd get a paternity test?"

"She probably thought if she crooked her little finger, I'd come running back. And if paternity ever came into question, Grandma Anna would already be gone."

"Why would she gamble with people's lives over *money*? Your life—our lives. And the baby! Oh, that poor little thing. What a terrible mother she's going to be."

"The word's also out that there's no baby anymore," Jason said quietly.

CHAPTER THIRTY-FOUR

Naomi had no feelings of uncertainty or confusion this time when she got off the plane in Lincoln and stepped out of the airport. It felt like coming home. To Nebraska, anyway. To Felix. She would have to get used to the fact the Hardys were living in Evelyn's house now. Of course, Jason's place was nice, but it wasn't the same. Not yet.

"Oh!" Naomi said when they reached the parking lot. "Where's my car?"

"*Now* you think about that?" laughed Jason. "I had Doc's son come and get it, so you wouldn't have to pay a fortune for parking. I knew I'd be coming back in ten days. But you," he said, leaning over and giving her a kiss, "I wasn't so sure of."

Marvilla, with a smudge of flour on her cheeks, hurried down Jason's steps as soon as he pulled into his driveway. She grabbed them both and cried, "If you aren't a sight for sore eyes, I don't know what is!" She hugged and kissed Naomi. Then Jason. Then Naomi again.

Jason put a stop to it by handing her a bag of souvenirs and telling her they should get inside and out of the wind so she could open them.

Jet lag wrenched them out of sleep while it was still dark. By the time the Uptown Café opened for business, they were ravenous and dying for pancakes. Of course, Heather's shenanigans, Naomi's hasty departure, and Jason's sudden trip to Japan had been keeping the town gossips busy. But thanks to Jason's detailed email to his assistant sent just before getting on the airplane, there'd be no need for further explanation. You could always count on Sharlene to spread the word. Naomi and Jason were together, and that was all that mattered. If people wanted to gossip about how happy they were, then let them.

They sat in a booth by the window and caught up on all the local news.

Raymond Roth's tomatoes had come in first place at the state fair.

Susan Smith's grandson had knocked his front tooth out in a skateboard accident.

Derrick Jones' sister from Florida had come up to visit and had a heart attack in the canned fruit aisle of the Husker Market. Her kids buried her in the cemetery here next to their father, whom they knew she didn't particularly like, rather than pay the money to send her to be buried next to her second husband, whom they knew she did like.

And on the young people's front, Sophie Brown was pregnant. But who the daddy was, she wasn't exactly sure.

Sheriff Tom stopped by their table to tell them that her poop on the porch incident would be shelved for now because there weren't any new leads. That seemed so long ago, Naomi had almost forgotten all about it.

Conversation in the Uptown Café ground to a halt when Jeremy walked in. If people expected Naomi to make a scene, they were going to be disappointed.

"How have you been, Jeremy?" Knowing that sooner or later, she was going to have to come to terms with the fact that her cousin and his family were now living in the place that used to be hers, she added, "I hope you are enjoying the house."

"Feel free to come by any time," he said sheepishly. "You're more than welcome."

Naomi nodded and said that she would like that, but they both knew she would never take him up on the offer.

On their second day back, Naomi got up early and walked around the town's perimeter and did a light workout in the school gym. When she got back, Jason was making French toast. She put her arms around him. "I'm so happy to be home."

"Maybe today," he said, "after we visit my dad, we could get the rest of your stuff out of the apartment. I know your rent is paid up for another few weeks, but why not make the move today?"

On the third day, Jason needed to go to the courthouse in Lincoln in the afternoon. He suggested Naomi come with him. He'd drop her off at the mall, and they could meet up later.

CHAPTER THIRTY-FIVE

"Well, if it isn't Jason Perry!" said a woman, stopping them in the household goods section at Target. "I'm so glad to run into you here."

"Uh… hi…"

"Sandy. Sandy Beemer, from Silver City."

"Oh, hi, Sandy. How're you doing?" Jason gave Naomi a look that meant he had no idea who this woman was.

"You don't know who I am, do you?" she laughed. "I knew your father from way back. How is Ron, by the way? I heard he's not doing so well."

Jason gave his standard reply, and then Sandy turned to Naomi. "I've heard all about you from Louise Letts. It's nice to meet you."

"It's nice to meet you, too." Naomi shook her hand and glanced at Jason, who seemed to have no idea who Louise Letts was either.

"Now let me see… There was something I wanted to talk to you about, Jason. But what was it?" Sandy tapped her fingers on her forehead. "Hang on, it'll come to me."

"Do you need any legal advice?"

"Oh, no. That's not it. Ever since I retired, my brain has turned to mush. It was something to do with the bank."

"The bank?"

Sandy took out her cell phone and checked her calendar. "Oh wait! Now I remember. You see, I retired last September to go out to California because my daughter was having triplets. You know, these days, if you can't get pregnant within that first six months of trying, you run off to the doctor and get a pill or something, and then, bam! You give birth to an entire litter!" She scrolled through a dozen pictures and held one out for them to see. "Take a look at these cuties. They're identical."

"Aw, how adorable!" Naomi gushed.

Sandy beamed. "They're natural triplets. No fertility drugs. And with two toddlers already, my daughter suddenly had five kids under the age of five. What else could I do but retire early and go out there to help?"

Jason looked at his watch and took Naomi's arm. "Yeah, they're pretty cute all right. Well, it was nice—"

"Oh, now I remember what I wanted to ask you. It was about Evelyn Johnson. You were her lawyer, weren't you?"

Jason became alert. "That's right. I was her lawyer."

"Well, to be honest," Sandy continued, "I had forgotten that she'd come into the bank because my retirement party was that afternoon. And the next day, I went to California and got busy with those babies. So, there was no way to keep up with the local news, and I didn't get back until a week ago. I was just too homesick to stay any longer. Nebraska people are just so much friendlier than those Californians, don't you think?"

"Um, Sandy, what was it about Evelyn you wanted to tell me?"

"Oh yes. Well, she and my mother used to be friends way back. I hadn't seen her for the longest time, but she came into the bank that day to have something notarized. I didn't think too much about it then, but yesterday I heard people talking about that probate trial. And you know, with the Hardys involved, I thought something sounded awfully fishy."

"Evelyn went to your bank in Silver City to notarize something? Do you remember when that was?" Jason's tone had become dead serious.

"Well, of course, I do. It was September 11th."

"September 11th! Are you sure of the date?"

"Why, of course, I'm sure. That was the day I retired, right? And who could ever forget anything happening on 9/11? Evelyn came in on the day I retired, and it was definitely that day."

"The bank is next to the Presbyterian Church, isn't it?" Jason's hand was clutching Naomi's elbow like it was about to get away from him.

"Well, almost. There's a drugstore in between."

Jason turned to Naomi, excitement in his voice. "That was the day Evelyn was on that Sunday school trip. She must have slipped out during one of the bingo games, and no one noticed. Otherwise, someone would've said something."

"Well, I remember she said she was in an awful hurry."

"Do you know what she had notarized?"

Sandy shook her head. "The manager took care of her. But I did the paperwork for her new safe deposit box."

"Safe deposit box!"

"So, you didn't know. I didn't think so. At the time, I thought it was kind of strange because you'd think she would've opened one up in Felix, right? I mean, how often would a woman her age go to Silver City to access it?"

"Did Evelyn strike you as being in sound mind that day?" Jason asked.

"Other than wanting to have a safe deposit box so far from home? Well, sure. Evelyn Johnson was always as sharp as a tack."

Sandy's phone buzzed. "Look, you two. I've got to skedaddle. That's my husband, and he gets upset if I spend too much time in Target."

Jason grabbed her hand and pumped it up and down. "You can't imagine how much help you've been, Sandy."

"Well, I would've told you about all this earlier, but you can just imagine how busy I've been with babies. All boys! But when I heard about that second will showing up, leaving everything to one of those Hardys, I just couldn't help but think that something was, well, you know what they say, rotten in Denmark." Before Sandy walked away, she placed her hand on Jason's shoulder. "My brother was one of the paramedics that day. Such a tragedy it was."

Jason nodded. "Thanks, Sandy. I might have to call you later about this, if you don't mind."

"Any time. I'm real glad to be of help."

Jason pulled Naomi away from their half-full shopping cart and out the door and into the parking lot. He fished his keys out of his pocket and tossed them to her. "Here. You drive."

"But Jason—"

"Shh. Let me call the bank." While on hold, he turned to her and said, "This could be it, Naomi, and—Hello? This is Jason Perry from Perry Law Office in Felix. I'm sorry to call out of the blue like this, but it's just come to my attention that…"

A few minutes later, Jason had all the information he needed. "Sandy was right," he said. "Evelyn did open a safe deposit box there. Let's hurry. We've got to get to the courthouse before it closes."

"The courthouse?"

"To get a warrant to open it up."

"But can't you drive?" Naomi wasn't sure she remembered how, after her two weeks in Japan.

"No, you have to. I've got to call the Hardy's lawyer."

Naomi made a face—the only person she disliked more than that Myron Silo was that Reverend Plank. And, of course, Donna.

He leaned over and kissed her cheek. "I don't want to get your hopes up, sweetheart, because it might be nothing at all. But I have a really good feeling about this."

CHAPTER THIRTY-SIX

"Well, I suppose everything is all in order," said Catherine Cole, the bank manager from Silver City, after examining the warrant Jason had obtained the day before. She slid the metal box out of its compartment and set it down on the table.

Jason held his breath as Stan Schwartz, Silver City's sheriff, opened it. Inside was a cassette tape labeled *Johnny Cash* and an envelope. When he saw "Will of Evelyn Johnson" scrawled in spidery cursive across the envelope, he was as excited as if the Cornhuskers were about to make the winning touchdown in the last seconds of the Big Ten Championship. When Stan pulled a single notarized sheet of yellow-lined legal paper out of the envelope in Evelyn's handwriting, Jason showed remarkable restraint by not jumping up and down and pumping his fists in the air.

Instead, he said, "Well, looky here."

"Of course, we will ask the court to investigate this further," Myron said, scowling after skimming the document.

"Let's go to the courthouse right now." Jason knew the judge was there waiting for them.

"Can't this wait until tomorrow?" asked Myron.

"Nope. I don't think so. I will also file an eviction notice for your clients."

"Now, Jason, is that really necessary?"

"Of course it is, Myron." Jason laughed and clapped him on the back, making him stumble forward a little. "And you know it is."

Jason and Myron stood in Judge Peters' chambers for what seemed an eternity before the judge peered up from his bifocals. "This will voids that cockamamie one that you," he said, glaring at Myron, "had to drag us to court for." He studied it carefully one more time. "I'd say this letter of Evelyn's pretty much spells it out. She never downloaded any will from the internet and the will drawn up by Jason still stands. Mike Johnson was, and always has been, her sole heir."

Jason nodded with a smile; Myron nodded with a frown.

The Judge turned to Jason. "It's a downright shame for your client that this didn't turn up earlier. It could have saved her a lot of heartache. Saved us from wasting our time."

"Judge," Myron said, "I will be filing—"

"What I want to know is this," Judge Peters interrupted, jabbing his finger at him. "What the hell were your clients up to? It doesn't take a rocket scientist to figure out that they were behind that phony will."

"But Judge—"

"Second-degree forgery is not something we take lightly in this courtroom. You might want to advise your clients to look for a defense lawyer. And," he added pointedly, "no ambulance chaser, either."

Then the judge picked up the cassette. "Trevor!" he called out to his clerk. "See if you can find something we can play this on, would you?" He turned to the lawyers. "I'm really curious, aren't you? Maybe it's good old Johnny singing 'Folsom Prison.' Now, wouldn't that be mighty appropriate?"

Jason couldn't help but enjoy watching Myron's discomfort when the judge chuckled at his joke. Things didn't look good for his clients. Or for him either, for that matter.

Trevor came in with a dusty RadioShack cassette player.

"Your honor," Jason said when the message on the tape turned out to be garbled. "I don't know if you remember, but I used to work for a firm in San Francisco. We could send this tape to their forensic specialist to see if he can recover anything. I'm pretty sure he wouldn't mind helping us out." It was all he could do not to smirk in Myron's direction.

"I see nothing wrong with that," said the judge. "Do you, Myron?"

Myron looked rather green but didn't disagree.

An hour later, Jason burst into Naomi's studio with an armful of flowers and a grin the size of Alaska. Letting out a wild hoot, he dropped the flowers, grabbed her, and danced her around the room.

"It's yours. The house. The farms. Everything."

He bent down to kiss her, but Naomi jerked away from him.

"What? What is it?"

"We've got to call Marvilla right this second. She'll kill us if she's not the first to hear!"

"Hop in the car. We'll go tell her."

CHAPTER THIRTY-SEVEN

Naomi was in Jason's kitchen, fixing her dinner while listening to J-pop on her phone and making a to-do list to prepare for her move next week. Every few minutes, she set her pencil down and sighed with happiness. Dear sweet Jason, was coming with her to Evelyn's. As much as he loved his home, he wanted to be with *her*. And besides, he had argued, those two widowed sisters who were keen to move to town and set up housekeeping together would be ideal tenants. He insisted his house would be in excellent hands.

Tonight, Jason was at his monthly poker game out at the Watson's farm, and Naomi was relishing her solitude. Let Jason enjoy his time with his friends over pizza and beer. She was planning to finish her last package of *natto,* fermented soybeans, defrosting on the counter. That, stirred together with a raw egg and a splash of soy sauce served over hot rice and topped with crispy *nori* seaweed, wasn't something she had when Jason was around. Namely, because he said it looked and smelled too disgusting.

At first, Naomi thought the rattling sound outside the kitchen door was caused by the wind brushing tree twigs against the window. When she heard it again, she pulled the gingham curtain back to check, and standing there was the last person in the world she wanted to see.

"Sorry I didn't come visit sooner," Andrea said, coming into the kitchen. "I was in Minneapolis at church camp."

"Oh, hi, Andrea." Naomi's voice was far friendlier than she felt. "Where's your car? I don't see it." Because if she had, she might have pretended not to be at home.

"Oh, that's because I walked over from Dan's. You know, Dan? My boyfriend." Andrea sat down at the table and picked up Naomi's sketchbook and started thumbing through it like she had every right to do so. "But I'm going to break up with him pretty soon. I need a smarter guy, don't you think? Someone who's college bound. He's not that smart. Even though everyone thinks he's super hot."

Naomi changed the subject. "Guess what? I got a book contract. For a children's book."

"Yeah, I heard. Congratulations." Andrea pointed at one of the sketches. "That one's my favorite. I love the way the colors mesh into each other here. It's beautiful. Will it go in your next book?"

"I just hope there'll be a next book," Naomi replied, flattered. "We'll have to wait and see how the first one sells."

Naomi poured two cups of green tea, and Andrea let loose a long string of chatter as if Evelyn's property had never started bouncing back and forth like a golden volleyball. About school, boys, the cheerleading squad, church camp. Naomi threw in a few responses but kept wondering if Andrea really was so naïve as to believe that they could ever be friends. The conversation switched to food, and when Andrea began hinting that she was hungry, an invitation to stay for dinner escaped from Naomi's mouth before she could harness it. There went her plans for her solitary feast.

"Oh, wow! Thanks! But it'll have to be quick because I've got tons of homework. "

The quicker, the better, Naomi was thinking. She plugged her iPhone into the charger on the counter, put her *natto* back into the fridge for later, and pulled out some vegetables.

"What's Jason up to tonight? Out with his ex-wife again?"

Naomi whirled around. "What?"

Andrea whacked her forehead with her palm. "I didn't mean that the way it sounded. It came out all wrong."

Naomi sighed. "I guess we all—what's that English expression? Put our foot—"

"—in our mouths? Yeah. Everyone says I'm always doing that. So, where *is* Jason, anyway?"

"Playing poker with Doc and some other guys."

"Oh, I heard those games can go on all night. I guess you're spending the evening all by your lonesome."

"I don't mind being alone." Naomi offered a smile, but wished she really was. "Now, you don't have a lot of time, so we'll make something quick. How does fried rice and salad sound?"

Fifteen minutes later, Naomi watched Andrea chomp her way through dinner and wondered if Lisa ever cooked the kid a proper meal. "There's some of Marvilla's lemon meringue pie in the fridge."

"Mmm. That sounds so yummy, but I won't be able to do cartwheels tomorrow during practice if I eat another bite. I wouldn't mind some more tea, though."

Naomi got up to boil more water. How could Andrea be so easy going after the way things had turned out for her family? At least when she had to leave Evelyn's house and turn over the farms to Jeremy Hardy, she still had what her father had given her. But Andrea and her family had nothing now. They couldn't even move back to their trailer home because their landlord had sold it to a family of Mexicans working at the chicken processing plant, and they hauled it off somewhere. Moving in with Donna in her tiny house certainly couldn't have been a picnic.

A wave of compassion swept over Naomi. "I'm sorry that things turned out how they did for you and your family. But no matter what, you have a bright future ahead of you. You'll get your scholarship. You'll go to college. Things'll be great. You're young and you've got everything going for you. You'll see." Naomi thought she sounded at least fifty years old.

"I suppose. I'm not worried about getting the scholarship. They always give them to poor smart kids like me."

"And maybe you could come to Tokyo with me someday. If your mother and father say it's okay." Naomi didn't mention the fact that Jeremy might be in jail. A full scale investigation for felony forgery was now underway.

"You mean stepmother, don't you? Lisa's not my real mom."

"Yes, of course. Lisa."

Andrea pointed at the kettle. "It's boiling."

Naomi got up and added fresh tea to the blue and white ceramic teapot she had bought in Kyoto, added hot water, and set it on the table. While the tea was steeping, she gathered the dishes, and rinsed them off in the sink. A minute later, she sat back down with a bag of Oreos.

"That dinner was delicious," Andrea said as they drank their tea. "Could I have the recipe?"

"Sure. Let me get a paper and pen."

Ashley was right—she had to stop being such a pushover and do things she didn't want to do because she was afraid of hurting someone's feelings. Why hadn't she just told Andrea the minute she showed up that she was too busy for company? But she knew she'd be nice until Andrea decided it was time to go and then kick herself for it later.

Naomi sipped at the second cup of tea Andrea had poured and jotted down the recipe on an index card. The way the girl was staring at her was giving her the creeps.

"Thanks." Andrea put the recipe into her bag. "So, when are you moving?"

"The day after tomorrow."

"I bet you can't wait."

While Naomi was thinking how to respond, she was gripped by a sharp pain in her gut, followed by a wave of nausea.

Andrea studied Naomi's face, nodding slowly. After a moment, she began to speak. "You've done pretty well for yourself here in America, haven't you? I mean, after all, you were just a nobody from Japan before, right?"

There was no way that was a joke gone wrong. "Look, Andrea—"

"A big fat nobody," Andrea repeated, this time in a sing-song voice. "And then you showed up. Completely out of the blue. No one knew you from a hole in the ground. And suddenly, you were like the Queen of Felix. 'Everybody *loves* Naomi. She's a *Johnson.*'" Hatred dripped from her voice when she added, "Well, la di da da. Look at you. *You* got the farms. *You* got the house. *You* got the money. You even managed to get the best guy in town while you were at it. And that's a total mystery, because Heather was a lot prettier than you, you know."

"You'd better leave." Naomi bent forward to relieve the cramping in her stomach. Her bowels felt like they might let loose, but she was suddenly too weak to stand, let alone get to the toilet.

"I'll be leaving, all right. But just not until I tidy up a bit first." Andrea carried her plates to the sink, washed and dried them, and put them back into the cupboard. "So getting back to the topic at hand," she said with her back still turned. "You were nothing but a nobody back in Japan, right? You weren't even smart enough to go to college. All you were was just some kind of bar girl, right?"

"Get out," Naomi moaned, as another gut-wrenching spasm hit.

"I kind of liked you, you know," Andrea said, wiping down the area where she had been sitting. "But you ruined everything. Evelyn's house and Evelyn's money and Evelyn's farms—they were going to get me through college." Mimicking Naomi, she said, "'Your scholarship will open doors and blah blah blah.' But I didn't want to just scrape by on a scholarship. I wanted the whole college package. A sorority. A junior year abroad. Maybe backpacking in Europe or Asia with friends. And a new car. Of course, a new car. I'm sick of being the poor, smart kid. You know, from the wrong side of the tracks—as they say. But thanks to *you*, I'll have to get a job in the cafeteria, and I'll have to wait on those bitches who were going to be my new friends."

Naomi tried to shift her focus away from her stomach cramps and back to what Andrea was saying.

"I planned everything for months and months and months. And it would've worked out just fine if you hadn't come along."

Through her pain, Naomi realized they had the whole thing about Evelyn's will wrong.

As if she could read Naomi's mind, Andrea snorted. "You can't possibly think my dimwitted father would have been smart enough to do anything like that. But I still don't understand how Evelyn figured it all out. I couldn't believe it when she came right out and asked me if I had been writing wills on her computer." Andrea gave a matter-of-fact shrug, and her grin stretched around her teeth when she added, "So you can see I had no choice, right? But still, it was pretty nerve-wracking when she didn't die."

Naomi's voice was losing its power. "You... killed... Evelyn?"

"No, silly. I didn't *kill* her. Nature was just going to take its course. I never dreamed that stupid Rebecca Mueller would show up after I helped Evelyn down those cellar stairs the fast way. Can you believe it? She went and called an ambulance. But God was on my side because Evelyn didn't remember a thing about our little conversation. After that, all I had to do was wait because I knew it was just a matter of time. And when Evelyn went to Jesus, all I had to do was wait a bit more. I needed to make sure the will fell into the right person's hands. You know, to make its appearance look completely out of the blue. And, to be honest, I was kind of worried about how Mike would take it. But then, hallelujah, he goes and dies. Now, don't get me wrong. I *liked* Mike, and I was sorry he died. But I thought he thought he was my grandpa and that he'd put me in his will. Then, I'd never have to pull out the phony one leaving everything to my dad." Andrea paused to eat one of the Oreos from the package, and while chewing, she said, "You can see why I'd be hesitant about that, right? My dad's so dumb he'd probably screw everything up. Still, that was better than nothing, and I figured I could always make things go my way later on. But then, with Mike out of the picture and with *me* getting his money, everything was going to be perfect." Andrea squinted at Naomi, her eyes hard and mean. "I never saw *you* coming, though. The long-lost illegitimate daughter turning up out of the blue. If it weren't for *you*, I wouldn't have ever needed to pull out my will. If it weren't for *you*, my life would be great."

Naomi's head drifted forward like a wilting flower on a stalk, and Andrea leaned across the table to brush the hair out of her eyes. "But since you and me are having such a good heart-to-heart, I'll let you in on a little secret. Mike isn't my grandpa, no matter what they say about him and my grandma. Because Jeremy's not my real father. Does that surprise you? Well, it's true. I read it in my mother's diary. Can you believe none of those fools ever thought to read it?"

Andrea stood, and her gaze helicoptered around the room until it fell on Naomi's iPhone upon the counter. Picking it up with the dishtowel, she moved it out of reach to the window ledge. "So, it seems my biological father was either a trucker from Des Moines with a flat tire who had some time to kill at the diner or a professor at some wedding in Lincoln she was waitressing at. Who knew that waitresses had so much fun? But then," she added with a sneer, "I bet you *do* know all about that, working in some sleazy bar."

Naomi let out a low, animalistic groan.

"My father had to have been the professor, don't you think? Considering how brilliant I am, that's the only logical explanation.

Personally speaking, though, I would've picked a more romantic spot to be conceived in than some dirty old handicapped bathroom."

Andrea reached across the table and patted Naomi on the arm. Her voice was eerily cheerful when she said, "Now, don't you worry. The arsenic shouldn't take too long. They say for most people it's just an hour or two, although I did read that for some, it might take longer. Let's just keep our fingers crossed that you have the easier time with it, shall we?"

"But... people... will... know... you're... here..."

"Nah. My car's over at Dan's, and technically, we're in his bed where I just finished jerking him off." Andrea giggled a little and added, "I'd certainly hate for *that* embarrassing bit of information to get around, especially since I'm the president of the virginity club. But what's a bit of humiliation when it comes with an iron-clad alibi? Just in case you're wondering, I'm still a virgin. And when the drug wears off, I'll be right beside Dan. Ready to do him again. With my mouth this time, I think. Since it's a special occasion and all."

"You... poisoned... him?"

"Oh no. I'd *never* do that. I just gave him a little sleeping pill, so you and I could spend some quality time together. But it's time for me to get back to him and leave you to it."

Naomi forced herself to stand, but pain knifed through her, and the power in her legs dissolved. She crumpled to the floor, bringing the china teapot down with her. The last thing Naomi heard Andrea say as she slipped out the backdoor was that she was going to miss Naomi's cooking.

A piece of the shattered teapot gouging into Naomi's shoulder reminded her she wasn't dead yet. When she shifted her weight, she remembered the phone she used just for local calls was in her jeans pocket. But it might as well be back in Japan for all the good that did her—she could barely move her arms. She ordered her eyes to remain open, knowing that once they shut, that'd be the end. She forced her body to shift, and with every last ounce of strength left in her, she got the phone out of the pocket and up to her mouth. She pushed the automatic redial button but fell into unconsciousness when her call went to voice mail.

■   ■   ■

Out at the Watson's place, poker night wasn't anywhere close to winding down, not while old Doc was ten dollars ahead. That evening, the major topic of conversation (as in every home in Felix) was how Jeremy Hardy had ever managed to pull off such a stunt. Motive, everyone agreed on. Who wouldn't want the farms and the houses? It turned out that Jeremy had plenty of opportunity as well, because he had been doing a variety of odd jobs for Evelyn in the months before she fell.

"But how," asked Sam Smith, the math teacher at the high school, "did Jeremy get into Evelyn's computer in the first place? And how did he convince her to sign that phony will?"

"Well, that's what I'm trying to find out," said Tom, laying his cards on the table and scooping the pile of quarters toward himself. "He says he's innocent, that he doesn't know a thing about any of that. That's his story, and he seems to be sticking to it."

It was Jason's turn to deal, but his phone buzzed in his pocket. When he saw it was the forensic expert from his old firm, he pushed back his chair and said, "Hey Steve. What's up?"

"Well, we could work out some of what was on that cassette tape you sent, and I'm sending the transcripts. That old lady was pretty certain that some high school kid had been monkeying around with her computer."

"Some high school kid?"

"Yeah, a girl who apparently had been hanging around all the time."

"Oh, Jesus!" Jason muttered into the phone before disconnecting and calling Naomi. She didn't pick up, but he saw she had tried to contact him from Evelyn's old phone. Instead of her message on voicemail, there was only faint, labored breathing.

He shouted to Tom, and they bolted out the door and raced back to town in the police car.

CHAPTER THIRTY-EIGHT

It was touch and go for the first three days, but the hemodialysis reversed the renal failure caused by the arsenic, and the blood transfusions helped flush it out of Naomi's system. The doctors expected her to make a full recovery, and after ten days in the hospital, she was on the mend and back in Jason's house.

People had been dropping by with casseroles, cakes, pies, and salads all day long. Naomi, weak as a newborn kitten, had no appetite but appreciated the love that went into each and every offering. Resting on the sofa, she simply savored the feeling of being alive.

Jason spent the day hovering over her, asking if she needed something to eat or something to drink. Or asking if she was comfortable on the sofa. Or maybe she'd prefer to be in one of the recliners. Or if it was too much for her, maybe she should go back to bed. Finally, Naomi told him what she needed was for him to sit still and quit fussing. She curled against him, burrowed under an afghan, and dozed.

Later that afternoon, the sheriff stopped by. "Don't get up, Jason. And *you*, young lady," he said to Naomi, "had us plenty worried." He helped himself to a cookie from the platter on the coffee table and eased into Jason's recliner. "I've come to tell you we finally found Andrea."

"Where was she?" asked Jason.

"At the church—in that little room where she'd been doing some work for Peter. She'd fixed herself one hell of an arsenic cocktail." Tom shuddered but didn't mention it was the smell of vomit and feces that made Peter Plank call him. "The doctors are doing what they can, but it doesn't look good."

"Maybe we should talk about something else," said Jason, glancing down at Naomi with concern.

"I want to hear," said Naomi, pushing herself off of the sofa.

"Sweetheart, shouldn't you wait until you're stronger?"

"No. I'm ready now. Tell me everything you know. Especially how Evelyn figured it all out."

"All right," Jason said, giving Tom a nod.

"Well, I guess," Tom began, "you could say it started with a conversation she was having with Mike about internet browser history. Remember, it was Evelyn's browser history that made the court decide in favor of that fake will? Well, believe it or not, she and Mike talked about that very topic in early September, when she was having some sort of problem with her computer slowing down. He told her she could fix it if she cleared her browser history. Remember, Evelyn was pretty proud of her computer skills, and she liked learning something new. So, anyway, when she opened her browser history, she saw all those links to websites about writing wills and about how to disinherit someone. Now, she knew she hadn't been visiting those sites, and the only other person using her computer had been Andrea. At first, she figured the kid was working on a school project. But then, why would those hits go back for months and months? Besides, there was nothing pointing to any of the other homework the girl had been doing. And that got Evelyn to wonder why. Then she started thinking about what had happened a few days before when Andrea stopped by, in tears, asking her to cosign a scholarship application. She couldn't find her parents, and the deadline was in about fifteen minutes. Well, Evelyn went out onto the front porch and signed the papers. Now, we all know Evelyn would never sign anything she hadn't read, but that day she couldn't find her reading glasses."

"I bet you anything," Jason said. "Andrea knew exactly where Evelyn's reading glasses were."

"I bet you're right about that," agreed Tom. "Anyway, Evelyn put two and two together. What exactly was it she had signed? And why were those other kids hanging around out front that day? She started wondering if those boys had been signature witnesses."

"Well, we never did track down those witnesses," said Jason, "They were probably just passing through town that day. I imagine Andrea gave them some sob story, and they believed her."

Jason spoke as if not being able to produce the witnesses had been entirely his fault. "I'm sure," Naomi said, "Andrea was very clever the way she got all that done."

Tom nodded and continued. "So, Evelyn decided to update her will right away. And make that cassette. She said she didn't want to make a fuss about anything until after Mike got back from some trip with his students."

"I guess we'll never know why she suddenly decided to have it notarized on that trip to Silver City," said Jason, "and why she left it in a safe deposit box there."

"But it was a good thing she did," said Tom, "because Andrea pushed her down the stairs the very next day. Evelyn was never the same after that."

"Andrea was always strange," said Jason, shaking his head. "But I never imagined she'd do anything like that."

"Well," said Tom. "There's more. Do you remember Lynn?"

"Andrea's birth mother?" asked Jason.

"Jeremy told me today that Lynn's brother was committed to Fulton State Hospital in St. Louis when he was a teenager. We can't say this any more, but it used to be known as the place for the criminally insane. Anyway, Jeremy never wanted Andrea to know that, so he kept it a secret. I called over there this morning, and it turns out the brother's still there—going on about thirty years now. It seems his parents were afraid he was going to move on from doing terrible things to barn cats to something more challenging. Like to women or children."

"Jeez," muttered Jason.

"So, maybe the acorn doesn't fall that far from the tree, or however that saying goes." Tom's phone buzzed, and he glanced down at the screen. "It's the hospital," he said, stepping into the kitchen. He came back into the living room, shaking his head.

Naomi reached for Jason's hand and swallowed back tears. Despite everything, she hadn't wanted this.

"At least Jeremy was with Andrea at the end," Tom said solemnly as he sat back down.

"I hope that gives him some closure," Jason said.

"Me, too. But now we also know why Lisa has been feeling so poorly the past year. Unless you're specifically looking for arsenic poisoning, it's pretty hard to detect. Especially if it's a small dose like what Andrea had been giving her. I'm going to have to go have a talk with that science teacher to find out what the hell kind of independent study lets a kid get her hands on arsenic."

Naomi closed her eyes and rubbed her forehead, thinking that there was something else. Something important. And even though she didn't want to remember the moment when she thought she was going to die, she forced herself to go back to that last conversation with Andrea. When it came to her, she shot up. "Hey! I just remembered something. Jeremy isn't Andrea's father."

Both men turned and looked at her.

"He was someone from a one-night stand. A professor."

"Are you sure?" asked Tom.

"I'm sure that's what Andrea told me. She said she read it in her mother's diary."

"I guess I'd better get back to the hospital to see about running some DNA tests. And see about finding that diary, too."

"While you're at it, would you mind running some tests to see if the rumors are true? You know, about Jeremy being my brother?"

"Are you sure you want to do that?" asked Jason. "Because even if he is, it won't change anything, you know."

"Maybe not. But I think it's better to know."

Tom stood up to go. "I'll see if Jeremy will agree to that." He was almost at the door when he turned around. "Oh, hell. I almost forgot to tell you guys the other thing. We were wrong all along about the manure on your porch. You weren't supposed to be the target. Dan Donovan was."

"Dan Donovan? Andrea's boyfriend?" asked Jason.

"Some idiot kids from Riley's football team—drunk as skunks at the time—thought it was a great prank."

Naomi gaped at Tom. "That was a prank?

"God only knows how they managed to pull it off without waking the entire neighborhood. When they realized they had hit the wrong house and people started calling it a hate crime, they kept their mouths shut. Until all the other shit hit the fan," Tom said, chuckling at his choice of words. "Then they got spooked and told their parents. And their parents called me. Those boys will do some community service, and I expect they'll be coming over in a day or so to apologize. But don't be too hard on them, Naomi. Because after that, everyone kept their eyes on your house. Andrea had to watch her step."

"Are you saying Naomi was safer because of those idiots?" asked Jason.

"She probably was."

"But it's all over now, isn't it?" said Naomi. "Everything is over."

"Yep. You can get on with your life. Both of you," Tom said, before closing the door on his way out.

Naomi settled back onto the sofa, talking and making plans with Jason until dusk fell across the Nebraska sky.

CHAPTER THIRTY-NINE

Seven months later

Naomi, Ashley, and Ashley's daughter Emily were admiring their reflections in front of the full-length mirror in the green room in Naomi's house.

"I just want you to tell me one thing. Are you sure that this is what you want? What you *really, really* want?"

Naomi looked at Ashley like she was crazy.

"Just joking." Ashley picked up the brush to smooth Naomi's hair one last time. "You look gorgeous."

Evelyn's wedding dress, which had also been worn by her mother, had been impossible for Naomi to wear as it was. Even if the silk hadn't deteriorated with age, it would have been much too small. But Marvilla told her to take it over to Ivy Burns, who could work magic with any piece of material. After combining the salvageable fabric with a few bolts of new silk, Ivy came up with a wedding dress that could rival any French designer.

"I'm so glad you're here," Naomi said, hugging her matron of honor.

"I wouldn't miss it for the world," said Ashley. "And I won't miss your next wedding, either."

Naomi smiled, remembering Jason's astonishment when she informed him that they had to have not one but *two* weddings. One in Nebraska and one in Japan.

"That's what it means to live with our feet in both worlds, Jason. We sometimes have to double up on stuff, whether we want to or not."

"Heck, Naomi, I'd marry you in a different place every single week for a whole year, if that was what you wanted."

"Don't worry," she had told him. "Two will be plenty."

"Are you ready?" Marvilla came into the bedroom in a floor-length purple silk gown, also made by Ivy Burns. When Naomi asked if she would act as the bride's mother, she took to the job like a pro. Marvilla was determined nothing was going to ruin Naomi and Jason's big day. Which was why she wasn't disappointed in the least when Peter Plank had been called to the General Assembly to answer questions about the inappropriate usage of church funds for his questionable projects. Or surprised either. Wasn't it her duty as a God-fearing Christian woman to voice her concerns in that detailed letter she sent to the Assembly several weeks ago? But more than her letter, it was probably Andrea's diary that concerned the Assembly the most. What that little psychopath had written about that nasty man in her diary may or may not have been true, but my-oh-my, the press certainly had a field day with it when it recently came to light.

Marvilla smiled. That Peter Plank had much more to worry about now than poking his nose into other people's business where it didn't belong. And besides, it was much nicer to bring Reverend Winkle out of retirement for the wedding. As long as everyone made sure he kept his pants on, he'd be just fine. He may have lost his marbles, but he was still the best preacher they ever had.

Naomi hugged Marvilla and planted a kiss on her papery cheek. "Yes, I'm ready. Ready as I'll ever be."

Marvilla drove the bridal party to the church. The whole town was expected to attend the wedding, and cars filled the parking lot and spilled out onto the street. The pews were packed, and latecomers had been directed to the fellowship hall, where they would have to watch the wedding on the television screen. Cake and refreshments were on the counter, ready to be served right after the wedding. In the evening, there was going to be another party at the steak house ten miles down the road. Samurai Sushi helped cater, and Kazuo Mori assured Jason at least a hundred times that there'd be nothing too slimy, too fishy, or too raw for the people of Felix.

The next day, they were going on their honeymoon.

"Anywhere but Denver," Naomi had insisted. "Call me superstitious, but I'm not gambling my honeymoon on Denver."

They agreed on New York. For *this* honeymoon, anyway. After their Japanese wedding, they planned to go to Bali.

"If you make me get married twice," said Jason, "then at least I get to have two honeymoons."

"No argument from me on that one," Naomi had replied.

"Hiroshi's up at the front with his iPad, and the Mori family is right behind him," Ashley told Naomi. "Your grandparents are already online with the one you sent them."

"What about Jeremy?" Naomi asked Marvilla.

"He and his dimwitted brother are both here. And Donna, too. God knows why you asked *her*."

But Naomi felt generous toward the Hardys after knowing without a doubt that they were *just* cousins. After all, poor Jeremy couldn't be blamed for what had happened. And Donna? Whoever said keep your enemies close was on to something.

Marvilla pulled Naomi to her one last time for one more gigantic hug. "Your father would be so proud of you." She wiped away a tear before taking Sheriff Tom's arm to be escorted to her seat of honor at the front of the church, right next to Jason's father, who was all spruced up in a coat and tie for the occasion and looking around in confusion.

"It's time." Ashley reached over to adjust the hair ornament that Naomi had asked her grandmother to send—the red and black lacquered one that she had worn for her own wedding in

Japan over sixty years earlier. She handed Naomi her bridal bouquet of pink and white roses, and they shared one last hug. She took Emily by the hand and led her to the entryway of the sanctuary. Just like they had practiced the night before, Emily moved ahead of Ashley down the aisle, dropping the rose petals from her basket with the concentration that only a three-year-old could muster up. After they reached the altar, Dorothy's organ rendition of Pachelbel's Canon in D began to fill the church, and the congregation stood and turned toward the entrance.

Naomi touched the cameo pin the Johnson women had all worn at their weddings for good luck and glanced down at Jason's mother's ring. She inhaled deeply, and with her head held high, she took her first step.

ACKNOWLEDGEMENTS

This novel would have never made it past the preliminary stages if it hadn't been for the valuable feedback I received from members of the Tokyo Writers Workshop.

I would also like to say thank you to friends who have read and commented on various versions of *Finding Naomi,* including Melissa Noguchi, Louise George Kittaka, Jennifer Nitta, and Margaret Yamanaka. Thank you so much for your support!

Special thanks must also go to Suzanne Kamata, Lea O'Harra, Karen Hill Anton, Thomas Kinoshita Lockley, David Joiner, and John Rucynski, Cam Torrens, Lena Gibson, and Niamh McAnally.

I'm honored to be a part of the vibrant expatriate writing community in Japan, and I have been inspired by so many wonderful writers here who write in various genres. I don't think I would have had the courage to turn to fiction without such great role models.

I'm also grateful for my husband, Shin Nagatomo, who always supported me in every way possible.

Thanks also go to Eric and Mariko Nagatomo, and to Alicia and Tony Guercio.

Thank you to my publisher Reagan Rothe and the incredible publishing team at Black Rose Writing for believing in me. I am particularly grateful for all the friendships and connections I have made as a member of the Black Rose Writing family. This was something so unexpected and delightful!

Finally, thank you to my family and friends who have always supported me in all of my dreams.

ABOUT THE AUTHOR

Diane Hawley Nagatomo was born in the UK and lived in Nebraska, Spain, Massachusetts, New Mexico, and California before coming to Japan in 1979. She is a semi-retired professor from Ochanomizu University and has written extensively on issues concerning gender, culture, and education. An avid reader her entire life, she turned to fiction with her 2023 debut novel, *The Butterfly Cafe.* While not teaching or writing, she and her Japanese husband of more than forty years spend time with their six grandchildren. *Finding Naomi* is her second work of fiction.

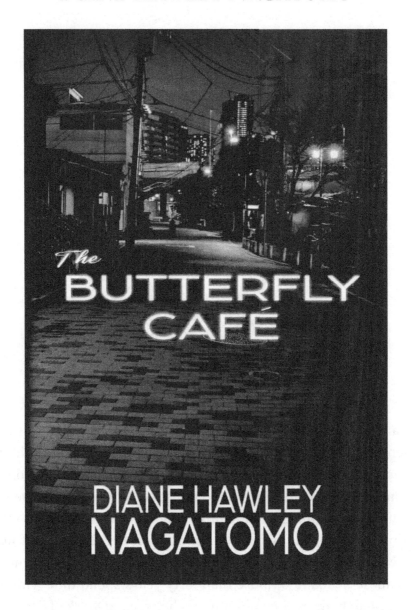

NOTE FROM
DIANE HAWLEY NAGATOMO

Word-of-mouth is crucial for any author to succeed. If you enjoyed *Finding Naomi*, please leave a review online—anywhere you are able. Even if it's just a sentence or two. It would make all the difference and would be very much appreciated.

Thanks!
Diane Hawley Nagatomo